The Gov and the Cowboy Promise

STAND-ALONE NOVEL

A Western Historical Romance Book

by

Sally M. Ross

SALLY M. ROSS

Disclaimer & Copyright

This is a work of fiction. Names, characters, places and incidents either are products of the author's imagination or are used fictitiously. Any resemblance to actual events or locales or persons, living or dead, is entirely coincidental.

Copyright© 2023 by Sally M. Ross

All Rights Reserved.

This book may not be reproduced or transmitted in any form without the written permission of the publisher.

In no way is it legal to reproduce, duplicate, or transmit any part of this document in either electronic means or in printed format. Recording of this publication is strictly prohibited and any storage of this document is not allowed unless with written permission from the publisher

Table of Contents

The Governess and the Cowboy's Promise 1
   Disclaimer & Copyright 2
   Table of Contents 3
   Letter from Sally M. Ross 5
Prologue 6
Chapter One 17
Chapter Two 24
Chapter Three 29
Chapter Four 44
Chapter Five 50
Chapter Six 62
Chapter Seven 73
Chapter Eight 82
Chapter Nine 90
Chapter Ten 105
Chapter Eleven 116
Chapter Twelve 121
Chapter Thirteen 126
Chapter Fourteen 134
Chapter Fifteen 139
Chapter Sixteen 145
Chapter Seventeen 154
Chapter Eighteen 166
Chapter Nineteen 177

Chapter Twenty 187
Chapter Twenty-One 197
Chapter Twenty-Two 201
Chapter Twenty-Three 211
Chapter Twenty-Four 220
Chapter Twenty-Five 226
Chapter Twenty-Six 232
Chapter Twenty-Seven 241
Chapter Twenty-Eight 246
Chapter Twenty-Nine 262
Chapter Thirty 267
Chapter Thirty 270
Chapter Thirty-Two 273
Chapter Thirty-Three 277
Epilogue 281
Extended Epilogue 286
   Also by Sally M. Ross 289

Letter from Sally M. Ross

"There are two kinds of people in the world those with guns and those that dig."

This iconic sentence from the *"Good the Bad and the Ugly"* was meant to change my life once and for all. I chose to be the one to hold the gun and, in my case…the pen!

I started writing as soon as I learned the alphabet. At first, it was some little fairytales, but I knew that this undimmed passion was my life's purpose.

I share the same love with my husband for the classic western movies, and we moved together to Texas to leave the dream on our little farm with Daisy, our lovely lab.

I'm a literary junkie reading everything that comes into my hands, with a bit of weakness on heartwarming romances and poetry.

If you choose to follow me on this journey, I can guarantee you characters that you would love to befriend, romances that will make your heart beat faster, and wholesome, genuine stories that will make you dream again!

Until next time,

Sally M. Ross

Prologue

Bartlett, Mississippi – October 1874

Mattie Walsh ran her fingertips over the calico fabric of her gown. Her hands shook unsteadily as a bolt of excited energy rushed through her. She admired herself in the looking glass, nodding approvingly at the delicate print of the dress she'd chosen for the evening.

She knew she had to look her best if she was to be on the arm of Lewis Mooney, and the dress that she had picked out allowed her to do just that.

Just the thought of her fiancé brought a dreamy sigh to her lips. Spotting a stray lock of caramel-colored hair tumbling down her shoulder, she skillfully reached up and pinned it back with the rest of her hair at the nape of her neck. Her thoughts never once left Lewis while she fixed the rest of her appearance by pinching her cheeks and lips to flood them with color, giving contrast to her pale features.

When she was finally satisfied, she glanced at the clock. It was six fifty-five in the evening. Lewis was set to arrive within the next five minutes to whisk her away to Bartlett's Town Hall for the dance that the town was hosting. She could see exactly how everything would go in her mind's eye, swept away on visions of spending the evening with Lewis in their small town.

Smack dab in the middle of Mississippi, Bartlett had a quaint charm to it that spoke to something within Mattie. She loved the familiar wood and tin buildings, even if they were a little ramshackle. She had grown up toddling in and out of them with her parents in tow. She adored the small General Store where she now worked and got to talk to her fellow townsfolk each day, the dusty roads, sitting on the porch with her brother, listening to the sound of cicadas singing on summer nights among the white oak trees, and the damp, humid air.

Mattie loved the flat, rolling meadows that spanned as far as the eye could see, blending into sparse forests covered in marshland. And more than anything, more than the buildings or the land or the smiling people that she passed in the morning, Mattie loved what her life was becoming now that she was engaged to Lewis Mooney.

A girlish giggle pulled itself from her lips all over again at the thought of him. Mattie still found it hard to believe that this man had chosen her, and she often found herself having to pinch her arm to be reassured that she wasn't trapped in some fanciful dream. Lewis was the most handsome man in Bartlett and had the eye of every woman in their town.

Just that morning, as Mattie had walked about the town square with Gilbert, her brother, she'd overheard some of the older biddies talking about Lewis and his fine features. Mattie had chuckled to herself as she'd walked past them, glad they'd be able to see her dancing the night away in his arms that very evening.

They had been engaged for going on six months, and she knew that soon it would be time to start preparing for their wedding, and she often lost herself in fantasies about what her wedding day would be like.

Mattie situated herself on the settee in their family room and tried as hard as she could not to watch the clock tick away the seconds as she anxiously awaited the knock on the door. She raised her hand, glancing with admiration at her engagement ring, turning it this way and that to watch the small gems inlaid in the band sparkle in the dim evening light.

She could hear her brother out on the porch, the tell-tale sound of his knife cutting through wood letting Mattie know that Gilbert was whittling. With a small smile, she looked toward the mantle beside the clock, where small wooden figurines decorated the space. She wondered if there would be a new one sitting with the intricately carved creatures by the time, she returned later that evening.

Almost of their own accord, her eyes darted once more to the clock, and Mattie noted that it was now past seven. Lewis had assured her that he would be there by no later than the top of the hour to retrieve her to walk to the Town Hall. A small spool of dread began to unfurl in her belly and the thought that perhaps something had happened to him filled her mind.

Visions began to dance in her mind of an overturned buggy, like the one that had claimed her parent's lives, or perhaps a fire. There were any number of things, each one more terrifying than the last, that could be the cause for Lewis' delay. Her palms began to sweat, and she wiped them on the fabric of her skirts as she pulled in a deep, steadying breath. Mattie quickly shook that thought away, not allowing herself to stew on such negativity.

But, as the seconds turned to minutes and the minutes turned into half an hour, she could no longer fight against the worry that filled her. Pushing herself up off the sofa, she stalked through the house and pushed open the heavy screen door that led to the front porch where her brother sat in his rocking chair, whittling in the fading evening light.

She cleared her throat as she approached Gilbert, and his eyes flicked to hers with surprise. Sometimes it caught Mattie off guard just how similar their looks were. He may have been six years older, but their fair complexion, bright green eyes, and shiny light brown hair were mirror images of each other.

Gilbert blinked in confusion, looking out at the setting sun before turning back to her.

"Gettin' a bit late," he surmised in his gruff, deep tenor.

"Lewis said he'd be here by seven," Mattie answered, fighting to keep her voice from shaking with worry. "Do you think something has happened?"

Gilbert grunted his dissent. Mattie loved her brother, and usually he was bursting with words and jokes. But when it was anything to do with Lewis, Mattie had learned that her brother did not have much to say.

Seven years ago, when their parents had died, she had only been fifteen, and he had been so young, barely twenty-one. But he had taken her in anyway, and he had done his best to raise her and help her through her terribly moody teenage years. Gilbert was the only family that she had left. And she knew it would remain that way until Mattie created one with Lewis.

"We'll walk to the hall and check there, see if maybe he arrived there first and got caught up with somethin'," Gilbert offered, pushing himself off of the wooden chair and standing to brush some of the dust off his pants. "You know that family of his, any opportunity to show off their prized pony."

Mattie had to fight from rolling her eyes at her brother as he sauntered down the front steps with her in tow. Gilbert wasn't overjoyed about her engagement to Lewis. He thought her future husband was nothing more than a pretty face. The Mooney family was the richest in town and had been for generations. Lewis was the sole heir, and as such, Gilbert hadn't really been in a place to reject the match when Lewis approached him to ask permission to marry Mattie.

But when Gilbert and Mattie were alone, he didn't hold his tongue on his thoughts about the man. He had made it clear to Mattie from the beginning that the only reason he was agreeing was because he knew she fancied Lewis and he could provide her with a life of comfort. However, he would have preferred her to fancy almost anyone else in Bartlett.

They walked swiftly through town, with Mattie trotting to keep up with Gilbert's long, assured strides. She tried as hard as she could to keep her focus on the streets and the comings and goings of the people around her, hoping that it would help to keep her thoughts from wandering to the doom and gloom of what might have happened to Lewis.

Before they had even rounded the corner for the Town Hall, the music that welled inside of it and the sound of the revelers within its walls rushed out to greet them. The large doors to the massive wooden building were thrown open, and a few people stood on the stairs to air themselves off in the breeze of the Mississippi autumn.

Through the gap in the door, she could see couples twirling across the dance floor, and she had no trouble imagining the chaos inside those four wooden walls.

She followed Gilbert up the steps, and he tipped his head in acknowledgement of the few people he passed that said hello. Mattie, however, kept her eyes peeled for any glimpse of Lewis or someone in the Mooney family. She stepped into the space, the sticky heat of so many bodies pressed in together greeting her just as surely as the strum of the fiddle. It was an eruption of color and sound, and it took her a moment to get her bearings.

As Mattie gazed around, her heart beating wildly, she wasn't sure if she felt disappointment or relief when there was no sight of Lewis in the crowd around them. Taking a few more steps into the building, the crowd surrounding the dance floor parted, creating a clear view of the couple that everyone stood around watching. And as Mattie's eyes zeroed in on them, her heart that had been pounding so ferociously just a second before, now seemed to stop entirely.

She must have gasped, or stumbled forward, or done something to draw Gilbert's attention, because he was immediately at her side. Her brother gripped the top of her arm, keeping her steady, but she shook him off. Mattie wasn't sure how to feel as she marched through the crowd.

A few of the townsfolk that she walked past shot her quick, sympathetic glances, while others avoided looking at her entirely, making Mattie sure that what she was looking at was real and not a figment of her tired, worried imagination. She pushed people to the side as she made her path toward Lewis and the beautiful, raven-haired girl that he expertly swung about in the center of the dance floor.

She didn't make a sound as she stood at the edge of the crowd, her chest heaving wildly from rapid her breaths as her palms began to sweat. Instead, rage and hurt thundered in her ears and Mattie began to shake, as her fiancé wrapped himself in the arms of another woman.

"You don't need to see this," came her brother's voice beside her.

She felt his hand clasp around her arm once again, and she felt the pressure of him trying to lead her away, but she resisted. Mattie planted her feet firmly on the wooden floor, locking all of her joints against the pressure Gilbert was applying, determined to take in the reality of what was unfolding before her. The truth of why Lewis had not shown up to get her crashing into her like a wave.

"I think I do," Mattie answered, and she hated how hollow her voice sounded but she did not know how to fix it.

She could feel the tension rolling off of Gilbert as he stood beside her, but she was thankful when he didn't try to pull her away again. Mattie was unsure of how much time had passed, it could have been seconds, it could have been hours, she would not have known the difference. But eventually, Lewis pulled his eyes away from the beauty he'd been dancing with and looked out at the crowd. When his eyes landed on her, his expression paled for only a moment before he schooled his features into one of casual disinterest.

She watched with abject horror as Lewis stopped dancing and leaned into the woman he held in his arms, much closer than Mattie would have liked, and whispered in her ear. The woman followed his gaze to where Mattie stood, a quick, sympathetic smile tugging at the corner of her lips as if it was Lewis who was the one who was being hurt by this encounter. It stoked Mattie's rage anew, and as the other woman gave Lewis a nod of understanding, Mattie wanted to begin screaming. She watched as he released the woman's small, trim waste and stalked toward Mattie.

She knew that they were drawing the eyes of the crowd, and she fought to keep her chin held high and to swallow past the lump that had formed in her throat.

"Mattie," Lewis said as he approached her, his velvet voice washing over her like honey. "I see you made it safely."

"No thanks to you," Gilbert cut in with anger and accusation dripping from every syllable, and Mattie was thankful for him.

Lewis nodded thoughtfully while she shot a pointed glance to the woman who was now retreating across the dance floor before her gaze landed back on Lewis.

"A word outside, if you will?" Lewis asked, waving his arm before him in an invitation for Mattie to lead the way.

There was a small part of her that wanted to argue, to say that she'd rather he said whatever he intended to say, right there, in front of all of those people. Perhaps if there were witnesses, he would be kind to her. Perhaps if there were witnesses, he would not leave her.

Because that is what she sensed was coming, and although she was currently seething with a bubbling, boiling rage, she also did not think she could bear the shame of him calling off their engagement. But she also knew better.

Lewis' pride and the weight that he put into his reputation would not allow him to talk to her now. If Mattie refused to go outside, he would insist, and then they would cause even more of a scene than they already were. And even though she knew that the ending of her engagement and the feelings of rejection that it brought with it might break her, she would rather try to walk away from this interaction with some of her dignity intact if she could.

She nodded at Lewis and then turned on her heel, stalking through the crowded hall. She felt the gaze of the other townsfolk on her with every step that she took. As Mattie approached the door, she caught sight of Gilbert standing by the threshold. He had waited on her, and the thought sent a flitter of appreciation through her for her ridiculous, often joking but currently grim and protective brother. But she pushed it down. She had no energy to think of anything right now, except for the conversation that was to come.

When they stepped through the doors, a slight breeze stirred the bottoms of her skirts, but Mattie hardly noticed. Lewis pushed past her, stalking a few feet away from those milling about on the steps, and then stopping. He shot an expectant look at Mattie, who approached with a hammering heart.

"What is happening, Lewis?" Mattie asked as she approached him, her brow furrowing in consternation. "Who was that woman? Why did you not come and retrieve me like you said?"

"I would have thought you'd have figured that out by now," Lewis said, studying his hands and refusing to meet Mattie's eyes. His tone sounded bored, but the rigid set of his shoulders and the grinding of his jaw in between sentences advised Mattie that he may not be as aloof about the matter as he seemed.

It was that more than anything, that cut Mattie straight to the bone. Lewis could see that he was hurting her, enough so that he was made uncomfortable by it. He knew about Mattie's past, about the feelings of inadequacy that she often struggled with, and as such, Lewis would be well aware of exactly how what was about to happen next would hurt her. And yet, it was not enough to stop him.

"Our engagement is off," Lewis continued, his voice hesitant, as if bracing himself for the blow he knew he was about to deliver. "To be fair, I should have waited longer to ask for your hand in the first place. You are kind and you are beautiful, but your family is not particularly wealthy, and it may seem cruel, but it is true that we both know you were aiming above your station."

His words hit Mattie like a fist, and she was suddenly finding it very hard to breathe. An uncomfortable look darted across Lewis' face as if he did not want to have to say these things to her, but knew that she deserved the truth, and so he would deliver it no matter how brutal.

"The woman you saw inside is the daughter of a very wealthy family from Chatham, the next town over. As you are well aware, my family has high expectations of me. Expectations that I have been recently made aware that you do not meet. Jane, however? Well, you have clearly seen her, and unfortunately, we are much more adequately matched."

Mattie looked down at her boots, his words falling between them. She did not want to meet his gaze as tears began dancing along the bottom of her lashes.

"There, there," Lewis said, his voice uncomfortable with the emotions that were threatening to overwhelm her. "Do not make a fuss, it will be easier for the both of us."

"Yes, it is so very important for me that I try to make things easier for *you*," Mattie hurled the words at him angrily, hoping that they would cut him, hoping that he would feel even a semblance of the hurt and pain that was roaring through her at that very moment. But Lewis did not flinch, did not blink, did not react to her words in the slightest. And his non-reaction caused Mattie's own anger to deflate, leaving her feeling hollow and defeated.

There was a brief pause in which he studied her, eyes roving over her from top to bottom, making Mattie feel like she was being looked at beneath a magnifying glass. She wanted to shy away from the scrutiny, but she did not want to give him any additional satisfaction knowing just how much he was affecting to her.

Finally, Lewis clicked his tongue at her, and then said nothing else as he turned on his heel and strode back into the building. When he disappeared fully into the crowd, and she could no longer see even a glimpse of his shirt, the oxygen left Mattie entirely. The corset under the fabric of her gown was too tight, and her breaths came in short, shallow gasps as the emptiness inside of her opened wide, a chasm that she feared wanted to swallow her whole. Her fingers clawed at her chest, working free the collar that now threatened to strangle her. Tears spilled over, rushing down her cheeks.

"Mattie."

Gilbert's low, steady voice cut through the din of her panic. She glanced up, her green eyes meeting their mirror. Her brother approached her with outstretched arms, and she didn't hesitate as she launched herself into them. She no longer cared that she was causing a scene, no longer cared about much at all. All that Mattie Walsh cared about now, was the fact that her world had crumbled around her.

Chapter One

Bartlett, Mississippi – April 1875

Mattie stared unblinkingly at the ceiling, partaking in her daily ritual of counting the wooden planks in the ceiling above her bed as she fought off the tears and melancholy that threatened to overwhelm her. It had been six months since Lewis Mooney had broken her heart in the middle of the Bartlett Town Square, which meant it had been six months since she had been able to leave her house without fear.

It had been easier during the winter when the colder temperatures tended to keep people inside. Even in a place like Mississippi, the sun needed a little bit of a break from shining so hot. And Mattie had taken full advantage.

But the days were growing warmer again, and she knew that Gilbert was getting tired of her being cooped up in the house all the time. She wished that she could convey to him just how painful the thought of having to venture into town was for her. Mattie had tried once, not long after her engagement to Lewis had ended.

But it had felt like only moments after she had gotten into the General Store to start her shift and had strapped on her apron that Lewis and his new fiancé, Jane Goodale, came traipsing in. Mattie had thought that she would be able to stand the sight of them together, but she had found out that notion to have been entirely incorrect.

As grief and hurt welled up inside her, Mattie had thrown off her apron and rushed home immediately. The second the door to the house had slammed shut behind her, she had collapsed into her bed in a heap of tears and wasn't able to get up for three days. Gilbert had been so concerned he'd called for the town's doctor, but much to Gilbert's chagrin there wasn't really a cure a doctor could give for a broken heart.

He'd been understanding at first, allowing Mattie to wail out her pain all hours of the day and night. But even her brother's previously endless amount of patience had soon worn thin. She had long since lost her job at the General Store. But, giving that it was where she had originally met Lewis, and then keeping in mind the last terrible sighting of him and Jane there, Mattie couldn't really bring herself to grieve the loss of her employment.

She knew that Gilbert would be just fine without the few pennies she scrounged up with her shifts. It wasn't like she was eating or doing much of anything that cost money, anymore.

Mattie sighed loudly, rolling over on her side and staring across her room. She had tried as hard as she could over the last couple months to at least keep up with the household chores, for Gilbert's sake. And most days she was at least able to pull herself out of bed and go through the motions.

But as with all grief, some days were better than others. And on that particular day she was having a very bad day. The sadness that she'd felt all those months ago crashed over her in waves as the hours ticked by, and still, she could not bring herself to move. The longer she laid in bed, the more she felt as if her limbs were pressing into the mattress; the weight of six-month's worth of grief pushing her farther into the straw until she felt she may never have the strength to claw her way back out.

The mirror across Mattie's room glinted silver, and her eyes darted to it. She caught a glimpse of her reflection, and a wince of pain at the ghastly sight darted across her face. Her once full and flush cheeks had grown gaunt, as if the grief over her loss and shame had sucked the life out of her. She feared that the melancholy that had dug its way into her heart had been sent by none other than the Devil, himself. Mattie had aimed too high in pursuing Lewis, and now she would reap the consequences of that sin.

Footsteps sounded against the floorboards as someone approached the door to her room, but Mattie hardly had the energy to glance in that direction, let alone stand to greet them. Whoever it was rapped on the other side of the door, three short bursts of knuckles against wood. She had to assume it was her brother, no one else would bother, not anymore.

There was a time when she had friends, or at least acquaintances, that would have come calling. And they had, at first. Once word had gotten out around town about the end to her and Lewis' engagement, there had been plenty of knocks at the door. Her friends had shown up with well wishes, with flowers and baked goods, all the things that Mattie used to find joy in. But now, the flowers only served to remind her of the ones that Lewis had brought her nearly every week whenever they were in season.

The desserts had turned to ash in her mouth and made her want to gag. And never once had she been able to muster up a simple 'thank you'. And so, the visits from her friends had become more and more infrequent, until they had stopped all together. Even then she could not find a single morsel of herself with enough energy to care.

Gilbert knocked on her door again, a quick rake of his knuckles against the wood. But still, she did not respond. She knew that he would come in eventually, if she didn't answer, and so Mattie did not waste any of the precious little energy that she had on inviting him in. And a few seconds later, the door pushed open and her brother stepped through the threshold, just as she had expected.

After a few moments of silence on the other end of the door, the handle turned, and Gilbert stepped into view.

"Mattie," Gilbert said, his deep voice hesitant and laced with concern. "This cannot continue."

She didn't answer him, opting instead to just follow him with her eyes as he crossed her room. There was a small wooden chair that she kept by a writing desk, and Gilbert grabbed it, drug it across the wooden floor before stopping directly by her bed and taking a seat. He placed his elbows on his knees and cupped his bearded chin, his green and gold-flecked eyes regarding her wearily.

Mattie hadn't paid much attention to her brother over the past six months, she had been too focused on keeping herself held together. But she realized now that there was a slight stoop to his shoulders that she didn't think had been there before, and she couldn't help but wonder how badly her melancholy had also seeped into him.

"I can't sit here and watch you waste away," he tried again, his gaze finding Mattie's and holding it steadily.

A lump rose unbidden into Mattie's throat, and she swallowed past it. She could not count the number of tears she had cried throughout the last six months. More than once she had wanted to explain to Gilbert just how much this had all meant to her.

She knew that her brother had watched when she was younger; a gangly, poorly looking thing that was teased by the other kids in their small town. They had badgered her, saying her teeth were too large for her angular face, that her knobby elbows and knees were sharp enough to cut. When she would pass too close, they would pretend to have been speared by her bony arms before falling into a fit of laughter when hurt and shame crossed her face.

She had been told that she had grown into her looks as she had gotten into adulthood, and the way that people had treated her had surely gotten better. She knew that Gilbert had thought Mattie had only cared for Lewis because of his handsome face and the status that a marriage to a man such as him could bring her. And she had never corrected him when he voiced his suspicions. But the truth was, being seen by Lewis, and the town knowing that someone like him could love her—it had *meant something.* To her, and to everyone around her. Once the news of their engagement had gotten out, so many people had treated her differently. She had finally been someone to the town, because of who Lewis was.

And then that all came crashing down around her six months ago. Not only had Lewis left her, but he had done so because Mattie herself had been lacking. She had not been pretty enough, or wealthy enough, or from a good enough family to hold his affections.

Mattie wanted to explain all of this to her brother. But the energy that it would require wasn't something she thought she could muster. And it also was not something that Mattie thought Gilbert would understand.

"I am not wasting," Mattie said to Gilbert, the sound of her voice thick and raspy with disuse.

"Have you not looked at yourself in the mirror?" he fired back, arching an eyebrow. "You are nothin' but bone pressed to flesh."

The image of herself in the looking glass just a few moments before flashed through her mind, and she had to fight against a wince. Had she not thought the same thing?

"I have chores to do," Mattie ignored his statement, pushing herself into a sitting position.

"No," Gilbert argued, halting Mattie as she attempted to climb to her feet.

"What do you mean, no?" Mattie fired back, a small spark of her old self coming back to life with his barked dissent.

She watched her brother as he extracted a folded piece of paper from the front pocket of his buttoned-up shirt. He smoothed it out, and she spotted scrawled writing across it, immediately marking it as a letter. Her eyes darted from the parchment up to her brother's face, wondering what on God's green Earth this could all be about.

"Remember James Murphy? Used to live here in Bartlett?" Gilbert asked, glancing at his sister and waiting.

"Of course I remember James," she said, her voice a little stronger and her sadness a little duller now that her interest had been captured. "How could I forget? He spent enough time at our house when the two of you were young."

"I've been corresponding with him as of late," Gilbert continued on, nodding his head toward the letter still clutched in his hands. "Since you remember him, I'm sure you recall he moved to Tennessee quite a few years back. His wife died not too long ago, leaving him alone with his baby daughter."

"I recall you telling me about his wife," Mattie answered, memories floating back to her. "You travelled to Tennessee for a bit to attend the funeral."

"Well, his previous governess is getting married, and now he's looking for a new one." Her brother gave her a long, pointed stare, and she began to put all of it together.

Curiosity welled inside of Mattie, and she began to work through the options she knew were going to be presented to her as her brother continued to talk.

"I was thinkin' that maybe you'd want to take up the job." Gilbert said in a rush, his words flying from him as if he was afraid if he stopped talking for even a moment, Mattie would not let him begin again. "You'd move to Mt. Juliet and help him take care of little Amy, she's only two, you see. And you could stay and work there as long as you'd like. It might give you the space you need away from this wretched town and all that Mooney business," Gilbert flushed with the last sentence, and a pang of guilt washed through Mattie.

She knew this all couldn't have been easy on Gilbert, watching her carry on like this all these months and feeling helpless. Mattie turned the idea over in her head, but she couldn't think of it as anything other than an offer of freedom. Freedom to heal, freedom to be somewhere that she didn't have to worry about seeing Lewis or Jane, or the pitying stares of anyone who knew what had happened. For the first time in a very, very long time, a feeling of peace washed over her as Mattie held her brother's gaze.

"I think that sounds like a grand idea," she answered him.

And when the soft smile that was positively filled with relief lit her brother's face, Mattie couldn't help but feel like this would be the best decision for both of them.

Chapter Two

Mt. Juliet, Tennessee – April 1875

James Murphy's steady, unhurried footsteps stirred up the dust as he walked from the post office back to his ranch house. He would usually have taken a buggy to get to and from town, but it had been such a nice day, he hadn't wanted to miss the opportunity to enjoy it a little bit, with the breeze tickling the whiskers of his beard and the sun shining warmly on his face, before he had to get back to work. He looked at the envelope he gripped in his hands as he walked, noting the familiar scrawl on the front of it.

This was the second letter he had received from his old friend, Gilbert Walsh, in less than a month. Figuring he could use the letter to pass the time as he walked back home, he opened it and took it out to read. Eyes skimming the page, he took in his friend's words of thanks for allowing Mattie to take up the role of governess to Amy. Gilbert had explained Mattie's situation in his very first letter, talking about her heartbreak and how he didn't think his sister would ever be able to move on if she remained in Bartlett.

James had tried to recall Mattie, but all he remembered of her was a gangly, awkward youth with large teeth who had loved to annoy her older brother. No matter how hard he tried, James couldn't picture what type of woman Mattie would have grown into. Though it didn't really matter. Because the one thing that James did understand was heartbreak.

And while his own earth-shattering grief was far different from Mattie's, he still felt the need to offer help to a kindred spirit that had been broken by love. Plus, he knew he would never fare well without a governess. Who better than someone he already knew, however vaguely he remembered her?

James finished reading Gilbert's letter, and by the end it confirmed that Mattie should be arriving in Mt. Juliet by the end of the week. It was sooner than he had expected, but he guessed that Gilbert wanted to get his sister out of the town that seemed to be draining her very soul. He hoped that Tennessee would be a good fit for her, especially since he knew just how vastly different it was from the hot, humid landscape of Mississippi.

James continued to glance at the letter, his eyes roving over it for a second time to make sure that he didn't miss anything. Which meant that he *did* miss the large form that sprouted up in front of him, not noticing the man until it was too late, and his body plowed into something solid.

James' breath left him with a woosh, and he blinked around him in surprise. His heart sank when he found himself face to face with none other than Hubert Bird. James had to fight back a grimace when he realized who was before him, and Hubert greeted him with a lazy, malicious grin.

"Well hello James," Hubert drawled.

"Hubert," James returned with a tip of his head.

"Beautiful day," the other man surmised, looking around them.

James didn't return the forced platitudes, instead he just nodded at the man again. They stared at one another, each man sizing the other up as the silence between them drawled out. Both James and Hubert were ranchers, running the two largest plots in the county, respectively. Both had inherited their lands when they were quite young, but where James had poured himself into his work, doing whatever was required to make sure that his ranch was a success, the same could not be said for Hubert. And each of them resented the other for the hand that they'd been dealt, among other reasons.

"How are things going at your little ranch?" Hubert asked with a sneer.

They were about the same height, but somehow Hubert still managed to look down his nose at James, and it set his nerves on edge.

"Goin' good," James said with a grunt. "Planting is coming along nicely. And we're gonna have a lot of calves born this spring."

He threw in those jabs, knowing that a lot of Hubert's own cattle hadn't fallen pregnant over the last breeding season. James saw the other man's face darken, his desired effect. He usually wasn't so needlessly cruel, but Hubert was always his one exception.

They shared a few additional words before Hubert finally wished James a good day, in a tone that let James know the niceties were not at all sincere. Then, Hubert brushed past him and continued on the dusty path into Mt. Juliet. James' enjoyment of the fair weather had ebbed after running into Hubert, so he hurried his steps as he made his way home.

He attempted to push his thoughts away from Hubert Bird and the overlapping past that they shared, just as he tried to keep his mind from wandering to his late wife. It would only serve to sour his mood, and he did not want his daughter, Amy, to pick up on it.

When he finally arrived home, he was immediately greeted by the sound of giggling coming from the parlor room in the large farmhouse. A smile crept over James' face as he stalked through the halls, following the sound of laughter to where his daughter sat, playing with her current governess, Josie.

Josie glanced up at him as he walked into the room, her round face spreading into a warm, platonic smile. He had always liked Josie; she was a kind woman who Amy had taken to almost immediately. And while he was happy for her and her soon-to-be-husband, he was incredibly sad to see her go.

She stood up from the floor, brushing down the wrinkles in her dress before walking forward.

"She's been fed and should be ready to sleep within the next hour or two," Josie said with a smile.

James blinked at her in confusion, and she must have caught on to it because she laughed and shook her head at him.

"You gave me the evenin' off, remember?" Josie chuckled. "I have things to do for the wedding."

It all came flooding back to him, and he nodded his head at her.

"Right, slipped my mind," James grunted.

Amy looked at him, raising her arms in a request for him to hold her. Her tight, blonde ringlets shone in the golden sunlight that spilled through the window, and her soft brown eyes glittered with love when she looked at him. She resembled Ruth so much, that sometimes it hurt his heart to look at her. But that was something he would never let her know.

He picked up the small toddler and held her, bouncing her as he walked Josie to the door, said goodbye, and watched as she strolled down the lane and finally disappeared from sight. Turning back to the empty house, James let a curse fall from his lips. He still had plenty of chores to get done, and it was time to go out and start the evening feeding process.

He knew that Josie had said Amy would be ready for bed soon, and he wondered if perhaps he could coax her to fall asleep early. He strolled to her room and placed her in her small bed, but after about twenty minutes of pleading and coddling, he was forced to accept that his willful toddler was not quite ready to fall asleep.

An idea popped into his head, and he placed Amy back on his hip as he strode out of the house. Walking into the barn, he quickly spotted a wheelbarrow and filled it with loose straw. He patted it around, softening it some before placing Amy's tiny body inside.

James looked around him, before grabbing a dried corn husk. Handing it to the happily babbling child, she took it with glee and began playing with it as if it was a doll. James wheeled Amy around with him as he made his way through the various barns, buildings, and pastures to feed the animals. As dusk began to fall around them, he stood beside the wheelbarrow, and looked out at the grazing cattle as the sun set along the horizon behind them. Amy had her chubby toddler's hand wrapped around his finger as she sat watching the cows graze lazily with him.

It was a moment before he realized how silent she had fallen, and when he glanced over at her, he smiled when he found Amy dozing peacefully in the straw bed with the dried piece of corn cradled to her chest. His heart swelled with love as he looked upon his daughter, and he picked her up gently and held her close.

She stirred for only a moment as he walked back to the house, but he quickly eased her back to sleep and laid her gently upon her bed. He closed the door to her room with a soft sigh and walked by lantern light through the rest of the vacant, quiet home. And as he did, he sent up a prayer to God; that Mattie would fit in well in the quiet life that he and

Amy had worked so hard to carve for themselves, as they healed from the loss of Ruth.

Chapter Three

Mt. Juliet, Tennessee – April 1875

Mattie's face pressed against the cool glass of the train window as it rattled. She raised her hand, drawing shapes in her breath as it fogged up the pane. When she had left Bartlett, she had watched as the swamplands of Mississippi sped past her window, the sparsely growing bald cypress trees slowly transforming into rolling plains dotted with yellow wheat and wildflowers.

But now, large, lush green trees that Mattie couldn't place sped by the window as massive hills larger than anything she had ever seen stood in the distance, and she wondered how long it would be until they finally reached Mt. Juliet.

At the beginning of her journey, there had been a small, delicate kernel of hope unfurling in her chest. When Gilbert had told her of James' letter, he had said Mt. Juliet could be Mattie's fresh start. And the closer she got to her destination, the more she had felt that it might actually be true.

Now, however, as the hours had passed and the glamour of travel had worn off, she found herself dismally bored and her heart hammering with anticipation for the sight of her new home. She took her head away from the glass, sitting up a little straighter as she glanced around the rail car.

Sitting across the seat from her was a young couple with a small child. They'd boarded the train one town after Bartlett, and upon noticing that Mattie was sitting alone, had asked if they could sit with her. Mattie had quickly agreed, glad to have company for at least a little while.

The baby, who she'd learned was named Eleanor, and the child's mother, named Alice, had both fallen asleep some time ago. But now, as she looked up and locked eyes with an alert Eleanor cradled in her mother's lap, her face broke out in a smile.

The infant returned it with a gummy grin of her own, and Mattie puffed up her cheeks and crossed her eyes, causing the baby to laugh. Stirred by the baby's laughter, Alice jolted awake and blinked wearily around the cabin before her eyes focused on Matie.

"How long was I asleep?" She asked, looking around wide eyed at Mattie and her husband, who Mattie had learned was named Thomas.

"About an hour," Thomas answered her as he gave Eleanor an animated face as well, forcing another round of joyous giggles from the child.

"I wonder how long it will be," Alice muttered, leaning forward to look out the window.

They wouldn't be getting off at the same stop as Mattie, but staying on until they made it to Kentucky. When Mattie had met them, she had hoped that perhaps they were going to Mt. Juliet and she would already have a friend, but unfortunately that would not be the case. At any rate, she was happy to have had companions her first time travelling by train.

She knew they must be getting close to her destination; Gilbert had told her that it should take less than half a day to reach Mt. Juliet. And she knew they were quickly approaching that marker.

Turning back to the window, a small gasp escaped her, and she leaned her forehead against the glass in an effort to take in more of the sight before her. The tree line had finally broken, and not far in the distance, she could see a town taking shape. With each second, it grew larger, and the hazy shape of the buildings began to take form.

It appeared to be more than double the size of Bartlett, and for some reason that surprised her. Gilbert had told her Mt. Juliet was larger, but she hadn't imagined it would have been by this much. From what she could tell, the buildings were made of stone and wood, some of them painted to bring the town to life. And maybe it was the rose-colored glasses of hope, but Mattie couldn't help but feel as if Mt. Juliet was welcoming her in and inviting her to find a home there.

"This must be it," Mattie whispered reverently, and Alice pressed forward to get a glimpse of the town as well.

"Oh Mattie," she squealed happily, "it's so quaint!"

The brakes of the train started to squeal as they began to slow, and Mattie's heart began racing as anticipation coursed through her. She tried, for what she imagined was the thousandth time, to picture what James looked like now. But no matter how much effort she exerted, the only image she could conjure was of the wiry teen who had just begun filling out before he'd left Mississippi.

She had found him handsome even then, and as Mattie smoothed down her skirts and ran her hands over her caramel hair to tidy it, she couldn't help but wonder if she would find him handsome still. She had never admitted it to anyone back then, but when they were children, she had fancied James quite a lot.

When Gilbert had first told Mattie about the offer of being James' governess, she had still been too lost in her grief to think of her old affections. But as the week had worn on, her departure date looming ever closer, that small kernel of hope had also begun to light things within her that had been dormant ever since that fateful night at the Bartlett Town Hall. And she had begun to get curious about James Murphy once more, a man that she had not seen in well over ten years, but who she would now be residing with.

Mattie knew that if her old crush reared its head while she was living with James it would only serve to complicate things. She had arrived at that conclusion early in her journey, when she had first boarded the train, and had squelched the thoughts every time they had risen. But now that she was closer than ever to seeing him again after all those years, she was finding it more difficult to banish those fanciful notions.

Steam floated past the window as the train finally came to a full stop, and the smoke momentarily clouded her view of the red brick train station they had pulled into. A few other passengers stood and began collecting their things, prompting Mattie to stand as well.

She bade goodbye to Thomas, Alice, and Eleanor and wished them well on the remainder of their travels. She stepped into the aisle with a twinge of sadness that she would likely never see them again. Nerves washed through her, and she began tapping her foot as she waited impatiently for the doors to open so she could start her search for James Murphy.

A car attendant appeared; his suit still pressed to perfection despite the hours of travel. He rushed forward and opened the door for them, and Mattie followed a small family as they rushed forward and stepped through the doors onto the platform. There were plenty of people milling about, some waiting for travelers in other cars, others waiting to board the train themselves.

She blinked in the bright light of the early evening sun, glancing from face to face as people walked past her, none of them even remotely familiar. A split second of panic rushed through her as she continued to look around and James was nowhere to be found. She realized that there was every possibility that they could run smack into each other and not realize it.

However would they find each other in this crowd, especially after all this time? Just as her worries were beginning to crescendo, a path opened through the small crowd, and all of her fears were dashed. Because there he was, standing on the platform with the sun shining down on him like a spotlight.

Mattie knew him immediately, and her heart hammered at the sight. His dark brown hair was longer now, swept back into a bun. And his face was bearded, where the last time she had seen him, he was clean-shaven. But even at a distance Mattie could see the same bright blue eyes, the exact shade as the vibrant sky above, framed with the long dark lashes that she remembered.

She watched as James eyed the crowd, his eyes roving over the people exiting each car. When they got to her, they swept right over her, and confusion rushed through her before she realized that he did not recognize her. He had been grown enough when he had left Bartlett that, while he had definitely filled out and changed since she had last seen him, he was still recognizable. But she had been just a child. An awkward and ugly one at that, so she couldn't blame him for not knowing her.

Mattie stepped forward, making her way through the crowd toward James. As she approached, his eyes landed on her again, and this time they did not move away. At first, they watched her with curiosity, and her heartbeat sped up the longer his gaze lingered.

Someone walked in between them, obscuring her view of him, and by the time they moved, and she was able to see his face once more, recognition had finally lit up his face. She closed the final few feet between them with a few, quick steps, and as she stood in front of him her breath began to come more rapidly as another bout of nerves washed over her.

"Mattie!" James exclaimed, his jaw popping open with surprise.

"Hello James," she greeted him with what she hoped was a polite smile, not wanting her anxiety to show through.

His voice was deeper than it had been the last she had seen him, and it washed over her like honey. She found herself wanting to lean in closer to him the more that he spoke.

"You look quite well. How were your travels?" His gaze was intense as it regarded her, and her cheeks flushed with pleasure at the compliment.

"They went well, thank you. Quite uneventful," Mattie gave him another small smile as she reminded herself that feeding into James' attractiveness could have disastrous consequences for her, and she shook herself internally to banish all thoughts on the matter.

James nodded and then looked up and down the train. Finally spotting the luggage car, he glanced back at her.

"I assume you had a trunk?"

"One steamer," she replied.

James simply dipped his head in acknowledgement of her answer before turning and striding confidently toward one of the porters by the luggage car. He did not motion for her to follow, but she did anyway, making sure to stay in the path his large body was carving through the crowd.

The porter looked up immediately and smiled at them, before beginning to help them locate her trunk.

"My carriage is this way," James said to the man when her luggage was secured, pointing toward the front of the station.

The porter nodded, pushing the trolley her trunk was loaded onto as he and Mattie followed James through the crowd. She tried not to stare as she exited the station and finally caught her first full, unobstructed view of Mt. Juliet. The dirt road that led through it was well maintained, and the buildings, while a little more worn up close than they had appeared at a distance, still gleamed in the early evening sun.

Mattie watched from a few feet back as the porter and James hoisted her trunk into the back of a modest wagon strapped to a large, brown workhorse. Once it was secured, James thanked the porter and sent him on his way before turning to Mattie.

"That everythin', then?" He asked her, his deep voice barely more than a grunt.

"Yes."

James nodded and then extended his hand, helping her up the two small steps. Mattie worked her hardest not to focus on the warmth of his hand, or the flush that it sent to her cheeks. Once she was situated on the long bench seat, he climbed the steps and plopped down next to her. Despite the sun beating down on them, he was close enough that she could still feel the warmth radiating off his body.

James reached forward, grabbed the reins of the horse, and gave them a quick, swift snap. As the large creature pushed forward, James guiding it through the roads of the town, Mattie took the opportunity to take in even more of her new home.

"What do you think?" James asked after a few moments and Mattie turned, finding him casting her hurried glances.

"It's much bigger than Bartlett," she said, and he grunted an affirmation. "The buildings are nicer, too. And there seems to be less dust."

"Less dust, more mud." He murmured. "But you're right about the buildings. At least this place doesn't seem like it was laid out by someone who'd drank an entire bottle of whiskey."

Mattie laughed at his candor, and another silence fell between them. But this time it wasn't an awkward one. She was content for a few minutes, to allow only the clopping sounds of the horse's hooves in the dirt, and the people bustling through the town to surround them.

Eventually, they reached the last row of buildings and the road began leading them through fields and pastures.

"How far away is your house?" Mattie asked him.

"Just another mile or two up the way," James said, keeping his eyes focused on the dirt road before them.

"Do you like living here?" Mattie asked him, hoping to get a conversation going between the two of them.

"I like it well enough," James said, his tone short and clipped.

He cast another quick glance in her direction, and he must have noticed her disappointment at his short response, because he continued only a moment later.

"I think you'll like it here, too." James offered, "Or at least, I hope you will."

Mattie blushed slightly, and then it was her turn to simply nod and not reply. She wasn't sure what would be an appropriate response to that. In the distance, a house began to take shape on the horizon.

"Is that it?" She asked, pointing at the structure.

"That's the hand's house," James answered. "My ranch hand, Elmer, lives there. It's where the beginning of my property starts."

"How large is your property?" Mattie's voice was wrought with curiosity.

"A couple thousand acres."

She started at his answer, not expecting it. She knew that his ranch was large, Gilbert had told her as much. But she hadn't quite expected it to be such a massive undertaking.

"That's quite a lot," Mattie couldn't help herself. "You manage it between just you and Elmer?"

"For the most part," James said with a nod. "When the busy season starts, we hire a few extra hands here and there. But we handle most of it."

Mattie stared at him for a moment in awe. She could not imagine how much work he performed.

"There are plenty of barns," he continued, not noticing, or not caring that she was still staring at him in surprise. He was pointing off to the side of the wagon as they jostled over the road, and Mattie squinted, spotting random dots in the distance that she assumed were the buildings he was indicating. "That way if any of the cattle or horses need shelter, they usually aren't far off no matter what pasture they're in. And then if the weather gets bad enough, we can also wrangle them in as much as we can."

Mattie just nodded, still staring off into the distance. A large, brown cow mooed at them as they rolled past, snapping her out of it.

"I bet it's quiet out here," she surmised, and James nodded his ascent. "Gilbert and I lived very close to town. Right on the edge, in fact. So, while we didn't get all the bustle of Bartlett proper, we weren't far removed from everything. This feels…"

Her mind scrambled for the right word, but James ended up offering it to her instead.

"Solitary."

She nodded before realizing he may think she meant that as a snub. Mattie hurried to amend her statement.

"Solitary but peaceful," she said in a rush, and was rewarded with the flash of an understanding smile from James.

Their conversation died out once more, and this time it didn't pick back up. As Mattie took in her surroundings, she tried to imagine what it was going to be like living this far from town but found that she still couldn't quite comprehend it.

Finally, another house came into view. This one much larger than the home James said Elmer lived in and Mattie's mouth popped open in awe as she gaped at it. It was beautiful; red brick and two stories high. Large windows paned the front of it, and they glimmered in the evening light. The shutters and trim were carefully painted in gleaming white, only serving to add to the house's charm. The wrap around porch not only had a wooden swing, that even at a distance you could tell had been built with care, but three large rocking chairs sitting side by side.

She thought back to her and Gilbert's house in Bartlett. With Gilbert's relative success as a cobbler, their home had been one of the finer ones in their small town. But James' made theirs look shabby by comparison.

"It's beautiful," she said, her voice low and reverent as they approached.

"It was my grandparents," he explained as he expertly guided the horse up the drive that looped around the front of the home.

A large young man with tanned, freckled skin and bright red hair came around the side of the house as they approached. He grinned widely when his eyes landed on Mattie, and then dipped into a low, exaggerated bow.

"Well, hello," the man said as he rose from his bow, his smile so large that Mattie was afraid it would split his cheeks. "This must be the darling Miss Mattie I've heard so much about."

He bounded forward, and something about his energy and his dancing, dark-brown eyes reminded Mattie of an overly excited puppy.

"Elmer," James warned as the young man approached, coming around the back of the carriage and stopping by her steamer trunk.

"What?" Elmer cocked an eyebrow at James, "all I did was greet her. And let her know that you haven't stopped jabberin' about her arrival for days."

James rolled his eyes at his ranch hand as they both reached into the wagon and lifted her large trunk. Mattie chuckled at them both, deciding right then and there that she liked Elmer.

The two men bantered back and forth as they carried her trunk the few steps across the yard and into the home beyond. Mattie followed closely behind, listening to them as they went.

As she stepped onto the porch, her boots clacking against the wooden planks, a breeze kicked up around her skirts and caused the rocking chairs to creak in welcome. Mattie smiled softly as she pushed open the door, and the sense of awe washed over her all over again.

The scent of freshly polished wood rose to greet her as soon as she stepped into the shade of the house, and Mattie stopped to inhale deeply. A large, gleaming staircase stood just inside the door, and a frazzled looking woman with her hands on her hips glared down at James and Elmer from the very top stair.

"Shhh," she hushed them, rushing down to the main floor. "I just got Amy down for a nap and your yappin' will wake her right back up."

James and Elmer's voices dropped, but they didn't stop bickering, carrying on instead at a whisper. The young woman stopped before Mattie, smiling kindly at her. She had mousy brown hair, and plain features. But her light, honey-colored eyes shone with a kindness that lit her up from the inside out, making Mattie unable to look away from her.

"You must be Mattie," the woman said, extending her hand for Mattie to shake. "I'm Josie, Amy's prior governess."

"A pleasure to meet you," Mattie answered, shaking the woman's proffered hand.

"I'm sure this is all a bit much," Josie gestured to the large house around them, and Mattie nodded. "I'll give you a tour while the little one naps and save you from those two upstairs. They bicker more than a married couple."

Josie shot an admonishing look in the way that James and Elmer had disappeared, before looping her arm through Mattie's and leading her toward an open doorway. The house was finely decorated, with an abundance of fireplaces, bookshelves, and stuffed chairs and couches.

When Gilbert had told her she would be living on a ranch, she had assumed that it would have been a small, family affair. But she was very quickly realizing that those assumptions had been quite wrong. With every new room they came across, she could envision her life here more and more clearly.

In the plush reading chair by the window in the drawing room, she imagined herself curled up with a book. She could see herself learning to play piano, tending the charming garden she caught a glimpse of from one of the windows. She imagined a small, adorable child tottering after her through the halls while they played and laughed. Mattie could see it all, and so much more as she and Josie roved through the rooms arm in arm.

"James must be quite successful," Mattie stated, glancing around her at all the beautiful furnishings.

"Oh, yes. He has the biggest ranch in three counties," Josie explained as they walked from a cozy reading room that held a piano to the kitchen. "The only person that even comes close to it is Mr. Bird."

The woman's voice hitched slightly at the other man's name, and Mattie made a mental note to figure out what that was about.

"James' letter to my brother said you were gettin' married?" Mattie asked, and the other woman blushed with joy as she showed her around the kitchen.

"Oh yes," Josie said, "my Jessup is a tailor and owns his own shop here in town."

"Congratulations!" Mattie smiled.

"Why thank you," Josie beamed. "I am very excited."

They continued their tour, and with each passing room Mattie felt more and more like she could be happy there. When they finally made their way upstairs, their first stop was at a bedroom. James stood in the center of it with Elmer nowhere to be found, and the first thing Mattie spotted was her steamer trunk resting at the foot of an incredibly comfortable looking bed.

"This will be your room," James said, holding his arms wide and indicating the space around him.

Mattie stepped forward, taking it all in. It was larger than her room back in Bartlett, and as with the rest of the house, it was much more finely furnished. The curtains were white, with small blue flowers stitched onto them, and they fluttered in the breeze coming through the open window.

The swish of the fabric put Mattie at ease as her eyes raked over everything else in the room. All of it was in the same white and blue tones, making the space seem tranquil and welcoming. She loved every bit of it.

"Thank you," Mattie said, looking at James, who held her gaze and gave her a slight nod.

Their stare lasted a little longer than felt necessary, and the intensity of his eyes as he regarded her made heat creep into her cheeks.

"There's one more person for you to meet," came Josie's voice from behind her, causing Mattie to eagerly divert her attention.

Josie gestured for Mattie to follow, and then they both turned and strode from the room. They crept down the hall, their footsteps padding on the rug that ran the length of the hallway.

"This right here is James' room," she said, pointing to the door that was cattycorner from Mattie's.

They arrived at another door two doors down from Mattie's own. It was partially ajar, and Josie turned to her with a smile.

"And this," Josie said, her voice lowered to just above a whisper, "is Amy's room."

Josie pushed open the door, and Mattie followed her into the room. There was a small, wooden child's bed on the far side underneath one of the windows. Josie stopped and motioned her forward, and Mattie padded across the plank wood floors with soft steps.

The sleeping child was beautiful, with round, rosy cheeks, shiny blonde curls, and a lovely, pouted mouth. Her dark lashes rested on her cheeks, and Mattie couldn't help but smile down at the small human softly slumbering before her.

As they exited once more, heading back to her now vacant bedroom to give her a chance to unpack, the small kernel of hope that had begun unfurling in Mattie's chest was now growing at full force.

Chapter Four

James placed a kiss to the top of Amy's head where she sat on the floor, playing with wooden blocks as Mattie watched over her. Satisfied that the two seemed to be getting on, James told Mattie he was going out to start his evening chores and strode from the room. Once he pushed open the screen door and stepped out onto the porch, he stood for a moment in the fresh air, inhaling deeply to calm his nerves.

From the moment his eyes had landed on Mattie at the train station, his entire body had been wound tight and he had felt restless. When he had first saw her approaching him on the platform, he had had no idea who she was. All he had seen was an outrageously beautiful woman approaching him, and it had confused and intrigued him.

But then, she had gotten close enough for him to notice her eyes, their light green hue with tiny flecks of gold the exact mirror of Gilbert's. He also noted the hollowness of her cheeks, and the dark circles beneath her eyes. Exactly what he would expect for a woman who had spent the last six months in hiding after a failed engagement.

The realization of who she was had hit him like a punch to the chest, and dread had followed quickly after. When he and his best friend had been writing each other to discuss Mattie's arrival, he had assured Gilbert that she would be safe with him, and that James would steer clear of any romantic notions when it came to Gilbert's younger sister. But when James had made those promises, he had not anticipated how much she would have changed since the last time he had seen her.

With his thoughts still muddled, James stepped off the porch and began walking across the yard toward the stables where the horses were kept. He hoped it would do his body, and his mind, some good to focus on his work for a while.

As he approached the barn, the sound of hooves on the ground rose up to meet him, and he turned to find Elmer approaching atop his white and brown speckled mare. He pulled on the reins when he arrived, his tanned, freckled face breaking into a wide exuberant grin.

"She getting settled in?" Elmer asked as he climbed down from his horse.

"She is," James answered with a nod, the two men walking into the stables shoulder to shoulder as was their routine. "Amy woke up not long after you left, seemed to take to Mattie almost immediately."

"Yeah, well," Elmer said with a shrug as he opened the door to the tack room and selected two pitchforks before handing one to James. "Amy likes anyone. She's the happiest baby I've ever met."

"How many babies have you met?" James chuckled and arched an eyebrow. "You don't have any siblings or friends."

"Don't need 'em. Not when I've got you."

James laughed despite himself, always amused by the younger man's antics. He had been a bit reluctant to hire Elmer, the boy had been so young when he first approached him. But he'd proven himself time and time again, and James now couldn't quite imagine running things without him. He had been more than happy to offer Elmer the other house on his property as a part of his payment, and even more excited when Elmer got engaged to a sweet girl from town named Laurah. Their wedding would be coming up in the next few months, and James made a mental note to increase Elmer's pay as a gift for the happy couple.

They fell into the easy rhythm that they had cultivated through the last year of working with each other. While one mucked out the stalls for the final time, the other filled the troughs with water and hay before whistling to call the horses in. They allowed them to eat as they started with the rest of their feedings, moving on to the hogs, and then eventually the cattle. The cattle were the easiest since they spent most of their time grazing. But it was still always an endeavor to make sure that their watering trough was clear and filled.

The sun crept closer to the horizon and then finally disappeared entirely behind the trees, streaking the dusk sky with orange and pink. When they finally finished everything up, he and Elmer bade each other goodnight, and James watched as Elmer rode his horse back across the pasture toward his home. James locked up the stable on his own before turning and following the same path he had taken earlier to make his way back to the house.

When he walked through the door, an odd smell greeted him. He scrunched his nose against the assault on his senses, following it all the way into the kitchen. When he crossed the threshold, he paused for a moment to take in the sight with amusement.

Amy was sitting secured at the table, babbling and watching with rapt attention as Mattie stood at the stove. There was smoke pouring from the skillet she stood in front of, and from that angle James found it impossible to tell what she was trying to cook. But whatever it was, it wasn't hard to figure out that it was well and truly burnt.

With a chuckle, he walked into the room. Amy noticed him first, her chubby toddler cheeks dimpling as she broke into a wild grin.

"Papa," she squealed at the sight of him, clapping excitedly.

"Hello darlin'," he smiled back at her and kissed the top of her head.

The commotion grabbed Mattie's attention, and she whirled to face him. Her beautiful features frozen with horror when she found him standing in the kitchen as she burnt supper.

"James," Mattie began stammering, "I'm so sorry. I started dinner and got distracted by playing with Amy, and then it all started smoking, and I…"

"Breathe, Mattie," James chuckled as he took a few quick steps to stand beside her.

Her cheeks were flushed with embarrassment, and there was a small part of him that hated that he noticed how pretty she looked. A few copper strands of hair had escaped from the plait she wore down her back, and he was shocked to find that he itched to reach up and tuck it behind her ear.

"It's alright," James said, clearing his throat and banishing those thoughts.

Mattie waved her hands in front of her face, clearing some of the smoke out of the way. James reached forward, moving to grab the skillet from the stove at the same time that Mattie did. Both of their hands came down on the handle, his large, calloused fingers wrapping around hers.

A warmth spread through him at the feel of her hand underneath his. He'd felt it earlier, too, when he had helped her into the carriage. James had wanted to recoil then, feeling as if noticing the way another woman's hand felt was a betrayal to Ruth. This time he did not allow himself to linger.

Mattie's eyes darted up to meet his when their hands made contact, shining with surprise. James wrenched back his hand at the same time as she pulled away. The pan fell to the floor with a clatter, the hot oil and contents splashing about, causing both James and Mattie to jump back to avoid being splattered.

Startled by the noise and all the sudden movement, Amy began to wail. James whirled to face his daughter, her cheeks already ruddy with her distress.

"I'm so sorry," Mattie began, pulling a rag off the counter and immediately crouching down. "I'm really making a mess of things on my very first day."

"It's quite alright," James said, keeping his voice light as he rushed forward to pull the squalling toddler into his arms. "I'll take care of Amy if you want to finish up with this?"

Mattie looked at him, her face still flushed with worry, but she nodded. He wanted, for just a moment, to stay and soothe her, too. She looked embarrassed and concerned. James felt as if he could see the doubt in herself shimmering just behind the depths of her eyes. But he couldn't concern himself with that now. Not while Amy was upset.

He turned and strode from the room, reminding himself that not only would getting too close to Mattie break his promise to Gilbert, but it would also serve to practically spit on the memory of his wife. She had only been gone two years, and the first woman that darkened their doorstep he was going to find himself enamored by? He wouldn't allow her memory to be so easily pushed to the side.

James bounced Amy as he walked, shushing and cooing to her all the while. He took her to the reading room, the one where the piano stood nestled between two bookcases. His daughter loved to hear him sing, and it was one of the few things that had an almost perfect success rate when it came to calming her down.

He plopped Amy onto the bench as he pulled it out, and then sat beside her. Already knowing what was coming,

Amy's previously torturous wails began to quiet, turning into small, tiny whimpers. James flexed his fingers, warming them up slightly before spreading them across the keys.

As he pressed down and the very first chord filled the air, Amy's tears began to dry entirely. His fingers danced along the keys quickly, and as he fell into the tempo of the song he began to sing. His daughter sat beside him, looking up at him with a wide, toothy grin, enraptured by the music. And James lost himself to it as well, letting the song overtake him as the words belted from his chest.

By the time the final chords were struck, and the echo of the notes died out, Amy no longer showed any signs of her previous distress save for the small paths her tears had carved down her cheeks.

"That was beautiful," came a voice from behind him, and he turned to find Mattie standing in the door frame.

"Thank you," James muttered, suddenly embarrassed.

James didn't particularly enjoy playing piano for people, and he definitely did not sing in front of them. He used to wait until Josie had left the house for the night before playing for Amy, or would sing to her when it was only the two of them outside doing chores or playing in the grass. Ruth had been his only real exception.

But with the way that Mattie was looking at him, eyes filled with tenderness and a delicate flush to her cheeks, he couldn't help but wonder if he eventually wouldn't mind making an exception for her too.

He tried to shake the thought. He tried as hard as he could to push it back into the farthest recesses of his mind. But he'd be damned if the thought also didn't make his heart jump, just a little bit.

THE GOVERNESS AND THE COWBOY'S PROMISE

Chapter Five

Mt. Juliet, Tennessee

Mattie blinked hazily as the early morning light began to stream through her bedroom window. With a low groan she rolled onto her back and threw her arm over her face, trying to block out the light. She hadn't even been here an entire day, and already she had managed to burn dinner, drop it on the floor, upset Amy, and embarrass James by hearing him sing. And now, she would be expected to get up and do it all over again.

Pushing herself up to a sitting position, she sat in the center of her bed and tried to gather her thoughts. Even for the few hours yesterday when she had been left to oversee things while James finished up his work with Elmer, she had found it exhausting. And she was finding it hard to believe that this was to be her life now, at least for the foreseeable future.

Mattie had never realized just how much Gilbert had sheltered her or how much he had protected her from working too hard. But now, with the previous day fresh in her mind and the prospect of Amy waking up at any moment to start her day, she was suddenly very aware that she would have her work cut out for her.

She finally worked up the courage to climb out of bed entirely, standing and stretching her arms over her head to limber up her body a bit. She had slept soundly and had been pleasantly surprised to find that the bed was as comfortable as it had looked. It was a sad endeavor to have to leave it.

Crossing the room, she stopped in front of the armoire and began rifling through it to select what she would wear that day. Her selection of clothing wasn't vast, just a handful of skirts, blouses, and gowns to choose from. But Gilbert had ensured that the clothes she had made were of quality material, so she was proud of each bit that she owned.

She took her time dressing, though trying as hard as she could to convince herself that she wasn't putting in that little extra effort to tighten her corset, and to ensure there were no wrinkles in her blouse. But, if perhaps she pinched her cheeks to bring color to them or bit down on her lips to redden them, all with the thought that James might enjoy it if she looked pretty—well no one but her needed to know.

She combed through her hair before beginning to work it into a braid. And while she did so, Mattie allowed her mind to wonder. She thought back to the day before, and to all the ways in which she had interacted with James and the ways in which he had interacted with Amy.

Mattie had to admit that she did not know the man that he had become. When they had been younger, James had been quick to laugh. He and Gilbert had always been pranking one another, and running amok throughout the town when they weren't working. But this James? He was more somber and intense.

Thinking about what it must have been like for him to lose Ruth in childbirth and then to look after Amy every day. She would be a living reminder of his pain, and Mattie could not blame him for allowing it to harden his heart and make him weary. She had to admit, though, that it suited him—the long hair, the beard, and the slightly gruff but somehow comforting demeanor. Mattie found herself intrigued by the thought of getting to know this version of James much better.

She took a final look at herself in the mirror, pleased with the results, before making her bed and turning to walk out of her room. In the hallway, she paused just outside of Amy's bedroom. Pushing open the door slightly, she peaked inside. The young child was still sleeping soundly, but Mattie wondered exactly how long that would last.

While Mattie adored children, she was only just realizing that she hadn't had much exposure to them, and perhaps she wasn't as prepared for the role of 'governess' as she had thought she'd be. When Gilbert had first told her about it, she had assumed her natural, caregiving instincts would take over. But in a very short amount of time, she had found there was much more to caring for a child than instinct.

The sound of someone clearing their throat behind her made her jump, and she was only just able to keep herself from gasping with surprise. She whirled in the direction of the sound, finding James standing in the now open doorway to his bedroom.

"James," Mattie whispered, shutting Amy's door just a bit more to block out the sound from where she stood, talking to James. "Sorry, I didn't know you were standing there."

"Nothin' to apologize for, I just walked out." James gave her a shy smile, and her cheeks flushed.

"I'll go get breakfast started," Mattie said, dipping her head and shuffling past him.

She darted down the stairs, unsure of why she was overcome by a sudden bout of nerves. By the time she made it to the kitchen, the somersaults her stomach were performing had died down marginally. She rifled through the ingredients in the pantry and came up with a quick idea for breakfast before getting it started.

She distracted herself with the steps of her breakfast preparations, hoping that James would busy himself until the food had been fully prepared. But, when a few moments later he walked into the room with a sleepy Amy perched on his hip, she realized that those hopes had been in vain.

Mattie waited as he sat Amy in her dining chair, securing the small table before her. She could hear James murmuring to the toddler in a low tone, coaxing her into waking up fully.

"That is a fine chair," Mattie said to coax a bit of conversation. "Did you make it?"

"I did," James replied with a small smile as he looked down at his daughter. "Ruth had her eye on one for a while, but none of them matched exactly what she wanted. So, I built her one she adored."

Mattie turned to watch him for a moment, taking in the almost reverent way he spoke about his late wife. He seemed to realize exactly what he had said and whom he had been talking about a moment after the words left his lips, and his face drained slightly of color. He cleared his throat once, and then turned his attention back to Amy, effectively shutting Mattie out.

She turned back to her task at hand, losing herself in the food preparations. When everything was finally done, she placed the eggs, potatoes, and the strawberries she had been shocked to find so early in the season into serving dishes and set them on the table before James. He eyed the spread hungrily before bringing his gaze up to meet Mattie's.

"Thank you," he murmured.

"You're most welcome."

She took the seat across from him, with Amy sitting in between them. For a moment, she found herself unsure of how to proceed. Did she feed Amy with James sitting right there? Or would he expect her to do it? How involved did he want her to be when he was around? Mattie knew that some fathers did not have any interest in child rearing, often dismissing even the most menial tasks as women's work. But from what she had observed so far, James was a rather hands on father. So, she didn't know how he would want to handle this.

Luckily, she did not have to ponder for long. Almost immediately James piled large heapings onto his plate and began to feed small bites to the toddler in between his own mouthfuls. Mattie readied her own dish and began eating, satisfied at the success of this meal, especially when compared to the disaster that dinner the night prior had been. As they ate, with Amy babbling happily to fill the silence, an idea struck Mattie.

"Would you be able to take me on a tour of the property today?" She asked James, and he pulled his eyes up from his plate of food to hold her stare.

"Today?" He clarified, his brow furrowing in thought.

Maddie nodded at him, eagerly awaiting his answer. If she was going to live there for God knows how long, it would likely be for the best that she knew whatever she could about what surrounded them.

"I don't think I can today," James answered after a moment's pause. "I have to head out to one of the far pastures, to repair a fence. It'll likely take me all day."

His eyes roved over her face, and Mattie's disappointment must have shown, because a moment later he said in a rush, "I can ask Elmer, though. I'm sure he'd be more than happy to get out of the hard work to show you around."

Mattie's spirits lifted a bit as she recalled the young, bright haired man she'd met yesterday. It may not be the same as spending the day with James, but Elmer's happy demeanor might be just the thing that she and Amy needed.

"What do you say, Amy?" Mattie cooed, turning her attention to the toddler whose face was smeared with strawberry. "Want to go on an adventure?"

"Venture!" Amy echoed, squealing excitedly, and forcing a laugh from both adults at the table.

They finished up their breakfast quickly, and then James kissed Amy before telling Mattie that he'd have Elmer ready the wagon and be up shortly. Mattie nodded, and then hurried to clear away and clean the dishes before rushing upstairs to get Amy ready for the day as well. Right as she finished getting the squirming toddler into her clothes, there was a loud knock against the screen door, announcing Elmer's arrival.

She swung Amy around, the small child giggling excitedly before Mattie plopped her on her hip and then strode down the stairs and toward the door. Elmer stood on the other side of it, a broad smile on his face.

"Mornin' Mattie," he said, before waving at Amy.

"Good morning," Mattie smiled at him, taking hold of Amy's hand, and waving it back at Elmer.

She stepped out onto the porch, and a slight breeze greeted her, ruffling the hem of her dress. The Tennessee day was warm, but it was nothing compared to the heat and humidity of Mississippi, and she found herself grateful for the reprieve. The same wagon that James had used to retrieve her the day before sat beside the house, hooked up to the same massive, brown work horse.

Elmer patted the animal affectionately as they walked past it toward the wagon seat before extending a hand to Mattie and helping her up into the bench. She placed Amy on her lap, bouncing the toddler excitedly as they waited for Elmer to climb aboard and lead them away.

As Elmer snapped the reins, spurring the horse into action, he began chatting excitedly. He told her all about the different pastures, when they were used and why, and all the comings and goings of the ranch that he and James operated.

Mattie listened intently, trying to keep up with Elmer's fast, excited speech, and not become too distracted by the infinite beauty around them. She was unsure of how long they remained like that, riding merrily together as Elmer talked. All Mattie knew was that with each passing moment, she fell more in love with the land on which she now lived; feeling a connection to the large, forested hills in the distance and the softly rolling pastures in between that she had never really felt in Bartlett.

By the time they made their final loop around, the sun was beating down overhead, and Amy had begun to nod off against Mattie's chest, and she cradled the young child against her. When the carriage finally rolled to a stop in front of the house, Elmer helped her down as she carried the toddler gently, trying as hard as she could to not wake her.

"Thank you, Elmer," Mattie said quietly. "For showing us around today."

Elmer raised a hand, waving off her thanks. "Don't mention it. The company was much better than if I was out working with cranky James."

Mattie chuckled as Elmer glanced at the sky, marking the position of the sun.

"Speaking of," Elmer said, "I should be getting back out there. He's likely cursin' up a storm by now. Have a good day, Mattie."

She told him to do the same as he climbed back into the wagon to bring it around to the stables, and then Mattie turned and strode into the house. Amy was still sleeping peacefully in Mattie's arms as she made her way up the stairs and then laid Amy softly in her bed. The toddler's small, peaceful snores filled the room as Mattie tucked her in, and she stood for a moment watching her as she slept, wondering what Amy might be dreaming about.

Her stomach gave a quick, swift growl that brought her out of her thoughts, reminding her that she would need to go into the kitchen to put together a quick snack. Amy would likely be cranky when she awoke, and would want something to eat.

Mattie turned, fully prepared to stride from the room, but the rays of sun that poured in through the window caught onto something across the room, making it flash. Mattie turned to look at it, spotting a small, silver jewelry box atop Amy's dresser. She stood for a moment, simply staring at it before curiosity got the better of her and she found herself across the room in a few quick steps.

Mattie stood before the dresser, staring down at the box. It had been polished meticulously, causing the metal to gleam in the sunlight. There was a small voice in the back of her mind telling her that this was not her business, but she quickly shushed it up. Reaching forward, Mattie ran her fingertips over the delicate box before lifting the lid. It was lined with soft, red velvet, and nestled inside was a beautiful silver hair pin in the shape of an intricate butterfly wing. It was stunning, and the sight of it stole Mattie's breath.

Without thinking, she reached up and plucked the beautiful pin from its box and pulled it out. She turned it this way and that in the sunlight, watching the way it glinted off the polished silver. Curious of how it would look tucked into her golden-brown strands, she reached up and placed it securely atop her braid. She then took a step with the intent of walking over to the large mirror that hung on the far wall of Amy's bedroom.

But the moment her foot made contact with the floorboard beneath it, a loud, riotous creak filled the room. Mattie winced, taking her foot back but it was already too late. Amy startled awake, a cry falling from her lips.

"There, there, sweet girl," Mattie cooed, rushing over to the child's bedside.

Amy cried harder, holding her hands out in front of her in a request for Mattie to pick her up. She did, cradling the child to her chest as she soothed her. It took a while, but eventually Amy's cries began to lessen, and she slowly drifted back to sleep. Once again, Mattie laid Amy atop her mattress, she straightened herself before backing out quietly from Amy's room. She hurried down the hall and then the stairs, before going into the kitchen to eat a quick snack and then begin the preparations for a full dinner.

She ate a large piece of bread, with a little bit of butter, which helped stifle the growling of her stomach. Then, with that satisfied, she began rifling through the pantry to decide what to make for their evening meal. She lost herself in her work, singing quietly as she went. Every so often she would pause and listen for any sound floating down the stairs that indicated Amy had woken up.

When she did, Mattie rushed upstairs to retrieve her, before placing her on the floor in the kitchen to play with her blocks as Mattie finished up. It felt like no time at all that she was taking the last of dinner off the stove and setting it on the table when James walked in the door.

Her eyes darted up immediately when she heard the screen door open, and through the window she could see that the sun was now slowly sinking toward the horizon, marking the time as mid-evening. She couldn't quite believe how quickly the day had passed.

"Hello little one," James said with a smile as he walked into the room, his eyes on Amy.

The child greeted her father exuberantly, immediately raising her hands for him to hold her, which he did gladly. He cooed to Amy, the toddler babbling at him happily before he turned his gaze back to Mattie.

"Did you have a good time on the tour?" He asked, cocking his head in question.

"We did. Elmer about talked our ears off though," Mattie said, crossing the kitchen and taking her seat.

James secured Amy in her chair before taking his own, chuckling all the while at what Mattie had said.

"He's good for that," he admitted as he scooted up to the table.

"He's a nice boy, though." Mattie admitted, thinking again of Elmer's easy smile and jovial laugh.

"Can't argue with you about that," James said, eyeing the food that she had laid out on the table.

Mattie had been determined to make up for the disaster that had been dinner the night before, and she was proud of the food she had prepared. She had even gone as far as to bake a pie with the leftover fruit from earlier that morning. She had heard Elmer say that the mild winter had caused the strawberries to ripen quicker this year, and she was grateful for it as the smell of the pie she had baked filled the air.

"Looks great, Mattie," James admitted as he grabbed a plate and began to place food upon it.

They chatted as they ate, Mattie asking him about his day and what all they had done to mend the pasture fence. She found herself fascinated by life on the ranch, and the more

James filled her in on what it required to keep this place afloat, the more she became in awe of him and of Elmer.

It felt like no time at all that the meal was finished and Mattie realized it was time for pie.

"Now I have a real treat for you," Mattie said with a smile as she pushed herself back from the table and stood.

She began walking toward the counter on the far end of the kitchen where she had sat the dish to cool, but James' voice brought her up short.

"Mattie, what is in your hair?"

At first Mattie was confused, wondering what he could be talking about. When he had spoken, his tone had been gruff, hardened in a way that it hadn't been just moments before. But then she recalled the hair pin from earlier in the day, the one she had placed in her hair before Amy had become fussy. Color rose in her cheeks as she turned to face him.

"Oh," her hand fluttered up to the back of her head, picking the pin out of where it was nestled at the top of her braid. "I saw this earlier in Amy's room, and I didn't think…"

James stood abruptly, knocking his chair back from the table and interrupting her.

"So, you thought that you would just what? Wear it?" He stepped toward her, reaching out quickly, and plucking the hair pin from between Mattie's fingers. "This was not yours to wear, Mattie."

James' face was flushed as a barrage of emotions flickered across it. Mattie could identify a few of them; anger, confusion, hurt, grief. She couldn't make sense of it all, though. He glowered at her, and she tried to stammer out an apology, but the entire time his face remained impassive.

Amy began to fuss, the tension in the room making her upset and James turned to take her out of her chair. Mattie wanted to explain, but at the same time she had no idea what she would say. She couldn't conceive as to why he would be so angry. And she feared that if she stood there any longer, she would surely begin to cry.

"You're done for the evening, I'll take care of Amy from here," James said, his voice devoid of all emotion.

He hadn't turned to look back at her, and for a moment Mattie couldn't do anything else but stare at his back as she fought past the lump in her throat. Not wanting the tears to fall while she was still here with him, she finally bowed her head and strode quickly from the room. She rushed upstairs, and when she was finally in the safety of her bedroom, she closed the door.

An errant tear leaked down her cheek and she hastily whipped it away. She had only been there two days, and on both days the only thing she had succeeded in doing was messing everything up. With a pit in her stomach, Mattie couldn't help but think that maybe coming to Mt. Juliet hadn't been the correct move for her at all.

Chapter Six

James laid in bed that night for what felt like hours, tossing and turning while sleep evaded him. He stared angrily at the ceiling, watching the shadows dance across his bedroom ceiling as he turned the events that had taken place earlier over in his mind.

He felt terrible about how he had reacted to Mattie at dinner when he'd seen that butterfly pin in her hair. To be quite honest, before James had seen her wearing it, he had all but forgotten that it had still been in the box on Amy's dresser.

After Ruth's passing, when he was still so lost in his grief that he could hardly see straight, he had thrown most of her things out so that he wouldn't have to look at them. But months later, after his heart had had a little more time to heal, he had stumbled upon that small, silver jewelry box tucked in the corner of their armoire.

James had been grateful when he had found it, immediately thinking that he would save it as something for Amy to wear when she was older. But whenever he was in Amy's room, for the longest time he had refused to look at it, terrified that it's mere existence would throw him back into a pit of despair. He guessed that after a while, his brain had made the decision for him to stop noticing it at all.

So, it had been a jolt to his entire system when he had seen it nestled just below the crown of Mattie's head. The sight of it had hit him like a horse's kick to the gut, and he'd reacted harshly. Too harshly, if he was being honest with himself. And now he couldn't sleep because of it.

With a sigh, he rolled over onto his side and tried as hard as he could to push his thoughts away from Mattie, away from the hairpin, and away from anything at all. Eventually, sleep pulled him under. But then he was caught up in dreams of Ruth, of silver hair pins, and of green eyes flecked with gold and filled with hurt.

When he woke with the morning sun, his eyes were still heavy with exhaustion, and he partly wondered if it would have been better had he not dozed off at all. James pushed himself out of bed and began getting ready for the day, his mind barely registering his movements as he pulled on a pair of trousers and the shirt he had asked Mattie to press the day before.

He looked out the window as he worked on his buttons, noting that the sun was higher in the sky than normal. He must have overslept.

Finishing with his clothes, James swept his long hair into a quick bun, securing it with a worn, thin piece of leather before stalking from the room. Amy's door was ajar, and as he walked past it, he was shocked to find it empty. James often joked that Amy slept longer than any grown adult that he knew, so if she was already awake, he must have overslept, indeed.

He stopped at the top of the stairs, listening to the noises of the house. He could just make out the sounds of Mattie preparing breakfast in the kitchen, and the sound of Amy making noises as she played. A pit formed in his stomach as he descended the steps, each time he raised his leg and brought it down it felt like it weighed a thousand pounds. James knew that he had to apologize to Mattie, but the truth was, he just wasn't sure how.

In order to apologize, he would first have to explain to her why the sight of the hairpin had upset him. And he didn't yet feel ready to discuss Ruth with her. But he guessed that he no longer had a choice in the matter.

As he turned the corner that led to the kitchen, he could smell the aroma of eggs, meat, and potatoes and he inhaled deeply, his stomach giving a soft growl. Mattie and Amy both had their backs to him, so he stood for a minute and watched them. He hadn't been surprised that Amy had liked Mattie almost immediately.

His daughter was an abnormally happy child who seemed to genuinely adore nearly every person she met. But the fact that Mattie seemed to have taken to her so quickly as well filled his heart with joy. And as he watched the two of them interact, he realized that that joy may prove to be dangerous.

After a few additional moments, James cleared his throat to announce his arrival as he strode further into the room. Amy looked at him, but this morning seemed to care more about the small, wooden toy that she was playing with than her Papa. That was alright with him, though. His attention right now was on the woman standing at the stove.

Her cheeks were flushed as she turned to look at him, her green eyes wide with worry. She was chewing the side of her cheek, and she looked so pretty in that moment that James almost forgot what he needed to do.

"James," she began, and the hesitant, worried sound to her voice jolted him, reminding him of everything he needed to say as she continued. "I'm so sorry. You were right that it wasn't..."

He held up his hand, and her sentence dropped.

"Mattie, you don't need to apologize," He explained, holding her gaze as the red of her cheeks deepened. "The hairpin belonged to Ruth, and the sight of it caught me off guard."

Her eyes widened further at the mention of his late wife's name, and she opened her mouth to speak, but he kept

THE GOVERNESS AND THE COWBOY'S PROMISE

going. If he stopped talking, even for a moment, he was afraid that he would lose his nerve.

"I reacted too harshly to you. You didn't deserve the way that I spoke to you last night, and for that I am truly sorry."

"I didn't know it was Ruth's," Mattie explained. "If I had, I never would have touched it."

"There was no way you could have known unless I told you. So, it is truly and absolutely alright."

They held each other's gaze for a moment longer before Mattie dipped her head in acknowledgement, both of them knowing that nothing more needed to be said. Mattie turned back to the stove, tending to the breakfast as he walked over to play with Amy. Before too long, they were eating. He and Mattie took turns feeding Amy, his daughter more than happy to be getting the attention of both adults in the room.

An idea struck him, and he turned to Mattie with a grin.

"What would you say to a trip into town today?" He asked, and her face lit up at the idea.

"Don't you have work to get done?"

"Elmer can handle it," James answered, waving off Mattie's concerns. "It's the least I can do."

Mattie's cheeks flushed once more, but she held his gaze and smiled.

"Then I think a trip to town sounds lovely."

James nodded at her, color rising to his own cheeks, and he found himself quite grateful that most of it would be hidden by his beard. When they finished up breakfast, he left Mattie to clean up while he went to ready the wagon and tell Elmer of his plans. The young man was already in one of the stables, mucking out the stalls. When James told him about what he would spend his day doing, he broke out into a wide grin.

"Just a little jaunt into town for the day? Slackin' already?" Elmer joked, his voice laced with mischief.

"Hush, now," James warned Elmer, but couldn't quite fight back his chuckle.

He filled Elmer in on the short list of things that needed done that day, which would not take him long. And then James told the young man to spend the rest of the day with his fiancé, he deserved the time off. Elmer had been taken aback by this and looked at him with mock horror.

"Only three days and Miss Mattie has already softened you up. I should buy her flowers to thank her." Elmer fanned himself dramatically, and James rolled his eyes at him before turning to leave.

He readied the wagon quickly, and in what felt like no time at all he was seated securely on the bench seat and guiding the horse up toward the house. Mattie sat on the front porch in one of the rocking chairs, with Amy perched in her lap facing her. Both were clapping their hands excitedly to the song Mattie was singing to her.

The horse whinnied loudly, making Mattie's head snap up and seek him out. Her eyes lit up when she saw him approaching, and he had to remind himself that it was because she was excited about going into town, not because she was excited to see him. James helped Mattie into the wagon, and waited for her and Amy to get situated safely before he climbed up with them.

The ride to town passed quickly, both of them chattering eagerly as he told her what stores he needed to go to in between bouts of her playing with Amy. When they pulled up in front of the farm supply store, Amy clapped her hands excitedly. James stood, jumping down from the wagon before turning to help Mattie and Amy down, and then they all clamored into the supply shop.

Matties eyes were wide as they walked through the threshold, the shade of the store cooling them down a bit from the heat of the Tennessee sun. James watched as Mattie looked around them, taking in the large bags of feed, the tools and equipment adorning the walls, and the long counter at the far end of the room where the shops proprietor, Mr. Tavers, stood regarding them kindly.

"Good mornin', Mr. Tavers," James said as he approached, and the other man dipped his hat.

"Who might this be?" The old man asked, leaning his elbows on the counter, and giving Mattie a warm smile.

"This is Mattie, she's Amy's new governess," James explained, gesturing between the two of them. "Mattie, this is Mr. Tavers. He owns this place."

"A pleasure to meet you, Mr. Tavers," Mattie said, securing Amy to her hip with one hand and extending the other across the counter for the old man to shake.

After the greetings were complete, James rattled off his list of items that he needed to purchase, and then walked with the old man to load them into the back of the wagon while Mattie and Amy observed. When he paid Mr. Tavers and said goodbye, he turned to Mattie.

"Now, I have an idea," he said, keeping his voice low and conspiratorial.

She leaned in closer to him, hanging on his every word.

"How about we go to the General Store, and you can decide whatever groceries and supplies you think the house needs."

Mattie's eyebrows shot up when he finished talking, an excited look playing across her face. James wasn't sure he had ever seen anyone get so excited over the prospect of shopping for food, and he had to fight back a laugh. Mattie nodded excitedly, and they climbed back into the wagon and headed down the road in the direction of the general store.

James was feeling much chattier as they drove through the town then he had two days prior when he'd picked Mattie up from the station. So, this time he decided to point out different shops, saloons, and things for her to see as they drove through. She asked him questions, and some of the townsfolk openly stared at them as they drove past.

He couldn't blame them, with Mattie's face alight with joy and the wonder of taking in the town around her, she was radiant. If he didn't have to focus on guiding the horse and wagon through the streets, he was sure that he'd find it nearly impossible to look away from her as well.

He shook himself slightly, banishing that thought from his mind with a reminder of his promise to Gilbert as they came to a stop before the General Store.

"It's so much bigger than the one I worked at in Bartlett," Mattie said as James helped her and Amy down from the wagon.

"You worked at the General?" James asked her as they turned and walked toward the shop.

"For a while, yes." Mattie nodded, shifting Amy onto her hip.

"Here," James said, holding his arms out for his daughter. "Let me take her so you can browse and make all the decisions."

She grinned at him as she handed him his child, and the sight of her smile made the day seem a little bit brighter. The large windows at the front of the store allowed her to see the shelves and shelves of goods, and as they walked inside Mattie began turning in circles to try and take it all in.

Barrels of nuts, beans, nails, and so much more were pushed along the walls. A long counter ran along the far corner, with everything from trousers to candy to tobacco piled atop the glass cases. Mattie darted around, looking at one thing and then another with breakneck speed. James watched her with fascination as she bounced from spot to spot, excitedly picking out what she thought they needed and reciting it to the store clerk.

He meandered over to the other side of the store, bouncing Amy on his hip, as he looked at some of the candy selections. He figured he'd buy Amy and Mattie a little something sweet while he could. James was no longer paying attention to Mattie as his eyes roved over the selection, and he picked out a few things then turned around. When he did, his heart sunk at the sight before him.

Mattie was standing to the side of the counter, immersed in conversation with a tall, broad-shouldered man. The man's back was facing James, but he would recognize that cocksure stature anywhere. Mattie was talking to none other than Hubert Bird.

James glowered at the man's back as he approached, their conversation growing clearer the closer that he got. He placed the candy he'd selected on the counter, next to the other items the store clerk was packaging that Mattie had selected, before striding directly up to the now chatting pair.

"...live on the ranch with James, taking care of young Amy," Mattie was saying as James approached.

She happened to look over at him then, catching his eye. Hubert followed her gaze, and when his stare landed on James, his expression soured.

"Hello Hubert," James said as he approached them, trying to keep any hint of malice from seeping into his voice. "Pleasure to see you here. I figured you'd be working on that ranch of yours."

"I could say the same to you," Hubert rebutted, his tone not nearly as controlled as James'. The man turned his gaze to Mattie, and James watched as his eyes roved over her slender frame, reminding him of a wolf sizing up prey. It made James' blood boil.

"But," Hubert continued, "it seems you have much better distractions than work these days."

"I'm no distraction," Mattie argued, seemingly oblivious to the animosity rolling off of the two men in front of her in waves. "We just needed to restock the pantry, that is all. And James was kind enough to let me pick out everything we needed."

He knew that Mattie thought she was doing him a favor, that proclaiming that to Hubert would be akin to singing James' praises. But if James knew one thing about Hubert Bird, it was that the man had a talent for turning anything that someone said into an insult, no matter how seemingly innocuous it was.

"How generous of him," Hubert said, his voice saccharine sweet and making James' skin crawl.

Thankfully, before James or Mattie could reply, the clerk announced that their order was ready. Mattie turned to

Hubert and bade him goodbye, while the two men locked eyes and simply tipped their heads to each other in acknowledgement before Hubert turned and strode from the store with James glowering after him.

"What was that all about?" Mattie asked, eyes darting from James to the door where Hubert had just exited. "Why were you acting so strange?"

"Hubert Bird is not a good man," James explained, carefully weighing how much he wanted to tell her.

"He didn't seem so bad," Mattie stated, rolling her eyes at him.

He wanted to argue with her more, wanted to spill out everything he knew about Hubert to her, if only to keep her far, far away from the man. But he also did not want to seem as if he was encouraging her to stay away due to jealousy. The fact that he had seethed with it the moment he'd turned to find Mattie talking to Hubert was irrelevant. No, this was about protecting Mattie from a bad man, that was all.

And the last thing he wanted to do was to push her closer toward him by protesting too harshly. Her brother, Gilbert, had quite a stubborn and defiant streak which had only gotten worse with age, and James would not be surprised if his younger sister carried the same gene. So, for now, he would allow her to think whatever she liked and he'd just have to keep an eye on the situation from afar.

He nodded at Mattie before passing Amy off to her so he could help the clerk load their groceries into the wagon. As he did, he could feel Mattie's eyes on him the entire time. But he did not look at her. Instead, he kept his eyes focused on the town, constantly scanning, and looking for any additional sign of Hubert.

It wasn't until they were seated in the wagon and making their way back to the ranch that James finally caught sight of the man once more. He was standing on the front porch of the most popular saloon in town, leaning against the wall as he spoke to one of his cronies. Hubert's eyes darted away from the man he was talking to and found them as they passed, his gaze darkening at the same time as a sly smile tugged at his lips.

James didn't react to Hubert's stare, instead he found himself scooting a little closer to Mattie on the bench seat and holding his head high as they drove down the lane. Mattie, for what it was worth, hadn't noticed Hubert standing there and instead was talking excitedly about what she planned to make with all of the groceries she had bought.

James tried his best to pay attention, but the farther away from town that they drove, there was only really one thing that his mind would allow him to focus on. And that was the fact that neither he, nor Mattie, had seen the last of Hubert Bird.

Chapter Seven

Mattie hummed as she worked, sprinkling a little bit more sugar on top of the fresh apple pie that she'd just taken out of the oven. After dinner, Amy had fallen asleep almost immediately, exhausted after their trip to town. James had to run out to shore up a few, final tasks for the night, and while Mattie knew that she likely should be horribly tired as well, she found herself invigorated instead.

The thought of heading upstairs to bed hadn't been the least bit appealing, and so, while the dusk fully faded into night, she found herself baking to pass the time. And now, as the pie cooled and she stood in the quiet house, her mind began to wonder.

She'd had a lovely time going into town earlier that day, and still she couldn't quite wrap her mind around how much better stocked the Mt. Juliet General Store had been compared to the one she had worked at. The only real thing of note that even slightly took away from her day was that strangeness between James and Mr. Bird.

From the moment that Mattie had caught sight of James walking up to her as she had talked to Hubert, she had known that something was wrong. Everything from the set of his shoulders to the hardness of his eyes had screamed disapproval as he had stalked toward them, and Mattie had found herself both worried and intrigued by the sudden change that had overcome James. Even when he had been mad at her for wearing Ruth's hairpin, he hadn't looked at her like that.

But, despite what James had said about Mr. Bird not being a good man, Mattie couldn't help but think that he had seemed perfectly fine. Nice, even. Not that she would tell James that. She could only imagine the look on his face then if she tried to further defend the man that he so clearly held disdain for.

At first, Mattie had wondered if it had been jealousy that had soured James' mood. But despite how much the thought had secretly thrilled her, his reaction to the other man had been too intense to be explained away by something that simple. No, Mattie knew that there was much more to the story between the two of them, and she was more than willing to wait to figure out exactly what that story was.

The creak of the front door opening brought her out of her thoughts, and Mattie turned around just as she heard it shut with a click. Footsteps echoed through the narrow hall, and soon James appeared in the doorway. He looked tired, and she wondered what all chores he had to complete this late that had taken him long enough for her to bake an entire pie.

"Something smells good," James said, sniffing the air appreciatively.

"Apple pie," Mattie explained with a smile. She gestured at his usual chair at the kitchen table and commanded, "sit, and I'll bring you over a slice."

He did as he was told, and Mattie almost made a comment about him following instructions for once. But she didn't want to sully the good day that they had had, or the strange new comradery that seemed to have blossomed between them over the last few hours. So instead, she turned her back and strode across the kitchen. Taking down two plates from the cabinet, she set them down and carefully cut two slices out of the still warm pie.

She chose the larger piece for James, hoping that it would be the final peace offering between them after the events of the prior night, as well as a thank you for taking her to town that day. Mattie grinned at him widely as she crossed the kitchen and set the steaming plate in front of him, before pulling out her own chair and taking a seat across from him. Vaguely, she noticed that even when Amy wasn't in the room with them, they still sat in the same spots, and something about the quickly established routine made her want to grin even wider.

Mattie watched as James eyed the pie appreciatively before looking up at her.

"Are you going to take a bite?" He asked, raising his eyebrows at her.

"You first," she said, still smiling.

James shrugged before grabbing his fork, picking up a massive bite of pie and putting it in his mouth. Mattie watched him hopefully, waiting for the moment when his eyes would close, or he'd groan over how good it tasted. But that moment never came. Instead, he chewed a few times before his mouth turned down at the corners, a look of disgust playing across his handsome features.

His eyes darted back and forth, panicked, before finally they landed on his plate and he leaned forward, spitting the bite he had just taken back out onto it. Mattie's heart thrummed in embarrassment, and she felt her cheeks flush as he grabbed his mug of ale in front of him and drank deeply.

"What is wrong with it?" Mattie asked in horror as he lowered his drink back down to the table.

"Hell if I know," James said with a laugh. "You try it and tell me."

"It can't be that bad," Mattie protested, picking up her fork and loading a bite onto it. "You're just being dramatic. I did everything perfectly."

"Oh, sure," James taunted her, eyes dancing with humor. "Then why does it taste rancid?"

"It does not!" Mattie whisper yelled, not wanting her voice to carry and wake up Amy. "You're just being a child."

"Show me then," James raised his eyebrows and looked pointedly at her fork.

"Alright then, I will."

With defiance in her belly, Mattie lifted her fork to her mouth. As her lips wrapped around it a horrid, strong flavor exploded across her tongue. She wanted to swallow it, she truly did, if only to pretend to James that he had been overreacting. But she couldn't bring herself to do it. In an action mirroring James', she leaned forward and spat her own bite back out onto her prank, appalled with herself at the unladylike action.

James nearly doubled over with laughter at the sight of Mattie's face as she scrambled to grab her own drink to chase the horrendous taste from her mouth.

"How did you make that pie?" James asked her, still sputtering with laughter.

"I told you," Mattie protested. "I did everything I was supposed to."

"Clearly not," he chuckled, pushing himself back from the table.

She watched as James crossed the room, walking over to the counter where a handful of ingredients still littered the surface.

"Is this what you used?" He inquired, gesturing while Mattie nodded. He dipped his finger forward, grabbing little bits of the ingredients to taste and bringing them to his mouth. When he reached the large, glass jar that contained a fine white powder, when he put his finger to his mouth and his expression soured, he also began to laugh.

"Mattie," he said, his voice laced with humor, "you used salt instead of sugar."

Dread filled her as she jumped up from her seat and stalked across the kitchen.

"No, I did not," she argued as she came to stand beside him.

"Yes, you absolutely did," he chuckled, picking up the container and holding it out to her.

She eyed the white substance in front of her wearily, before dipping her finger in, grabbing a few granules, and then bringing them to her lips. Just as James had said, the taste of salt danced across her tongue, and her cheeks heated as the realization washed over her.

James laughed again, a real laugh that pulled straight from his belly. The sound of it made her heart feel light and caused knots to dance in her stomach. The longer it went on, the better she felt, despite the very real fact that he was laughing *at* her. Soon enough, she found herself chuckling with him, and then, that chuckle turned into a full, hearty laugh of her own.

"You should have seen your face," he shook his head when their laughter finally began to subside.

"My face?" Mattie exclaimed. "When you first bit into the pie I wasn't sure if you were going to cry, or vomit."

That sent them both into another fit of giggles, and they doubled over, clutching at their stomachs as they locked eyes. Mattie couldn't remember the last time she had laughed like this with someone. She knew for sure that it had been well before everything that had happened with Lewis.

At the thought of him, her laughter died out and she stood up straight. James, noticing the quick change in her demeanor, also let his laughter fall while he regarded her wearily.

"Is everything alright?" He asked, his brow creasing with worry.

"Yes," Mattie lied, tucking a stray strand of hair that had escaped from her braid behind her ear. "I just…"

She glanced around wildly, the house suddenly feeling a little too small.

"I just need some air," she finally said.

James nodded. "Go out to the front porch. I'll get rid of the pie."

Mattie nodded and turned on her heel, not looking back as she strode from the house. As soon as the front door closed behind her and she stepped out, the fresh air of the night surrounded her, causing her to feel immediately better. A cool breeze danced around, sending shivers skittering across her flesh, but she didn't mind it.

Stepping a little further out onto the porch, she leaned forward and looked up at the night sky. The stars shimmered and the full moon glowed, casting the beautiful terrain of the ranch in a silver light. Mattie wrapped her arms around herself, trying as hard as she could to banish all worry and thoughts of Lewis Mooney from her mind.

She heard the door to the house open behind her, but she didn't turn. She knew who had joined her. Mattie heard James' footsteps as he crossed the wooden porch, and then felt the heat rolling off his body as he came to stand beside her. They stood in silence for a few moments, and Mattie appreciated the extra time for her to collect her thoughts.

"Thank you," Mattie said at last, her voice low enough that she wondered if he would even be able to hear her.

"For what?" James asked, turning to face her.

"Today. The trip to town. The offer to move here to Mt. Juliet." Mattie raised one shoulder in a half shrug before letting it drop. "All of it."

James studied her face for a moment, and she could see that his blue eyes were laced with concern.

"Do you remember the summer that me and Gilbert got caught chasing cats through town in the middle of the night?" James asked, and the abrupt change of subject caught Mattie off guard.

"What?" She said with a laugh, shaking her head.

"Ok, so you don't remember?" James cocked an eyebrow at her, and Mattie rolled her eyes. "There were these feral cats that lived behind the Bartlett General Store. Some of them were nice, and those ones we always tried to feed whenever we could. But then there was another group of 'em, mean as all get out. They'd come up and try to steal the food we'd lay out for the others."

His face transformed as he spoke, and Mattie could have sworn she was finally getting a glimpse to the James that she had known all those years ago. But better, somehow.

"So," James continued, unaware that both he and Mattie had moved much closer to each other. "Gilbert and I would sneak out in the middle of the night if we suspected the tom cats were out and about, and when they were, we'd chase them through the streets. They kicked up such a ruckus though, spitting and howling as they ran. One night, Harvey Winters came storming out from his place above the shop and started throwing things at us. You know that scar that Gilbert has right by his hairline?"

He paused, waiting for Mattie to answer, so she nodded vigorously. She did remember it. One morning her family had woken up, and when Gilbert had come down for breakfast, he had had a gash on his forehead. He'd refused to tell them how he'd gotten it, and no one in town had ever spoke up. So, it had remained a mystery all these years.

"Well, Old Man Harvey had thrown a tin pan at us, and it smacked Gilbert in the head as we'd run. That's how he got it."

Mattie's mouth popped open in surprise at the revelation, "why didn't Old Man Harvey ever say anything?"

It wasn't hard for her to recall the man, he had been the owner of the General Store when she'd worked there, too. He was a crotchety old fellow, always complaining about the goings-on in the town. Something like that would have been right up his alley to spread around to the other townsfolk of Bartlett.

"I don't think he knew for sure that it was us," James explained with a grin. "If you recall, Gilbert went to work on one of the farms a little over a week after for the rest of the summer. So, no one from town ever saw the gash on his head, and word never got out."

Mattie threw her head back and laughed, picturing it all in her mind exactly as James had told it. When her laughter subsided, she glanced at him only to find him watching her. In the silver light of the full moon, his eyes seemed to glow as he regarded her, and Mattie felt warmth spread through her under the weight of her gaze.

She glanced at the space between them, marking that throughout their conversation they had moved quite a bit closer to one another. Close enough that she could feel the heat of his body radiating off him.

Something about the way that James was looking at her made her pulse spike. His eyes darted down, focusing on her lips, and Mattie got the sense that he was contemplating whether to kiss her. A thrill ran through her at the thought. She had never kissed Lewis; it wouldn't have been proper. But she had always dreamed of what it would be like when her lips finally pressed against a man's, and something about the thought of her first kiss being with James seemed right.

She leaned forward a bit, preparing herself for the moment where his lips touched hers. His eyes darkened slightly, and she could have sworn that she saw a glimmer of want dancing behind his gaze. Suddenly, James shook his head as if clearing it, and he took several steps back from Mattie.

Her cheeks flushed, this time with embarrassment as he retreated from her.

"It's getting late," James said, his voice gruff with some emotion that Mattie couldn't quite place. "Amy will likely be up early; we should get to bed."

Mattie nodded, and James didn't wait for her before turning and striding into the house. She followed him slowly, taking care to close the front door before making her way up the steps. By the time she got to her bedroom door, James' own was firmly shut, and not a single sound escaped from the other side.

"What were you thinking?" Mattie whispered to herself as she walked into her own room and closed the door.

She prepared herself for bed, trying as hard as she could to tell herself that she had imagined it all. That there was no way James Murphy had been contemplating kissing her as they stood on that front porch. But even if that was true, Mattie had to admit to herself that it didn't change the beautiful, horrible fact that she had wanted him to.

Chapter Eight

James ground his teeth together as he lifted the sledgehammer with both hands and drove it down onto the post he had been working on. There hadn't been much rain the last week, and it had made the ground hard and unyielding as he struggled to construct the border for another pasture. He welcomed the grueling work, however, especially after the almost misstep with Mattie the night prior.

No matter how hard James had tried, after leaving her on that porch, he had not been able to shake the image of her looking up at him with her green and gold eyes burning with affection and desire. It had taken all his will power to walk away from her and to lock himself in his room.

When he had finally cooled down from the events on the porch, the guilt had washed over him in waves. Guilt over what Ruth would have thought if she could have seen him in that moment pining for another woman. Guilt over what Gilbert would have thought if he knew his best friend had come so incredibly close to kissing his sister; a sister that James had promised to protect and watch over as if she were his own kin.

All of that had roared through him as the shadows danced on his ceiling and night turned into dawn. And by the time the first rays of sun had started to streak through the sky, he was still entirely unsure of how to proceed with Mattie. So, he climbed out of bed, careful to tread on silent feet as he dressed himself and then crept through the house toward the kitchen.

Opting for a breakfast of bread, butter, and cheese, the moment the last bite had passed his lips he had left the house, glad to have done so without rousing either Amy or Mattie. He'd been out in the pasture ever since, working himself ragged, in an effort to push the thoughts that threatened to overwhelm him out of his mind.

With one more grunt of effort, he brought the sledgehammer down atop the fence post with a resounding *thunk* and the earth beneath it finally gave way, allowing it to sink the last few inches to its desired depth. James straightened himself and stretched his back before wiping his brow clear of the sweat that dripped from his dark brown hair and down to his brow. Elmer was a few feet away, working on a post of his own, and James took a moment to breathe and watch him.

By the time Elmer had arrived that morning, James had already secured three of the posts on his own. The young man had been shocked, but hadn't commented on the relentless, frenzied way that James had gone about his work, and for that he was incredibly grateful. He took his gaze away from Elmer and glanced up at the sky, marking that the sun was now almost directly overhead.

His stomach gave a quick, swift growl, letting James know that he was definitely due for his midday meal. In his haste to leave the house quietly that morning, he had not stopped to gather anything to bring out in the pasture with him. It was something he regretted, but he still wasn't ready to face Mattie just yet.

James turned against the sun to glance in the direction of the house and was shocked to find a figure walking across the expansive yard directly toward him and Elmer. He watched as they approached, taking in the familiar walk and the glint of sun off of caramel hair and a knot formed in his stomach. As Mattie's form became clearer, walking with Amy perched on one hip and a basket in her other hand, that knot travelled north to form a lump in his throat.

"I thought I'd bring you both some lunch," Mattie called as she approached, flashing a warm smile that sent shivers down James' spine.

The sound of her voice grabbed Elmer's attention, and his spine straightened. As soon as he spotted her, his face lit up and he jogged over to greet her. James shook his head as he set down his sledgehammer and walked over to join them, pushing down a twinge of jealousy at the sight of Elmer and Mattie easily talking.

It's a good thing that they're friendly, he reminded himself as he approached them, shaking off the negative thoughts. *It's good for her to have friends, plus Elmer is engaged and is no danger.* He forced himself to smile at them both and hoped it didn't come out as a grimace.

"Thank you, Mattie," James said, finally meeting her eyes.

"I also brought a blanket and thought perhaps we could have a picnic," her eyebrows shot up and her face lit with hope when their gazes landed on each other.

For a moment he thought of dismissing her, of just taking what she had packed for lunch and telling her that they were too busy to pause for a picnic. But the thought of the way her face would fall when he crushed that hope wasn't something he could bear. Plus, he needed to figure out how to behave around her despite his growing attraction. If he couldn't, then it was never going to work and her living with them would become torturous.

"Absolutely," he said, keeping his voice light and unassuming. "It will be good to spend time with Amy, anyway."

James held out his arms to reach for his daughter, trying not to pay attention to the quick flash of confusion that crossed Mattie's delicate features at his casual disinterest. He took Amy's squirming body as Mattie began arranging the blanket and the food, assisted by an all too eager Elmer. James deliberately waited, stalling as he tried not to watch the two of them work together to assemble their lunch.

When Mattie and Elmer first sat down, each of them facing the other on opposite sides of the blanket, James realized with a jolt that he would be forced to sit by Mattie. Unsure if he could handle the proximity, he glanced at Elmer.

"Elmer, would you mind scooting toward Mattie," he asked, the words threatening to catch in his throat on the bundle of nerves, "I would like to have a spot for both me and Amy."

Elmer looked confused but obliged, and James couldn't bring himself to glance at Mattie as he plopped onto the blanket and sat Amy beside him. He spent his time focusing on his daughter, helping her as she picked the heads off dandelions. Each tiny yellow bud that she handed him, he helped her braid into a small, delicate flower crown to place atop her head. Every time he caught a glimpse of Mattie, his heart leapt in his chest followed by a rush of guilt and confusion. So instead, he did whatever he could to avoid paying attention to her more than was necessary.

"What do you think, James?" Mattie's voice broke through Amy's babbling as she handed him yet another yellow headed weed, and James was forced to turn his attention to the woman in question.

Her brow was furrowed as she regarded him, and he wondered how apparent it had been that he was ignoring her.

"What do I think about what?" He asked, not having heard what she and Elmer had been discussing.

"About me trying to make another pie soon, to make up for the terrible one last night," Mattie explained. "I just finished telling Elmer all about it."

At the mention of the pie, a smile tugged at the corner of his lips, remembering the look upon her face when she'd first put the bite in her mouth. It wasn't something he would soon forget, and he couldn't recall the last time he had laughed that hard with another. But he also knew that to dwell on that would only end up causing them both insurmountable pain. It could not continue. He reminded himself of Gilbert and Ruth and shoved his feelings once more to the side.

"Another pie sounds good," James answered, keeping his voice polite, but not inviting.

"Perhaps this time I'll get to try a slice," Elmer joked as he shot James a questioning look, clearly having picked up on his reluctance to engage in conversation.

"You're lucky you didn't try the one last night." Mattie smiled at Elmer, but James noted that it did not fully reach her eyes.

The rest of lunch passed uneventfully, with only a few errant comments thrown James' way. Other than that, Mattie and Elmer seemed perfectly content to talk to one another, with Elmer telling her the entire story of his bride-to-be, Laurah. Eventually, Amy began getting cranky and showing signs of needing a nap, which was Mattie's cue to pack up lunch and head back to the house.

She bade both James and Elmer goodbye and James planted a swift kiss to the top of Amy's head before Mattie turned and walked back across the pasture toward the house, with Amy nuzzling into her as they walked. He could feel Elmer staring at him, but James turned back to his work and tried to ignore him.

"What was that?" Elmer demanded.

"What are you talking about?" James asked, without looking away from the post he had picked up from the ground.

"The awkwardness between the two of you. Your distant attitude. All of it. I've never known you to be unkind, James. Not to those who don't deserve it. And while that may not have been downright rude, it was quite close."

James let out an exasperated sigh as he brought his forefinger and thumb to his temple, rubbing it gently to ease the tension that was building there.

"Let it lie, Elmer," James warned.

Something in his voice must have told Elmer that James was serious, and this was a matter he wasn't willing to discuss, because the other man just shook his head at James and then stomped back over to where he had been working.

They worked like that for the remainder of the day, only speaking to each other when necessary and James constantly warring with himself. He knew that he had to find a way to co-exist with Mattie, to keep things friendly without falling into the trap he was currently so tempted by. The problem for James was that he didn't know how.

Later that evening, as he headed across the lawn with his shoulders bent from a day of hard work, the beginning of an idea started to take shape. He opened the screen door and stepped inside. He could hear Mattie and Amy in the kitchen, and James took a breath to steel himself.

He walked through the house, his boots making loud thuds with each step to announce his arrival. Amy was strapped into her dining chair, playing with an assortment of blocks when he entered, and he ruffled her hair. Mattie turned to greet him, a hesitant smile flashing across her face.

"Did you get the fence finished?" She asked as she gathered up a few serving plates and brought them to the table.

"Almost, we'll have to go back out tomorrow. But it should only take us about half a day."

"That's good then." Mattie's tone was short and matter of fact.

James knew that he had no right to feel hurt by her sudden distance, not after the way he had behaved throughout the day. But as they took their respective seats, he still couldn't help the twinge of sadness that flitted through him from the chasm that had opened up between them.

An awkward silence fell, with only Amy's babbling to fill it. Both James and Mattie served themselves, spooning out helpings of the green beans, carrots, potatoes, and stewed meat in gravy that she had concocted.

"Alright," Mattie said after a few, tension filled moments. "What's happening? You've been distant and all but ignoring me the entire day."

She placed her fork beside her plate and crossed her arms as she glared at him across the table. He regarded her for a moment, taking the time to weigh how he should answer, before shaking his head.

"What do you mean?"

"You've barely spoken to me," Mattie accused, her eyebrows shooting up so high they almost disappeared into her hairline.

"We're speaking now, and we spoke at lunch," James argued back.

He knew his attempt was feeble at best, so he shook his head and tried to continue.

"I'm sorry, Mattie," he began again. "There is just quite a lot on my mind, that's all. But I assure you, there is nothing wrong."

She narrowed her eyes at him warily, and he could tell she sensed the lie that fell from his lips. But thankfully, she did not push it farther. Mattie just nodded and leaned forward, digging back into her own meal. For the rest of their time eating, he made much more of an effort to behave normally. And by the time Mattie began clearing away the dishes and James offered to take Amy up and put her to bed, they'd fallen back into some semblance of comradery.

James held Amy close as he carried her up the stairs, the sound of dishes clinking together as Mattie scrubbed them fading with every step that he took. As he filled a small wash basin and toweled off his squirming toddler, he thought about what he could do to help temper what was occurring between he and Mattie.

A thousand ideas swirled through his mind, but there was one that kept coming back to him. It was his least favorite that he had conjured, but it was also the one that made the most sense. Should Mattie find someone to court her, James would no longer have to worry about his own desires.

So, he would introduce her to some of his friends. She was so beautiful, there was no conceivable way that they would not fancy her. Knowing them, she would likely be able to choose whoever she wanted and have them all eating out of the palm of her hands. And once Mattie had fallen in love, he would be able to wipe all notions of himself falling for her from his mind.

Chapter Nine

"Oh, Amy," Mattie cooed at the fussy toddler as she tried to change her diaper. "What are we going to do now?"

Amy squirmed and protested while Mattie wrapped the cloth around Amy's tiny body.

"Noooo," Amy stated defiantly, locking eyes with Mattie.

"Sweet, silly girl. We have to get you all clean, don't we. Can't have you walking around with a soggy bottom."

Amy stopped squirming at the final words, giving a slight giggle at Mattie's last few words. A grin tugged at the corners of Mattie's lips.

"Do you think that's funny, little one? Soggy bottom?"

Amy gave a full, hearty laugh as Mattie said the two words over and over again, before finishing by blowing a raspberry on Amy's tummy, causing a flurry of high-pitched squeals and laughter.

When she finally got the child changed and settled, Mattie pulled Amy's dressing gown back over her.

"Alright," Mattie said as she picked Amy up and began walking through the house. "Now it's time to ponder our question of the day—which is will your daddy be abysmally grumpy again? Or will he be charming and pleasant? Only time will tell."

The toddler babbled back to Mattie; her chubby, sweet face animated.

"You know, Amy," Mattie answered the toddler. "I think you're quite right."

Amy, seemingly satisfied that her toddler-speak had been understood, distracted herself by playing with the braid that ran down Mattie's back as they made their way to the drawing room. Sitting Amy down on the rug and giving her toys to busy herself with, her mind turned to James for what felt like the thousandth time.

He'd claimed at dinner the night prior that nothing was wrong, and he had seemed amenable enough after that, but deep down she had known he'd been lying. But the distance between them had returned that morning, and it made her heart weary. She had seen him at breakfast, but only long enough for him to grab a piece of bacon and bread, and a few small items for a lunch and head out the door. He'd barely even paused to say goodbye to Amy before leaving in a huff.

Mattie could feel it in her bones that it was tied to the night with the pie. And now, convinced that it had not all been in her head, based off James' reaction, she was frightened that her willingness and desire to kiss him had been an overstep on her part. And she had no idea how to begin to make it right.

Amy looked up at her, her chubby cheeks bouncing as she tried to repeat the word that Mattie was saying to her.

"Block," Mattie said, annunciating the word carefully as she held the tiny wooden toy aloft.

"Bock," Amy parroted with a giggle and Mattie cheered for her.

They'd been working on her words every day, and Mattie was happy that while the Amy's speech was primarily a garbled mess of words that were hard to understand, she was still making loads of progress. Putting the block down, she considered for a moment what they could do for the remainder of the afternoon, to pass the time. She had been in the house for too long, and even her foray into the pasture yesterday hadn't been much help.

An idea struck Mattie, as she thought of the large, wooden baby carriage that rested along the wall in one of the drawing rooms. She stood, placed Amy on her hip and then marched out into the pasture.

She ran into Elmer first and let him know that she was taking Amy to visit Josie in town. She figured the baby would like to see her prior governess, and it would be good for her to get out of the house. Josie had told Mattie exactly where she lived and that she could stop by any day that she liked, so she was good and well going to take her up on it.

Elmer agreed hesitantly to tell James when he saw him, and Mattie went back to the house with a newfound purpose lengthening her stride. The wooden pram was beautiful, but not the easiest to navigate over the dirt road that led to town.

Eventually she got a handle on it, and Amy seemed to enjoy being jostled about in the bassinet that sat atop the wheels, clapping her hands excitedly every time she heard Mattie grunt with effort as she pushed the contraption farther down the road.

Despite the effort it took, Mattie enjoyed how it felt to actually leave the house and do something. And they made it to town in no time at all. Mattie looked around for the saloon that Josie had told her she lived near, as they walked along the main street of Mt. Juliet, and after a little while of searching her eyes fell upon a whitewashed building with a run down, almost derelict look about it. She figured that was the saloon. It was the only building in Mt. Juliet that she could tell wasn't being kept up to par.

She followed the road just past the saloon, as Josie had indicated, and then, exactly as the other woman had described, she saw the small Tailor's shop that Josie told her about Jessup owning. Mattie was glad that he was a tailor. She'd noticed a bit of wear on some of James' work trousers, and wondered if she might be able to purchase a bit of fabric for a patch from Jessup before she left.

Mattie walked to the stairs that led up to the apartment above the shop and extracted Amy from her pram. She tucked it under the shade of the stairs, where it would be hidden from the road or passersby, then headed up toward the door.

She rapped her knuckles against the wood three times, hoping that Josie was home and that she hadn't made the trip for nothing. Thankfully, she only had to worry for a moment before the door was pulled open by a smiling Josie.

On her walk into town, she had wondered if Josie would recognize her since they had only met the one time. But thankfully, the moment her eyes landed on Mattie they lit with recognition and warmth.

"Mattie! Amy!" Josie exclaimed as she opened the door wide and then stepped back to allow the woman and child to walk through the threshold. "What a pleasure to see you both."

The two women gave each other a quick embrace in welcome before Josie led both Mattie and Amy to a small, wooden kitchen table.

"I have a few toys here for the little one," Josie said quickly as she bustled out of the room before returning with a small basket of wooden toys.

With Amy sitting on the floor, babbling happily at the toys she had been given, Josie handed Mattie a coffee mug and then sat with her at the table.

THE GOVERNESS AND THE COWBOY'S PROMISE

"How have you been? How are you settling in?" Josie asked Mattie, her face alight with interest.

"Things are going well," Mattie answered, and then decided to add honestly. "James has been in quite a mood the last two days. But we'll manage."

"Ah." Josie nodded her head knowingly as she brought her mug to her lips to sip. "He can fall into fits of melancholy, that's for sure. I always suspected it was when he was thinking about Ruth a lot."

Mattie considered this, letting the information wash over her. Could that be it? Could it have nothing to do with what had occurred, or almost occurred, between the two of them at all, and actually have everything to do with him missing his wife? She supposed that it would make sense.

"Don't take it personally, Mattie," Josie said when she noticed Mattie's contemplative expression. "He means well, I promise. And he's a very good man. He'll come around."

She reached across the table and gave Mattie's hand a quick pat. Amy let out a squeal of delight as she waved a large, pink ribbon in the air, distracting the two women momentarily. They watched her for a moment, both of them chuckling at the glee on the toddler's face. Mattie found herself wishing that she was that easy to entertain as well.

The two women sat there a little while longer, nursing their coffees and watching the small child before them. When Mattie turned to Josie and asked her about her wedding, the other woman's face lit up with delight.

"Oh, darling," Josie clapped her hands together excitedly. "It's been lovely. Don't get me wrong, Jessup has a terrible habit of taking his boots off and leaving them in the worst places imaginable. But it's been a grand adventure getting to live together. And the wifely duties quite make up for it."

Josie looked at Mattie knowingly, waggling her eyebrows and giving her an exaggerated wink. Mattie felt color pool in her cheeks at what Josie was insinuating, and the other woman collapsed in a fit of giggles at Mattie's expression.

"Don't worry," Josie waved a hand in the air once her laughter subsided. "I won't give you the details. But just know that married life, well it's worth every bit of waiting and of heartache. I will, however, tell you about the day of the weddin'."

Josie leaned forward, placing her elbows on the table, and resting her chin in her hands as she spoke excitedly. She began filling Mattie in on exactly where they got married, the flowers she wove into her hair and the bouquet of wildflowers that matched. By all accounts, it had been a lovely, happy affair.

Mattie chewed on the inside of her cheek as Josie spoke, a question burning inside of her. She wondered if she could ask the other woman, before deciding that she didn't have anything to lose.

"So, James..." Mattie began during a lull in conversation, and then her words cut off, wondering how to phrase the next bit of it. "Has he courted anyone or fancied anyone since Ruth passed away?"

Josie's eyes roved over Mattie's face, and Mattie wondered for a moment if she had overstepped. But there was no judgement to be found in the other woman's expression. Instead, it turned pensive as she wracked her memories. After a few moments, Josie gave a slight shake of her head.

"I don't think so," she answered. "Nothing that I can recall, anyways. But to be fair I'm not sure if I would have noticed a thing like that, and he's too much of a gentleman to talk about it openly."

Mattie nodded, not wanting to press further.

"So, tell me about your old town," Josie said excitedly. "Barnet, James said it was called?"

Mattie shook her head and chuckled.

"Bartlett," she corrected. "And it's small. Quite a deal smaller than Mt. Juliet."

"Well, I don't know how that's possible," Josie scoffed, forcing another laugh from Mattie.

"It's hotter in Mississippi, so hot that sometimes you can feel the air around you. And the bugs are an absolute nuisance. But oh, when the cicadas start singing in the summertime or when you're by the marshlands and the frogs are peeping?" Mattie closed her eyes, picturing it all and a feeling of calm rushed over her. "There's a lot that I could say about Bartlett, and not all of it is kind. But, until recently it was the only home I had ever known. And that has to count for somethin'."

When she opened her eyes again and glanced at Josie, the other woman was nodding solemnly, and Mattie could have sworn that there was something like understanding dancing in the depths of her gaze.

"Have you always lived in Mt. Juliet?" Mattie asked tentatively, hoping to find another kindred spirit in Tennessee. One that had left behind a home that they once loved but felt like it no longer held anything for her.

"I have." Josie nodded and Mattie felt that small kernel of hope deflate.

Seeming to sense the other woman's shift in emotions, Josie reached across the table and patted the top of Mattie's hand, where it was resting by her mug of coffee.

"I do understand though, what it's like to feel torn between two places," Josie explained. "It's how I felt when I moved from my parent's house to here on my wedding night. It may not be as extreme as what you did, moving so far away. But I feel like it'll always be strange when you're forced to live somewhere new and figure out a way to make it home."

Mattie felt a wave of gratitude rock through her. She brought her coffee mug to her lips, and as she took a sip of the still warm liquid and forced herself to swallow past the newly formed lump in her throat.

"So," Mattie said when she set her drink back down on the table, giving Josie a wide, open grin. "Tell me more about Mt. Juliet."

With that, Josie began gushing once more, their tender moment left on the table between them. It felt like no time had passed at all before there was the sound of footsteps on the stairs outside and then the door opened. A tall, lanky man with dark hair and kind, brown eyes walked through the door. He startled to a stop at the sight of Mattie sitting at the kitchen table and Amy playing on the floor.

Josie stood from the table and blinked in confusion.

"Jessup," she said with shock lacing her voice. "What are you doing up here so early?"

"It's past three," Jessup answered with a good-natured laugh. His eyes took in the scene before him, roving over the newcomers and lighting with recognition when his gaze landed on Amy, and he put the pieces together.

"You must be Mattie." Jessup gave her a kind, wide smile as he stepped into the apartment and extended a hand for her to shake.

"I am," Mattie answered as she greeted him. "A pleasure to meet you, Jessup. Josie has told me so much about you."

"Likewise." Jessup grinned before turning to Amy. "And you!"

He bent down to pick her up, tossing her lightly in the air as she giggled with glee. Mattie and Josie smiled as they watched him interact with the child, Amy lighting up and grinning widely at the man in front of her. Then, something that Jessup had said registered with Mattie.

"Did you say it was past three?" She asked in a hurry, and Jessup answered her with a nod. "I didn't realize it had gotten so late. We should begin heading home."

"Are you sure?" Josie asked, "you're more than welcome to stay longer. I can cook a little extra for supper."

"That is very kind, thank you. But I didn't prepare anything for James, and he'll be coming in from the fields soon. I would need to get started on his dinner."

Josie nodded understandingly as Jessup passed the baby to Mattie. They all said their goodbyes before Mattie walked down the stairs and pulled Amy's pram from the shadows. She nestled the baby into the basket on top, and Amy blinked around before settling into the folded-up blanket that Mattie had placed inside.

Mattie wasn't surprised that almost immediately upon pushing her down the road, the gentle rocking lulled Amy into a deep sleep. She gazed down at Amy affectionately as she walked up the road before turning by the saloon to head in the direction of James' ranch. However, she was brought up short by the sound of someone calling her name.

She turned, wondering who in town would even know her, and then it was all made clear when she spotted none other than Hubert Bird walking toward her with long, confident strides. Mattie smiled at the man as he approached, and he dipped his hat to her in greeting as he closed the final few feet between them.

"Pleasure to see you out and about, Mattie," he drawled, the corner of his mouth pulling up in a grin.

"It's a pleasure to see you as well, Mr. Bird," Mattie answered him with a smile of her own.

"Hubert, please," he corrected with a wave of his hand.

"Fine, Hubert."

"What brings you into town?"

"We just came to see Josie, you know, Amy's prior governess." Mattie gestured to the side street behind them that lead to Jessup's shop and their shared apartment.

"Ah," Hubert said with a nod of recognition. "Good people, those two."

"Very good. Josie's been quite kind to me since I moved here."

"Glad to hear it. I'd hate to have to pay her and Jessup a visit if they were giving you a hard time." He winked at her, forcing a peal of laughter to fall from her lips.

"Are you headed back to the ranch, then?" Hubert asked, leaning forward to spot a sleeping Amy nestled up tightly.

"We are," Mattie answered. "it isn't too far of a walk, thankfully."

"Let me join you," Hubert offered good naturedly.

Mattie considered saying no for a moment, recalling the reaction that James had to the man when they had seen him at the General Store. But, with the way that James had behaved toward her over the last few days, she found that she did not particularly care to take how he would feel about it into consideration at the moment. And if Mattie were being honest, she would like the company.

"Ok," Mattie said with a nod.

She gave the pram a push, and it jostled over the uneven road. Hubert, noticing her struggling, extended a hand and stepped toward her.

"Allow me," he said, placing his hand on the handle of the pram as Mattie scooted out of the way.

She knew that James wouldn't like him pushing Amy, but she also didn't want to fight with pushing the buggy over the road if she could avoid it. And she was quite tired, so she promised herself that she would only allow him to push the baby carriage until they got close to the house. Then, Mattie would insist on taking over.

"Where did you move here from?" Hubert asked as they walked.

"Bartlett, Mississippi."

"You're quite a ways from home, then."

"I am." Mattie nodded as images of her past in Bartlett filled her mind. "It's nice though, being here. Having something different. A change of pace."

"So Bartlett was a fast-paced town?" Hubert grinned as he turned to glance at her sidelong, forcing a chuckle from Mattie.

"Not exactly," she answered with a shrug. "There were just some things I wanted to leave behind, and I'm glad I did."

"I assume you don't want to tell me what those are, then?"

Mattie's heart picked up pace a little as she gave him an apologetic glance and said, "you assume correctly."

There was a moment of awkward silence filled only with the sound of their shoes against the packed earth and the turning of the pram's wheels. But soon, Hubert cleared his throat and began speaking once more.

"How do you know James, then?"

"Oh, he was friends with my brother before he moved to Mt. Juliet. They're still quite close. And when he told Gilbert, that's my brother, that he needed a new governess… well they both thought I would be a good fit."

"Since you wanted to leave things behind?" Hubert raised his eyebrows in question.

"Precisely." Mattie nodded.

"I bet you have loads of stories about James as a child."

"Tons." Mattie chuckled as some of them popped into her head.

"What was he like back then? I have a hard time picturing it."

"Well, he was stubborn, which I'm sure comes as no surprise. And cantankerous, but in a funny sort of way. He and my brother were always off fishing or getting into some kind of trouble with the other townsfolk when they weren't working. But he was kind, too, just like he is now."

Mattie flushed after her last sentence, suddenly consumed by the feeling that James would not appreciate her discussing his childhood with Hubert Bird.

"Now you've heard all about me," Mattie said, trying to change the subject.

"I'm a rancher," he explained, his face wearing a wide, proud grin. "Cattle mostly. Have one of the largest ranches in the county."

She wasn't shocked to find that he was a fellow rancher, and the thought crossed her mind that perhaps that was where James' surly attitude surrounding Hubert stemmed from. Could it be as simple as mere competition?

Quicker than she expected, Mattie looked around her and found that they were already coming upon the ranch. Just before they got into view of the main house, Mattie took over pushing the pram, and was thankful when there were no objections from Hubert.

The screen door opened as they approached, and a figure stepped out onto the front porch, shielding their eyes against the sun. Mattie recognized the rigid set of the shoulders, the dark hair that was swept back in a low bun, and the beard that donned his face. James watched them warily as they got closer.

"Hubert," James said, his voice laced with irritation, as they crept into earshot.

"Hello James," Hubert returned, giving him a wide smile. "I just saw Miss Mattie here walking home alone and offered to escort her. Didn't want anything bad to happen to her."

James' gaze weighed on Mattie, and she felt heat rise to her cheeks underneath it.

"We went to town to see Josie," she explained and was disappointed that her voice came out timid.

"Elmer let me know," he said with a nod of dismissal.

She glanced at his face, and his expression was cold and filled with disappointment, sending a wave of shame rocking through her.

"Now that I've delivered her home safely, I'll take my leave." Hubert dipped his head to Mattie and then James in turn, giving them both a subtle goodbye before tucking his hand in his pockets, turning, and strolling back down the lane.

Mattie, wanting desperately to get back in the house before James' irritation boiled over, picked a still-sleeping Amy up from the basket of the pram and tucked her to her chest.

"I'll come back out for this," Mattie said, pointing to the stroller before walking into the house to lay Amy in her bed.

Mattie figured that by the time she tucked Amy in and had her settled in her bed, some of James' annoyance at Hubert escorting them home would have worn off. But, when she descended the stairs just as he was closing the door behind him, she could immediately tell that that hope had been misplaced.

"What were you doing with Hubert Bird, Mattie?" James asked, his voice low and angry.

Mattie furrowed her brow in confusion. Annoyance and irritation she had suspected, and that had been a part of the reason she had accepted Hubert's offer after James' cold distance over the last two days. But anger? That was something she had not anticipated.

"He told you himself," Mattie answered him, straightening her spine under the weight of his gaze. "He saw me walking home and simply offered to escort me. It was a kind thing to do."

"It was not a kind thing to do, because he is not a kind man." James swallowed once, and Mattie got the suspicion that he was working to control his volume.

"He seemed perfectly fine to me," Mattie argued back as her brow furrowed with stubborn consternation.

"Yes, and so did your ex-fiancé. But we both know how that turned out."

A gasp pushed past Mattie's lips as her thoughts began reeling. Before she had a chance to respond he continued.

"You will not see him again."

Her temper, stoked by his comment about Lewis and his subsequent demand, roared to life deep within her belly.

"How dare you," She took a step toward him, pointing a finger directly at his chest. "How dare you use Lewis against me when you know nothing about the matter. And as for Hubert, you have no right to demand that of me. You all but ignore me for two days straight and then demand that I not accept an act of kindness from one of the only other people I have met in this town. You are not my brother, and you are not my caretaker."

Mattie's breaths were coming out fast and ragged, her emotions and worry that had been raging since the night on the porch finally bubbling over.

"I am not *yours* to command, James Murphy, and I am free to speak to whomever I like," Mattie hurled the words at him, and she was satisfied when she saw some of his anger abate, replaced by a look of contrition. "Now, if you would excuse me, I have dinner to prepare."

She stormed past him, never once looking back but she could feel him gaping after her until she disappeared into the kitchen.

Chapter Ten

James raked his fingers through his hair for a final time as he tried to brush it into submission. He had not really spoken to Mattie since the previous afternoon when Hubert had walked her home. He had eaten dinner quickly and then dismissed himself, heading back out to the barn to muck out the already clean stalls in an effort to get his mind off things and work through his feelings. By the time James had gotten back to the house, both she and Amy were already tucked away in bed for the evening.

Over the course of the next day, as James worked to understand the situation from Mattie's point of view, his anger about it had completely dissipated. He couldn't believe that he had allowed his anger to get the better of him and that he used her ex-fiancé against her. That thought alone filled James with an overwhelming sense of guilt. He knew he needed to apologize, knew that he owed her that much. But, for the life of him he couldn't figure out how to do it.

A bead of water ran down the nape of his neck from where he had brushed it into his ear, sending a chill down his spine and wrenching his thoughts away from Mattie and back to the present. He paused in his room, listening to the sounds of the house. He could hear her in the kitchen, singing loudly as she cooked.

A smile tugged up the corners of his lips as he secured his hair in a bun with his usual strip of leather and then strode from his room. His socks muffled the sound of his steps as he trudged through the house, and he paused at the doorway of the kitchen to listen to Mattie sing for a moment.

He hadn't heard her sing before, not in the way she was now. And James found the sound lovely. He glanced to where his daughter was sitting, enraptured in her dining chair, and he could tell she thought so, too.

Not wanting to get caught watching her, he stepped into the room and cleared his throat. A squeak of surprise left Mattie as she whirled to face him, her hand fluttering to her chest as her breathing became rapid. The look on her face was so shocked, James couldn't help it as laughter pulled itself from him.

"Careful, Mattie," James chuckled as he approached the kitchen table and took his seat. "Don't want to have to call the coroner because you had a heart attack."

"It's not my fault you snuck up on me," she protested. "Go sit, dinner is almost ready."

James was still laughing to himself as he pulled out his chair and sat beside Amy. He played with her while he waited for Mattie to bring the food to the dinner table, and then she sat in her usual spot across from him. A thick, awkward silence descended upon them, and as James loaded food onto his plate and a small one for Amy, his mind began to whir with everything that he wanted to say.

The silence drug on, filled with nothing but the clinking of cutlery and Amy's happy babbling as she attempted to feed herself. It swelled and swelled, until finally, James could no longer bear it.

"Mattie," James said at the same time as Mattie gave a quick, exasperated, "James."

They stared at each other for a moment before James shook his head in an effort to clear it.

"Mattie," James tried again, his throat suddenly thick with nerves. "We need to talk."

"Could it perhaps wait until after supper and when Amy is in bed?" she asked, looking up at him through her long, dark lashes.

"If that's what you want," He said, gulping down another bite and finding it hard to swallow.

"It is," Mattie confirmed before turning her attention back to Amy.

Silence spread between them, as James pushed food around his plate. After a few, torturous moments, Mattie cleared her throat and gave him a hesitant glance.

"What did you and Elmer work on today?" she asked, and James could tell she was trying for nonchalance.

"Moving some of the cattle to a new grazing pasture," he explained. "If they stay in one pasture too long, they can do a lot of damage to the land. So we try to move them around whenever we can."

He watched Mattie's face as he spoke and noted the spark of interest that lit her gaze. It hadn't escaped him that she loved learning about the ranch. Before things had gone so terribly wrong, he had liked teaching and telling her about what it took to run it. He wondered if they would get back to that again.

"How was your day? What all did you get done?" James asked, hoping that their conversation wouldn't stall.

Mattie opened her mouth to speak, but they were both brought up short by

Amy.

"Ma," the toddler said clearly.

James' eyes snapped to his daughter and his heart began hammering nervously as his mind struggled to make sense of what was happening.

"Ma," Amy screeched happily, looking at Mattie. "Ma, ma, ma."

Her small syllables began to blend together, the word Mama ringing out loud and clear. He couldn't believe what he was hearing, his daughter calling her governess Ma. When Ruth had been pregnant, he had imagined what it would be like when their child looked at her with love filled eyes and declared her *mama*. In his fantasies, it had been a sweet, love filled moment. But now, all it did was fill him with dread. James' gaze darted to Mattie, and he found her sitting ram rod straight, her face devoid of color.

"Mattie," James said as he turned his attention back to his daughter as he wiped his sweaty palms against his trousers in an attempt to dry them. "That is Mattie."

He pointed at the woman, saying her name again. But Amy wouldn't be swayed.

"Ma, ma, ma."

Finally, Mattie shook herself and some of the terror that had leached into her expression began to fade.

"Silly girl," she cooed, and James noticed that her voice was shaking. "My name is Mattie. Mat-tee. Mat-tee."

She annuncrated slowly, her finger pointing at her own chest. Slowly, Amy's babbles died down, and her mouth started working to copy the way Mattie was forming the words.

After a few miss pronunciations, she finally gave a loud, proud, "Att-eeee!"

Amy pointed her chubby, toddler fingers at Mattie.

"Att-eee!" She said again, pride filling her face as Mattie grinned widely at her.

"Yes!" Mattie cooed, clapping. "Mattie! That's right, little dove. You did it!"

James' heart began to slow as Amy continued to repeat Mattie's name over and over again. He finished the last few bites of his meal in silence as Mattie distracted his daughter for a few more moments before clapping her hands once and proclaiming that it was time for bed.

As Mattie disappeared from the kitchen, cooing to an excited Amy, James leaned back in his chair and exhaled slowly. Raking his fingers through his beard nervously, suddenly unable to sit still, he pushed himself back form the table and walked out on the front porch in the hopes that the fresh air would clear his head.

Knowing that if he stayed on his feet he would just begin pacing, he sat in one of the rocking chairs and looked out over the yard. The moon was waning, but still full enough to cast the property in a beautiful, silver haze. He let the soft back and forth motion of the chair soothe him as he waited for Mattie to return.

Eventually, he was roused by the sound of the stairs creaking under her weight as she came back down them. He pushed himself to his feet and padded back in the house. Mattie's head snapped up at the sound of the door creaking open, and then her face flooded with relief when she realized that it was just him.

"I didn't realize you had gone outside," she said breathlessly.

"Just needed a bit of air," he explained.

There was another brief pause where they both studied each other, and Mattie chewed on the inside of her cheek.

"Would you like to sit in the family room?" She asked, and he nodded.

James turned on his heel, walking toward the cozy room that was furnished with a comfortable, stuffed settee and sofa. Mattie walked ahead of him, heading straight for the settee that sat in the window. There was enough room on it for both of them, so as soon as she situated herself on it, James lowered himself to sit beside her.

He wondered briefly if he should bring up what had just occurred with Amy. But he quickly dismissed the idea. There was too much to talk about as it was.

"Mattie," he began as he met and held her vivid green eyes. "I need to apologize for how I have behaved."

Mattie blinked at him slowly as she took in his words, and he watched as color flushed prettily across her cheeks.

"First, I want to start by saying I had no right to bring up your ex-fiancé in that manner. There is nothing I can say to excuse that, and I am truly sorry. Your brother only told me a bit about what happened, just enough to explain why he thought you getting out of Bartlett was a good idea. And I never, ever should have used that against you." James paused for a moment as he grappled with how much to tell her. "When I saw you with Hubert yesterday, well.... I think you've figured out by now that I don't trust that man. But I'd like to tell you why, if you're keen."

He paused again, waiting for her to nod before continuing.

"My grandparent's owned this ranch, and I would come up from time to time to help my grandfather with some of the work. I met Hubert when we were quite young. His father was a rancher, too. And they were the only ones even close to competing with ours. Hubert was awful, even then. But he was bearable."

James shuddered as he prepared himself for the next part of the story, closing his eyes for a moment to steel himself against the onslaught of memories that threatened to overwhelm him as he spoke.

"When I moved to Mt. Juliet for good, we butted heads, but it was nothing major. Not until the night I met Ruth. We were at a town dance…"

"They have those here?" Mattie interjected, her voice hopeful.

"They do. Even better than the ones in Bartlett," James chuckled at her excitement before continuing with his story. "Anyways, we were at a dance, and she had been dancing with everyone. Ruth was the life of the party. She was actually dancing with Hubert the first time I saw her, and the way she lit up the room, well I just had to talk to her. When the dance ended, I approached her and asked if she minded sparing me a dance. She had, and Hubert had been spittin' mad."

James smiled softly at the memory of Ruth, "we danced the entire rest of the night. And by the time it came to an end, I knew that I wanted to marry her. Hubert felt slighted, you see. He couldn't stand that she'd chosen me over him. And he's had it out for mc cvcr since."

He cut the story there, leaving out some of the worse suspicions about things that Hubert had done and said over the years in an effort to get back at him for 'stealing' Ruth. He hoped that it was enough to deter Mattie from engaging with Hubert further, but he knew that only time would tell.

Mattie contemplated his story for a moment, and then she nodded at him.

"Thank you, for telling me," Mattie said as she studied his face. "She must have been some beauty, your Ruth."

The sound of her name coming from Mattie's lips stirred something in James. He hadn't been able to talk about Ruth in so long, not to anyone. But Mattie had never known her, had no preconceived notions of what his marriage had been like. All Mattie knew was James, and the man that he had been in his past and who he was now. He found himself wanting to open up to her about it.

"She was," James admitted with a nod. "She had the kind of beauty that could bring a room to its knees. And she was kind. Funny, too."

"I hope that Amy is like her," as soon as the words left Mattie's mouth her hand flew up to clap over it, as if she hadn't meant to say it.

"I do, too," James answered with a smile, letting Mattie know that what she said was alright. "She already looks so much like her. And as she grows, I see Ruth in Amy more and more."

"Good," Mattie said, her gaze raking over the room before turning back to James in earnest. "I forgive you, by the way. For what you said."

James studied Mattie, reading the sincerity in her face, and decided not to press it further. A question danced in the back of his mind, one that had bothered him for quite some time, but he wasn't sure how to broach.

"I don't want to pry," James started, hoping that Mattie wouldn't take offense to his line of questioning. "And I understand that this might be too soon to talk about after everything that has happened. I just can't help but wonder... what actually happened with your ex-fiancé?"

"Gilbert didn't tell you?" She cocked her head at him in question.

"He did," James admitted sheepishly. "And that level of heartbreak was something I understand, so it's what led me to invite you here as Amy's governess. But I'd like to hear the story from you if you don't mind."

Mattie's cheeks flashed crimson, and for a moment James was worried he had pushed too far. But, when she began to speak with a tentative but honest voice, that worry vanished.

"His name was Lewis Mooney," Mattie explained, holding her chin high and proud.

"Mooney?" James interjected, the name ringing a bell from the time he had spent in Bartlett. "Not the Mooney family that owns half the town?"

"One and the same," she said with a nod. "I was working in the General Store when we met. He came in and immediately caught my fancy. He was so charming, and he kept coming in, openly admitting that he didn't need anything, he just wanted to come in and see me."

Her eyes flicked away for a moment, down to her shoes. And something about the reverence in her voice let James know that being wanted by Lewis, being wanted by *someone* in that manner, had meant quite a large deal to her. A large part of him wanted to reach out and touch her, simply a comforting brush of the arm, but he knew that that would be too much for him to bear.

Mattie continued speaking, completely unaware of the affect the conversation was having on him. "We were courting for a year and got engaged. I wanted to marry quickly, but he did not. And I was so happy to be engaged to him, so enamored with the beauty and the promise of what our life could be together, that I agreed to wait, even though it wasn't what I desired. I would have done anything to keep him, and I think he knew that and took advantage of it. Six months later, we were supposed to attend a Bartlett town dance. He never showed up to take me. When I walked in with Gilbert, he was dancing with another woman."

Her voice broke slightly, and she cleared her throat before continuing.

"Lewis told me that night that our engagement was off. That he had chosen another better suited for him and the station provided to him by his family."

Mattie's voice trailed off as she finished the recounting of the events, and James stared at her lovely face. So many emotions warred within him, anger at the man who had hurt him, confusion over how someone could deliberately hurt her, sadness at the heartache that Mattie must have experienced.

"He is a fool," James said without thinking. "Any man would be a fool to have you and then willingly lose you."

Her eyes widened with shock as the words left his mouth, but then the look on her face changed. Mattie's green eyes became heavy lidded and the air between them grew tense. James' pulse spiked as he looked down at her, and an almost overwhelming urge to lean down and press his lips to hers threatened to overtake her.

He heard Mattie's breath hitched, and her eyes fluttered, on the verge of closing. His eyes darted down to her lips, and he marveled at how easy it would be to close those last few inches of space between them. But then, the thought of Ruth and of Gilbert rushed into him and his blood ran cold.

James jumped up from the settee, backing away from her. Mattie's eyes sprang open with the sound of his feet shuffling across the floorboards and hurt and confusion flitted across her beautiful features.

"You should go to bed, Mattie," James advised, his voice low and thick with the effort it took to speak. "Before we both do something that we'll regret."

Mattie shuddered but then nodded, and James watched as she stood, crossed the floor of the family room, and disappeared beyond. He listened intently, hearing the creak of the stairs and then the sound of her door shutting softly. It was only then, when he knew she was safely secured behind the door of her bedchamber that he let out a sigh of relief and sank down to sit on the sofa across the room as he worked to regain his composure.

He wished that he could go to her and explain that he wanted to kiss her, that she had not misread the situation at all and that her confusion in the matter was not at all warranted. But to do so would be to admit something incredibly dangerous to the both of them. He had both a promise and a vow to keep, and he would not allow himself to lose sight of either of those things. No matter how much his affections for Mattie seemed to be growing.

Chapter Eleven

Mattie scrubbed the already clean dish a little more, glad for the distraction that cleaning was providing her. James had not come to breakfast the morning after she had thought he was going to kiss her again, and she was struggling to fight against the shame and embarrassment that threatened to overwhelm her.

She could hear Amy behind her, where she had set her up with her small, wooden toys. The toddler was gabbing with her typical, childlike babble, but the words they had been working on for the past week had been interlaced.

Now, woven into the endless stream of random noises was a "bock," as she called blocks, or "Att-eee" as she now referred to Mattie after the disastrous "ma" incident. She tried to focus on the child's words, to lose herself in the nonsense that Amy threw about, but she couldn't peel herself away from her own inner turmoil no matter how hard she tried.

Mattie wasn't sure if she would ever forget the look on James' face as he told her that they would both regret what almost happened the night before. It had been so similar to the pained look that Lewis had worn when he'd ended their engagement, and those same feelings of inadequacy and abandonment crashed over her in wave after wave.

Tears pricked at the back of her eyes as she continued to stew on it, cleaning up the few dishes from what she and Amy had prepared. Mattie had barely been able to eat, opting instead to push the food around her plate after only a few, quick bites. Anything that passed her lips just turned to ash in her mouth, and she could hardly bring herself to swallow.

Finally, she could no longer justify scrubbing anything in the kitchen, she'd worked so diligently to clean it all already.

Mattie turned to Amy, hands on her hips as she swallowed past the lump in her throat.

"Well, little one," Mattie said aloud, startled by the rasp of her own voice. "what are we going to do today?"

Amy looked at her, her soft brown eyes wide as she babbled. Mattie caught onto a few words, one of which, "side", gave her an idea.

She glanced toward the windows, marking how beautiful a day it was and decided that Amy was right.

"Good idea, sweet girl." Mattie cooed as she walked over and bent to pick the child up.

Placing Amy on her hip, she walked through the house and then up to Amy's room to find a bonnet for her head and a parasol to block the sun. Once all the items were secured, she strode from the house.

Mattie recalled from her tour the day she arrived at Mt. Juliet that not far behind the house there was a moderate plot of land that James had converted into a vegetable garden. She knew that he and Elmer had their hands full with readying the pastures for the summer season and hadn't been able to tend the vegetables as much as they would have liked. So today, she was going to do that for them.

She tried to recall just how far back the plot of land was, but it only required a little bit of searching before she finally stumbled upon it. Mattie set Amy down as she prepared a blanket, the parasol, and a few of the toys that she'd brought for the child to busy herself with as Mattie worked. Once she was satisfied that the child was well situated, she turned and looked at the garden with her hands on her hips.

Rows and rows of crops spread out before her, each in need of quite a lot of care. Mattie's mood lifted at the sight of it. It would be more than enough work to keep her busy for the day. For the next few days, if she was being honest with herself. And if things with James continued to be as awkward as they had been, she would be in dire need of the distraction.

Mattie stepped forward and into the first row before dropping to her knees and beginning to yank at some of the weeds. It didn't take long before she realized some of the plants also needed pruning and would need to be watered as well. She stood, glancing around, and wiping her dirty hands on her skirt.

She noticed a small, wooden shed not far from the garden, and she was sure it would contain everything she would need.

"Amy, stay right there," she commanded, pointing at the toddler who smiled widely at Mattie as she sauntered over to the shed.

She pulled at the handle and the wooden door opened with a loud creak. It was dark inside, and as Mattie stepped through, she had to pause for a few moments for her eyes to adjust. As they did, items lining the walls came into better view.

Spotting a watering pail, shears, and a handheld rake she quickly grabbed them up and made her way back out to where she had left Amy. Thankfully, the toddler had not moved at all, not that Mattie had expected her to. And Mattie quickly returned to work.

It didn't take long before Mattie was covered in sweat, beads of it dripping down her brow and onto her nose. She constantly had to straighten herself to catch her breath and wipe the sleeve of her dress against her face to clear it of the moisture. But even though the work was hard, and the day was hot, Mattie found it satisfying as well. Her muscles were already groaning, and she knew that tonight, for the first time in days, she would sleep soundly.

The sound of shoes crunching across the grass caught her attention, and Mattie sat up straight to look across the yard at who would be approaching. They were silhouetted against the sun, and Mattie shaded her eyes, trying to make out who they were as they got closer.

The first thing she noticed was a large, colorful bouquet of flowers and her brow furrowed. Was this James' way of apologizing for all that had transpired between them over the last few days? Then, the figure took another step, and she was finally able to make out their face and her heart sank. Hubert Bird.

"Hello there, Miss Mattie," Hubert said with the dip of his hat.

Mattie returned his greeting with a smile, one that she hoped didn't betray the now conflicted feelings that were rushing through her.

"Hello Hubert," Mattie returned, "what brings you all the way out to the ranch?"

"I saw these just this mornin'," he extended the large bouquet of flowers to her, "and just had to bring them out to you. Give you something beautiful to brighten your day a bit."

Mattie stood and once more brushed her hands along her skirt, not that it was much use. Pretty much all of her was covered in a fine layer of dust and sweat.

"They're lovely, thank you." She said as she reached forward and wrapped her hand around the delicate stems of the blooms.

Everything that James had admitted to her about Hubert the night before rushed through her mind. All of her experiences with Hubert thus far had been nothing short of pleasant, but she knew that James would not lie to her. Not about something such as that.

"Mattie, are you alright?" Hubert asked, his dark, sun kissed brow knitting together in concern.

"Quite," Mattie said in a rush. "Just busy, is all."

She gestured behind her to the garden that she had hardly made a dent in. Hubert nodded, taking it all in and then his gaze roved back to her face. He must have seen something written within the lines of her features, because his gaze suddenly darkened.

"Did James speak to you about me?" He asked, his voice taking on a tone of anger that she had not yet heard in it.

"No!" Mattie protested much too quickly, and she knew Hubert sensed the lie within it.

"I see," his voice was quiet and contemplative. But Mattie could tell by the set of his shoulders and the way his jaw clenched and unclenched that he was upset. "I guess I'll just have to go have a talk with Mr. James Murphy."

Before she could stop him, he turned on his heel and strode out toward the pastures. Mattie blinked after him for a moment, completely overwhelmed by the turn her afternoon had taken. Knowing that she needed to hurry after him, she quickly darted forward and grabbed Amy off of the blanket, following in Hubert's footsteps. But she couldn't keep up with his quick pace, not with a baby on her hip. She only hoped that she found them before it was too late.

Chapter Twelve

James grunted with effort as he held up the beam that Elmer was working to secure in the barn. The sound of the hammering echoed through the small space and out into the world beyond, a sound that had been serving to help distract him all day.

He had not been able to face Mattie that morning, had not even been able to contemplate being able to see the still lingering hurt on her face over his dismissal the night before. And so, he had risen with the sun and went out to work as early and as quietly as he could. It was the cowards way out, he knew. And he had opted to take it too many times already for his own liking. But it was the only option he had.

James' stomach had been in knots all day as he contemplated what had occurred. He couldn't lie to himself any longer, he wanted Mattie. His affections for her only continued to grow with each passing day, and he would be a fool to try to deny that fact. But it was also a fact that James had made a promise to Gilbert that nothing would happen between the two of them.

That he would take care of her as he would his own sister. And Gilbert had been too good a friend for too long for James to even consider betraying that trust. No, James knew that he needed to work harder to stifle the kernel of desire that was sparking between them and push his own feelings to the side.

"Murphy!"

The sound of a male voice yelling his name pulled James from his thoughts and the sound of the hammer that Elmer was using came to an abrupt stop. Still holding the beam aloft, James wasn't able to turn immediately. Instead, he glanced up and watched as confusion and then recognition danced over Elmer's face at whoever had just walked in the barn. The color drained from the young mans tanned skin, and suddenly James had a sinking suspicion of who he would find standing behind him.

He heard the sound of shoes on dirt as whoever it was walked into the barn, and James looked around for something to prop the beam on so he could turn and confront what was coming. Elmer stayed where he was, shooting James a questioning look as James worked to take the beam from his shoulder and secure it on a large piece of wood he'd scooted over with his foot.

"Hubert," James said when he turned and marked the figure now stalking toward him with angry strides. "What did I do to deserve the pleasure of you on my property two days in a row?"

James couldn't help the sarcasm that leeched into his tone, and the other man's scowl deepened.

"Did you tell Mattie to stay away from me?" Hubert demanded, his face beet red with emotion.

"Why would I do a thing like that?" James taunted as he cocked his head. He knew it was cruel, but he found himself reveling in the other man's anger. It felt good to focus on something other than his own emotional distress for a change.

"You know why," Hubert pointed a finger at his chest. "Stay out of this, Murphy."

Just then, Mattie rushed into the barn, her cheeks flushed pink from the effort of making it to the barn. Amy was balanced on her hip, and at the sound of the raised voices her face screwed up in distress.

"Hubert, you will not raise your voice around my daughter," James growled, advancing a step. "And as for Mattie, I will do whatever I damn well please. She is the governess to my child and my best friends' little sister. I have promised to take care of her as I would my own sister, and that is a promise that I intend to keep. You and I are both aware that Mattie has no idea the real depths of your depravity, but she is a smart girl. I don't need to warn her to stay away from men like you. She has worked that out for herself."

Hubert gaped at James, at the vitriol that fell so readily from between his lips. The man glanced from Mattie, to James, to Elmer, and then made it's rounds again. Mattie was cooing to Amy, doing the best she could to quiet her amid all the tension in the air. James wasn't sure how it was possible, but Hubert's face turned an even deeper shade of red, and his dark brown eyes narrowed.

"Stay out of this. What Mattie and I have is none of your business," Hubert hissed before turning and stalking from the barn.

Mattie gaped at them all, her head whipping wildly from watching Hubert as he marched across the property and then back to James, who stood in the middle of the barn with his chest heaving.

"I'm just going to go get something from the shed," Elmer's voice drifted from behind James, steeped with caution.

He listened as Elmer's footsteps sounded through the barn and then faded with his retreat. All the while, James could not take his eyes off of Mattie.

"So, we discuss Hubert last night, I tell you about everything that happened, and you still decide to entertain him?" James' heart was racing at the thought, at the fact that he had opened up to her and she had dismissed it all so readily. But he refused to show his hurt.

"I did not entertain him," Mattie protested, stepping forward with her eyes wide and pleading. "He showed up with flowers and I didn't know what to do, so I..."

"So, you told him that you couldn't speak to him because of me, was that it?" James interrupted her, not wanting to listen to her excuses. "You didn't think it would be sufficient for you to not want to talk to him yourself, you had to allow me to take the blame?"

"James," Mattie's voice rose with hurt. "No, you don't understand."

"I understand plenty." He held out his hands, gesturing for Amy. "Hand me my daughter."

Mattie blinked at him for a moment, and he watched the confusion and hurt flit across her features before she extracted a marginally calmer Amy from her hip and passed her to James. James wrapped his arms around his daughter, pressing her small, warm body to his as his brain worked to make sense of everything that had just occurred. He knew he couldn't do that, though, not with Mattie standing before him.

"I'll bring Amy back inside in a little bit," James said in a dismissive voice.

He didn't look at Mattie as he spoke, but he didn't need to. James knew that his words would hurt her, and he also knew that if he saw the flash of pain dance across her features it would weaken his resolve. For the moment, at least, he just wanted to be mad.

Mattie didn't say anything else to him as she turned and walked from the barn, and James bounced Amy in the air and played with her as he listened to her retreating footsteps.

When Elmer came back inside, his ranch hand shot him a confused look, but something in James' expression deterred him from asking any questions. James set up one of the wheelbarrows for Amy and placed her in it, wanting to have her near him while he worked. It brought comfort to him, hearing his daughter laughing and entertaining herself, and living a happy life despite lacking the presence of her mother.

By the time he and Elmer finished up for the day, Amy was snoozing in the wheelbarrow amongst a fresh bale of hay. He said goodbye to Elmer and told him where to meet him on the property for the work they needed to do the next day. He picked up Amy and roused her carefully as he walked back to the house, giving her a few minutes to wake herself up.

By the time they walked into the house, Mattie was setting the table for dinner. James tucked Amy into her wooden dining chair and loaded up food onto both of their plates. An awkwardness filled the air, but James refused to be the first one to dispel it. And as dinner continued, neither he nor Mattie spoke.

Chapter Thirteen

Mattie tossed and turned, staring angrily up at her ceiling. For the entirety of dinner, James did not speak one word to her. When he had dismissed her from the barn, she had hoped that after a few hours of work he would have calmed down about everything that had happened to Hubert, but it seemed that he did not.

Mattie had wanted to yell at him, her own frustration bubbling just below the surface. It wasn't as if she had asked Hubert to show up to the ranch with flowers in hand. This was not her fault, and she was so incredibly angry at James for making her feel as if it was.

She wanted to tell him that he was acting like a child, and that his anger would be better directed at Hubert himself, and not at her. But she knew that trying to bring it up would only end in another fight. Especially while the feelings of the day were so fresh in both of their minds. And so, she had held her tongue.

It had felt good to lay Amy down for the night, to tuck her in and watch as she drifted off to sleep before Mattie turned into her own room. At her wash basin she had used a strip of cloth and water and a sparing bit of soap to scrub the last bits of dirt from her face and arms.

She had washed her hands upon returning to the house to begin dinner but removing the remaining layer of grime prior to bed had felt almost heavenly.

Mattie had hoped that the act of scrubbing her skin, the way she rubbed the cloth methodically to remove the most dirt possible, would have distracted her mind. But it had not. And so, she had laid in bed throughout most of the night while sleep evaded her. More than once she wondered if James was awake too.

At one point, she had thought of possibly storming across the hall and knocking on his door, demanding that he speak to her, and they end this anger and hurt before them. But Mattie hadn't been able to work up the courage to do so. She was upset with James, yes. But she also did not want to risk deepening his anger to the point that he sent her back to Bartlett, dismissing her as no longer worth the trouble.

She had only been able to doze for a couple of hours by the time the sun began to rise. When the first rays broke through her window, rousing her from the light sleep she had fallen into, she laid on her back and stared absently at the same ceiling she had glared at for half the night.

Mattie heard when James finally rose. Across the hall she could hear his scuffling and moving about as he made his bed and dressed for his day. Not wanting him to rush out before breakfast once again, she pushed herself out of bed and dressed in a hurry. She made it downstairs and to the kitchen just as James opened the door to his room.

Taking out the food she needed for breakfast, Mattie busied herself with dicing potatoes as he strode into the room. His footsteps stopped abruptly, and Mattie assumed that he was surprised to find her already in the kitchen.

She whirled to face him, finding that he was already attempting to back out of the room.

"None of that," Mattie demanded, using the knife she held for chopping to motion to his usual seat at the table. It came off more menacing than she intended, but when his eyes widened and he obeyed her by pulling out the chair and taking a seat, she couldn't bring herself to regret it.

"We need to talk," Mattie began, turning back to her chopping.

"Do we?" James said in a cool, even tone.

"You know that we do." Mattie threw the potatoes in the pan and began to crack open the eggs. "You had no right to speak to me the way you did yesterday."

James was quiet a moment as Mattie whisked the eggs in the bowl and then poured them in a separate pan. For a while, only the sound of the cooking eggs and the crisping potatoes filled the air. She turned her back on the stove, eyeing James across the kitchen. Underneath his beard, she could see his jaw working back and forth in contemplation, and his bright blue eyes were watching her wearily.

Finally, James dipped his head in agreement.

"You're right," he admitted. "I was angry and hurt. I took it out on you, and I should not have."

Mattie had expected more of a fight, had believed that he'd find some other way to blame her for Hubert arriving at the ranch yesterday afternoon. And now, with his apology floating between them, the heat of her anger began to cool, but only slightly.

"You have to stop doing that," Mattie said sternly. "Blaming me for things that aren't my fault. It is unkind, James. And I don't deserve it."

James nodded again as he glanced down at the table. She wanted to admonish him for looking away, or command that he bring his gaze back to hers. But, instead, she just carried on.

"I did not invite Hubert here yesterday, and I think you well know that. I did not ask him to bring me flowers. And I surely

THE GOVERNESS AND THE COWBOY'S PROMISE

did not ask him to go traipsing across the property to yell at you in front of Elmer and Amy."

"I know, Mattie," James sighed.

"Then why did you yell at me for it?" Her voice came out harsher and louder than she had intended, but all of the emotions that she'd had over the course of the last few days was bubbling inside of her. Speaking about it all felt like a flood gate had opened up, and she now felt as if she had no way to stop her words from pouring out of her.

"Because..." James began, pushing up from the table as his blue eyes flashed at her. His chest rose and fall rapidly, and she wondered what he could possibly be thinking. "Do you care for him, Mattie? Do you fancy him?"

The question caught her off guard and she narrowed her eyes at him.

"Why would you even ask me that?"

"You know why!" James exclaimed, his own voice rising to match hers.

The thought that they were risking waking Amy tickled the back of her mind, but she squelched it down. The fight they had both been dancing around for days was finally upon them, and she was going to see it through one way or another.

"Hubert is sweet," she admitted to him, and James' face fell slightly. "He is attentive. And to be quite honest with you I don't mind the attention."

She paused for dramatic effect, watching as the weight of her words washed over him before continuing.

"But no, I do not fancy him."

The relief that James felt was almost palpable, and another bout of annoyance overcame her.

"Why do you care, anyway?" Mattie narrowed her eyes at him. "What does it matter to you if I fancy Hubert Bird?"

James stared at her, his mouth popping open with a bit of surprise at her direct line of questioning. But Mattie couldn't fathom why he would be perplexed that her frustrations were finally bubbling over. Twice now she had thought that James was going to kiss her, and twice he had done nothing more than use that moment to embarrass her. The same rejections time and time again. First from her classmates as they taunted her, then from Lewis, and now, possibly worst of all, from James Murphy.

James who had known her for most of her life. James who was handsome and good and kind. James who trusted her to take care of his daughter, to clean his home, but somehow did not seem to find her good enough for anything more. Mattie couldn't take another moment of it.

Hurt swelled within her as James' ice blue gaze raked over her. Her hands were shaking under the weight of his gaze, but he seemed to not notice.

"It is all just an act, Mattie." James' voice was soft, as if he believed the fight was already behind them. "Hubert is putting on an act to try to impress you. You deserve so much better than him."

"By better, do you mean you?" The words left Mattie's mouth before she could stop them, cruel and harsh.

James recoiled at them, shock dancing across his handsome features. She wanted to continue, to throw out at him how much his rejections had hurt her both times he had hurled it at her. But she refrained, opting instead to stand there and wait for him to respond.

The fight seemed to leak out of James, and he looked down at the floor, studying his hands, his shoes, the floorboards, looking anywhere than at Mattie herself.

"You know that I don't mean that." His voice was not unkind, in fact, Mattie could have sworn there was a hint of regret hidden within them. But they cut her deeply all the same. "You and me? It would not be right."

Mattie took a quick step back until she came in contact with the counter. The eggs made a popping sound, and she was reminded that she still had food on the stove. With gratitude, she turned and stirred the breakfast. It was slightly burnt, but salvageable. And Mattie made a big show of getting the food out of the pans and onto serving plates.

"Mattie," there was a pleading note in James' tone, but she did not want to hear it.

"Breakfast is ready," she said in a hollow voice, setting the plates on the kitchen table.

She could tell that James wanted to say more, but she was saved from his further rejection by the sound of cries coming from Amy's room.

"I'll go. Stay and eat," Mattie commanded, not stopping to look at James as she turned and strode from the room.

Her heart was racing with hurt and the sting of James' rejection once more as she climbed the stairs and opened the door to Amy's room. Upon seeing Mattie, Amy's cries ceased, and she smiled up at her happily. A lump formed in Mattie's throat as she rushed forward to help Amy out of bed and begin dressing her.

She cooed softly to the child, letting her comforting presence wash over her as the sting of James' final rejection washed over her anew. She hadn't expected it to hurt this much, hadn't expected to feel the sting of it all the way in her bones. And yet, here she was, trying not to cry over James' words.

"It would not be right," He had said to her. And she knew what he meant. It wouldn't be right for him to allow himself a few moments of pleasure to kiss her, when he knew that it would mean more to her than it would to him. It would not be right, because he did not care for her. Not in the same way.

She swallowed hard, trying and failing to blink back the tears that threatened to spill from her eyes. Amy blinked at her as Mattie pulled the child's dress over her head, and then reached up her chubby toddler hand to wipe away one of the tears slowly falling down Mattie's cheek.

Mattie smiled at the toddler, laughing gently at the affection that Amy so readily gave. She pressed a kiss to Amy's tiny fist, grateful for the small child. She took as much time as she could to get Amy ready for the day, drawing the strings on the toddler's dress together much more slowly than she usually would, and taking extra care with her stockings, and bonnet.

When Mattie knew she could delay no longer, she picked up Amy and walked out of the room. She descended the stairs carefully, taking care to list to any noise coming from any other part of the house. But when she made it into the kitchen, she realized that that was in vain. The room was empty, and it appeared that James had done most of the dishes for her.

All but the serving plates that still contained the food that Amy and Mattie had yet to eat had been washed and placed on a drying rack. Mattie felt a quick rush of gratitude, then regret over how she had spoken to him, followed by another bout of sadness over the rejection.

With a sigh, Mattie placed Amy in her highchair before sitting down beside her. She spooned food onto a plate and began feeding both herself and Amy. And she knew without a shadow of a doubt that the conflicting emotions warring inside of her wouldn't be letting up any time soon.

Chapter Fourteen

The fabric gave a faint *snap* as Mattie shook it out to rid the garment of wrinkles before bringing it up to the clothesline and pinning it securely in place. The morning had passed quickly, and the sun was now shining directly overhead.

After her foray in the garden the day before and the sodden clothes that James had piled in the laundry basket from the last few days on the ranch, Mattie had known exactly what her morning would be spent doing from the moment she had finished breakfast.

The sound of the door to the house opening and closing grabbed her attention, and she turned to glance in that direction. Striding across the yard was Elmer, his bright red hair gleaming in the sun, and something white held in his hands. As he got closer, Mattie's eyes were able to better focus on whatever it was he held, and she quickly made it out as an envelope.

"Hello Elmer," Mattie said with a genuine smile as the young man approached.

"Mornin' Mattie. Got some mail for ya," he extended his hand to her as he got close, and Mattie looked at it confused for a moment. Noting her confusion, Elmer explained further. "James sent me in town to the post office to gather everything for him."

Mattie nodded and reached a hand forward, plucking the envelope from between Elmer's fingers.

"Thank you," she said as she turned it over, noting her brother's familiar scrawl across it.

She and Elmer made a few moments of small talk before he wished her good day and made his way back out into the pasture. The laundry long forgotten, Mattie quickly opened the letter, and her eyes devoured every word her brother had written her.

It was her first piece of mail she'd received since arriving in Mt. Juliet, and Mattie was excited to see how things in her hometown were faring. She walked over to the blanket and parasol where Amy was playing and sat down beside her, and her brother's voice sounded through her mind as she read on.

Dearest Mattie,

I hope that everything is going well in Mt. Juliet. Things are going very well here in Bartlett. There have been a few more dances, and they repainted the General Store. It's a bright, vibrant red, and I think you would have loved it.

I received a letter from James, and he said that you were fitting right in in Tennessee. And it made my heart so incredibly glad to hear it. I had worried how you would fare when I placed you on that train, but to know that you are flourishing there makes all the worry worth it.

I wanted to remind you, though, that it is alright for you to go out and still live. While you moved to Tennessee to become a governess, that does not have to be your entire life. Visit the town, make friends, maybe fall in love, and force James to give you a night off and take some time to yourself. You do not have to be chained to the house all hours of the day. I know you have always prided yourself on the way you can work, but work is not all there is. Find some happiness for yourself while you're at it, Mattie.

Hopefully I'll hear from you soon.

Your brother,

Gilbert

Mattie's eyes burned with unshed tears as she finished the letter, deciding to read it one more time. Her brother was not one who took showing emotion lightly, and the fact that he had taken the time to sit down and write out those beautiful words touched her deeply.

"Live, Mattie," he had written, and it had resounded deep within her. She would do exactly that.

Hurriedly, Mattie hung the final pieces of laundry and double checked the clothes pins to ensure they were secure. Then, she turned to pick up Amy from the ground, packed up the parasol and blanket, and then strode into the house. Walking into the drawing room, she opened up the drawer in the writing desk and extracted a piece of paper. Quickly, she scrawled on it exactly where she was headed so James would not worry if he came back before her, and then went to grab Amy's pram.

In no time at all, she and Amy were firmly nestled within the buildings of Mt. Juliet, and Mattie paused to appreciate for a moment the sounds of life and of people milling about. The ranch was beautiful, but its relative seclusion made it quiet. And she hadn't realized how much she had been craving a little bit of noise.

A little way up the road, Mattie spotted a lilac painted building with a beautiful, white sign that marked it as the local haberdashery. Excitedly, Mattie pushed the pram toward it a little more quickly, before pulling it up along the façade of the shop and taking a peek through the windows.

Row after row of gorgeous dresses for women and suits for men, followed by shelves holding glamorous hats, scarves, and even some jewelry. It had been a while since Mattie had bought herself anything of note, and so she extracted Amy from the basket atop the pram and held her tightly as she walked into the shop.

The large windows at the front of the building allowed for quite a bit of natural light to illuminate the space, and the moment that Mattie stepped into it she was instantly carried away on the tides of luxurious fabrics.

She was greeted briefly by the clerk, and then took to roaming between the beautiful clothes and shelves of accessories. Mattie dreamed about owning something as grand as what was on display but knowing that she'd never have any use for it, she quickly waved away the notions. Then, as she was walking through the final aisle that was stocked with hat after hat, Mattie's eyes fell on something that absolutely stole her breath.

The hat was white cotton pulled tight over its structure. It had a delicate, sweeping brim, and beautiful, pale blue flowers interwoven on the crown. A plume of blue ribbon fanned from the back of it, cascading down so long that it would have passed the wearers shoulders. Her hands reached out of their own accord, and she ran her fingertips over it.

She set Amy down on a small chair only a foot or so away, and then plucked the hat from the shelf. Mattie nestled it softly onto her caramel locks before turning to study herself in one of the many looking glasses around the shop.

"That looks beautiful on you," said a voice beside her, causing her to jump with a start.

Hubert Bird stood only a few feet away, smiling at her warmly. Images rushed into Mattie's mind of the last time she saw Hubert, red faced and yelling at James with barely controlled anger. Unease washed through her at his proximity, and she shifted uncomfortably on her feet.

"Thank you, Hubert," she said kindly, hoping that she would be able to wave off the conversation soon. "It is a very beautiful hat. I'm sure it would look lovely on anyone."

Mattie reached up to take the hat from her head just as Amy let out a wine of frustration. Placing the hat back on the shelf, mattie rushed over to grab Amy, who was now begging to fuss quite a bit. Mattie cooed to her, trying to get the fussy child to calm.

"I am so sorry, Hubert," Mattie said in a rush. "It is past time for Amy's nap. I must get going."

Afraid that he was going to offer to walk her home again, Mattie rushed from the shop and left Hubert in her wake. She did not want to seem cruel, but she also did not want to spend any additional time in his presence if she could avoid it.

Not now that she knew not only the full story behind his history with James, but also how deeply it would hurt him. Plus, she had not liked the anger that had flared within him when he suspected that she had been warned to keep her distance. Mattie knew from some of her friends' back in Bartlett that a man's temper could sometimes prove to be quite dangerous.

Mattie settled Amy back into the basket of the pram as quickly as she could before pushing it down the road. The rocking motion of it as she guided it down the road calmed the fussy child, her whines getting quieter until finally they stopped all together and Amy drifted off to sleep. Mattie walked more quickly than she normally would as she made her way back to the ranch, casting a glance behind her every so often to ensure that Hubert had not followed.

When the ranch house finally came into view, she let out a sigh of relief, feeling a sense of safety wash over her.

THE GOVERNESS AND THE COWBOY'S PROMISE

Chapter Fifteen

The screen door creaked loudly as James pulled it open and stepped into the house. His muscles screamed in protest as he bent to take off his boots. As soon as he kicked them off, a sigh of relief escaped him. The smell of food floated to him in the air, and he followed it to the kitchen where Mattie was just finishing up supper.

Another wave of emotion washed over him at the sight of her. James had been battling with his feelings for Mattie throughout most of the day. On one hand, he felt glad to have told her that nothing could ever happen between them. She did not need to know the reasons why, and it was probably better for them both if she didn't. In order for her to understand that he would first need to admit that he wanted her but could not have her. And knowing that would only serve to hurt her farther.

On the other hand, James hated that he had to disappoint her. It was good that she knew not to get her hopes up, but he also knew just how much Mattie had been hurt in the past, especially after she had opened up to him about it the other night. And now James was just another name on the list of people who had hurt her. He despised that fact, but he knew it was for the best.

As James stepped into the kitchen, Mattie looked up and gave him a tentative but warm smile. They had not spoken since the night before, as he had rushed out of the house that morning before she had risen. He had been worried that the hostile and awkward air that had surrounded them for the past few days would remain. But if Mattie's smile was any indication, she had decided not to hold a grudge.

James pulled out his seat at the kitchen table and plopped down into it, feeling better than he had in days.

"Pop pop!" Amy squealed when her brown eyes landed on him.

"Hello little one," he said, leaning forward to give her a quick, swift kiss on the top of her head before she diverted her attention back to her toys.

"How was your day?" He asked Mattie hesitantly, wondering if her seemingly warm mood would translate well to conversation.

"I got the laundry done, I just brought it in off of the line," Mattie answered as she placed the food in the center of the table. "Amy and I went into town for a little bit, and I browsed the haberdashery."

"Did you buy anything?"

"No," Mattie's answer came a little too quickly, and James wondered what that was about. But the tentative peace that had descended between them felt too fragile, so he didn't press any further.

"It was a good day for the walk to town. Hopefully you enjoyed it," James opted to say instead.

The conversation felt stilted and awkward; both he and Mattie walking on eggshells around the other so as not to descend into another argument like they had so many times recently. However, James still felt hopeful.

"I received a letter from Gilbert," Mattie said, and James looked up to meet her eyes.

They were bright and excited as she talked about her brother. He wondered how much Gilbert had told her about the letter that James had written him. He had tried to be vague and not allude to the fact that he had been developing feelings for Gilbert's little sister. Instead, he had opted to tell him about how Mattie was getting along well with both Elmer and Josie, and that if she got out a little more, he felt sure that she would make a few friends.

"Did he?" James raised a brow. "And what did he have to say?"

"He gave me a few updates about Bartlett. Apparently, they painted the General Store bright red. And then he said you'd told him I was fitting in in Mt. Juliet," she shot him a pointed look at this before continuing on. "But then, he encouraged me to get out more. To go into town, to make friends and maybe…"

She hesitated, and James leaned forward slightly as he chewed his food, wondering what she was about to say.

"Maybe fall in love," Mattie finished, her tone soft and unsure.

A bolt of surprise rushed through James, followed by a small, quick pang of jealousy. He quickly fought to stuff that down and keep his face arranged in one that conveyed pleasant, platonic interest.

"That's a fine idea, Mattie," James hated the words the moment they left his lips, but he knew he needed to pretend to be happy and supportive of this notion. "Gilbert is right."

"Is he?" She said as she studied his face.

"Of course," James paused to swallow down a bite of his stew. It felt thick in his throat and it was hard to make it go down now that his stomach has been soured by the news. "In fact, there is a dance coming up at the Town Hall in a few days. There will be plenty of people there for you to meet. Perhaps we should go."

Mattie lit up at this news, her face becoming animated.

"Are you sure?"

James chuckled at her excitement, all awkwardness and hostility between them now entirely vanishing in light of the news.

"I'm sure. In fact, if you're going to be there with the intent to fall in love, as you put it, you'll need something new to wear. You won't be impressin' any fellas in those dresses you've been wearing to pull weeds in."

He winked at her to let her know the joke was good natured, and he was rewarded by Mattie rolling her eyes at him.

"Only if you're sure," Mattie answered, looking at him seriously.

"I am." James gave her a quick, firm nod. He hoped that his face did not betray how much he hated the idea that he would have to see her on anyone else's arm but his.

"Ok then," Mattie said with a grin.

They fell into easy conversation at that, with Mattie chatting away about the dance and how excited she was. James informed her that Josie is who would be decorating the Town Hall and helping with the preparation, and that if she'd like, he would speak to her about Mattie helping out.

Mattie had positively glowed at the idea, and it had almost completely stolen his breath. By the time that dinner was finished, and he had taken Amy up to put her to sleep while Mattie cleaned the kitchen, James had accepted that he would have to tread very carefully over the next few days to manage his jealousy and emotions.

He slept fitfully that night, tossing and turning and filled with dreams of Mattie dancing with other men. The next morning after breakfast, he had readied the wagon and they had set off toward town. As they'd past Elmer's house, James had pulled the wagon to a stop and walked to the door, letting Elmer know to take the day off and spend time with Laurah. Elmer had been more than happy to oblige James' command.

By the time they arrived in town, Mattie was practically vibrating on the bench seat with excitement. James pulled on the reigns, bringing the horse to a stop before the seamstress's shop. He wasn't excited to go shopping, but he was glad to see the joy that was bursting from Mattie.

James helped Mattie climb down from the carriage, careful not to focus too much on the feeling of her hand in his as he did so. Mattie, oblivious to the inner turmoil that James was working through, rushed into the shop on a wave of excitement.

"Do not worry about the price," James had told her as they'd ridden into town. And he had meant every word. Mattie had tried to argue with him, tried to assure him that she would keep the price of her gown low and that she would pay for it out of her governess wages, but James had waved her off. It warmed his heart to do this for her. And he knew that his opportunities to bring her joy would be limited, so he had to take them where he could.

Mattie talked excitedly to the seamstress as the woman took her measurements and they browsed through fabric together. By the end of it, Mattie had selected a gorgeous, sage green corseted gown, with delicate yellow flowers stitched up the bodice. When she had put on the gown and walked out into the show room, it was all James could do to keep his mouth from dropping to the floor.

"You will for sure find your husband in that," James said jokingly, trying to imagine what Gilbert would say to her.

Mattie's face had scrunched up for only a moment before she turned and told the seamstress that they would take it. The gown needed only a few alterations, and they scheduled when she could come back and pick it up.

Before they headed back home, they decided to stop and see Josie and spend a few moments chatting with her while she played with Amy. Josie was delighted at the thought of Mattie helping her ready the Town Hall for the dance when James brought it up, and after they left, it was all Mattie could talk about the entire ride home.

James hated that he now had to put on a concerned, brotherly act. The way he had to behave toward Mattie chafed against his skin. But he knew that if he wanted to keep his promise to Gilbert, it was what he had to do. As they finally pulled back up in front of the house, he told Mattie and Amy to go on into the house, and he would take care of putting the wagon and the horse away. He took a few moments to take deep breaths and calm the nerves that were racing through his body. And sent up a quick prayer that he was making the right choice.

Chapter Sixteen

Mattie smiled to herself as she followed the well-worn road that led into town. The afternoon sun beat down on her from overhead, while a breeze ruffled her skirts around her ankles. She stopped for a moment to smell a patch of wildflowers, before continuing on her way to help Josie ready the Town Hall for the dance.

She never would have imagined when she woke yesterday morning that her fight with James would have turned into all of this. Mattie had been disappointed by James' reaction when she told him about Gilbert's letter, and about her brother's recommendation that she try to fall in love. But, when he had told her about the dance and that he would be taking her to buy a dress, her mood had quickly improved.

Mattie had hoped that when he saw her trying on gowns, that perhaps he would see her in a different light. But, based off his kind and almost brotherly words of encouragement while they were with the seamstress, she had no such luck.

Waving the thoughts away, Mattie decided to focus instead on the day ahead of her. She was excited to spend the morning decorating with Josie. In the limited time that she had spent with the other woman, she found that she very much enjoyed her company. And she was glad to spend more time with her that day.

As the town came into view, Mattie was overcome with another bolt of excitement, and she hastened her steps. Following the directions that James had given her for locating the town hall was simple enough, and in no time at all Mattie found herself standing in front of the large, whitewashed wooden building.

It was double the size of the Town Hall back in Bartlett, and when Mattie pulled open the large, heavy wooden door, her mouth popped open in surprise. The inside was stunning, the rich, oak that made up the building was polished and gleaming on the inside. Large, iron hooks hung out of the walls with large lanterns that illuminated the space in a rich, comforting glow.

Josie was standing in the middle of the large room, her hands on her hips as she turned about and looked at everything. At the sound of Mattie's feet on the wooden floors, Josie's eyes flitted to Mattie and then lit up with joy at the sight of her.

"Mattie," Josie exclaimed, rushing forward to pull her into a quick, warm hug. "I'm so glad you made it! I almost talked Jessup's ear off the whole night about how excited I was you would be helpin' today!"

Mattie laughed, "I'm excited to! What all is there to do? The place is already so beautiful."

"Well, we were able to get a ton of flowers that we're going to put in vases and decorate the tables. Some ivy vines to wrap around the pillars, you know. That sort of thing."

Mattie nodded along as Josie spoke, trying to envision all the ways that the two of them would bring the building to life.

"The wagon carrying everything should be here in just a minute," Josie said just as a loud whistle sounded through the open doors. "Oh, that'll be them now. Come on!"

Josie hustled forward and Mattie had to all but jog to keep up with the woman. Josie may have been shorter than Mattie, but her quick, fervent strides more than made up for it. When Mattie stepped outside, she stared in surprise. Josie hadn't been kidding when she said there were a lot of flowers for them to use. The men driving the wagon climbed down, and began bringing them in in droves, setting them on the tables that Josie indicated. In no time at all, the hall was awash in a flurry of activity.

As the men continued to carry in the blooms, Josie had Mattie start putting them in bundles. She instructed her on which flowers made up which bouquets, and then left her to her own devices to begin putting them together in the jars and cans they were using as vases.

It took Mattie a moment to make sense of it all, how to add balance to the bouquets that she was building. But, with Josie's expert instruction, she got the hang of it in no time at all. And, before long, Mattie found that she quite liked the work. There were plenty of wildflower patches in the pastures on the ranch, and Mattie made a mental note to take Amy out to pick some and to start building bouquets for the kitchen more often.

After all the flowers, vines, and everything else that they needed were unloaded, Mattie and Josie wasted no time finishing up the bouquets for the centers of the tables and then instructing a few other helpers on where to drape the vines and streamers.

It took a few hours, but when everything was finished, Mattie and Josie walked to the front of the room that had been left clear for the dance floor and surveyed their work. The place had already been beautiful when Mattie had arrived, but with the added decoration the place had come alive. The bright yellow, white, and green of the flowers and foliage popped against the golden wood of the building.

"It's beautiful," Mattie exclaimed as Josie nodded her agreement. Needing a break, both women walked over to one of the tables, pulled out a chair, and took a seat. Breathing heavily, Mattie and Josie looked at each other while they rested, both women wearing a broad, satisfied grin at all of the things they'd been able to complete.

"So," Josie said as she settled into her chair, her expression contemplative. "There will be a lot of bachelors at the dance tomorrow."

Josie wiggled her eyebrows at Mattie knowingly, and Mattie couldn't help but laugh.

"That's what I've heard."

"Oh really," Josie placed her elbows on the table between them and leaned forward, propping her chin in her hands. "From who?"

"James."

Josie's eyebrows shot up at Mattie's answer. "That's surprising."

"How so?" Mattie cocked her head.

"I just didn't think he'd want you talking to other bachelors. Perhaps I was mistaken."

Mattie shrugged noncommittally. "So, who might these other bachelors be?"

"Oh," Josie giggled, and her cheeks flushed crimson. "Well, there are plenty. Vance Tavers, for starters. He's a right looker, that one. His Pa owns the feed and farm supply shop in town."

Mattie nodded at that, recalling the old man she'd met right after arriving in Mt. Juliet.

"There's William McTavish, owner of the saloon. He's a bit rough around the edges, loves him a good stiff drink. But he's kind enough, and quite handsome." Josie counted off on the tips of her fingers with each new name that she listed.

Mattie recounted what Josie was telling her, trying her best to commit the names to memory. As her friend talked, she looked around the room and tried to imagine herself out on the dance floor with the men that Josie was describing to her. A thought occurred to Mattie, and she turned her gaze back to the other woman.

"What about Hubert Bird?"

Mattie knew James wouldn't approve of her asking about him, and she didn't have any intention of dancing with him or giving him more than just a polite 'hello' when she saw him next. But it wouldn't hurt to get someone else's opinion on the man. Just in case.

"Hubert Bird?" Josie asked, contemplatively.

She glanced down at the table they were sitting at and seemed to chew the inside of her lips.

"You can be candid," Mattie said to the other woman, sensing her reluctance to discuss it further. Josie nodded once before meeting Mattie's gaze once more.

"Hubert can be... exuberant in his pursuits." Josie's voice was hesitant as if she was weighing each word as she spoke it. "He can be kind when he wants to be, and his family is well established, and he's handsome enough. So it isn't that he'd be a bad match. But he doesn't always know how to react when his affections are not reciprocated."

Mattie considered Josie's words, comparing them to what she had already learned about Hubert from James and also her own experiences with the man thus far. Everything that Josie had said rang true, and Mattie made a silent promise to herself to do everything in her power not to encourage Hubert going forward.

Glancing at the large clock that adorned the mantle on the massive fireplace at the back of the room, Josie let out a small squeak of surprise.

"Oh my!" Josie pushed herself back from the table and stood, smoothing down her skirts. "It's later than I thought. And look at me, just gabbin' away. I need to get back to the shop to help Jessup with a few things to wrap up the afternoon."

"I'm so sorry to keep you," Mattie said, but her apologies were quickly waved off by the other woman.

"Nonsense, I've loved having you help out, Mattie. Please don't be a stranger. And at the very least, I'll see you tomorrow night."

Mattie smiled at Josie, for the first time feeling as if she might have finally found a true friend in her new town. The two women bade each other goodbye as they exited the building, Josie locking up before they went. Mattie strolled in the opposite direction of Josie, taking her time to look at the varying shops as she made her way back to the ranch.

Along the main road that ran through the center of town, she spotted a quaint bakery. The smell of bread and fresh baked goods floated through the air on a breeze as someone strolled out the door, and Mattie's mouth watered enticingly. Giving in to temptation, Mattie crossed the distance to the front of the store and pulled open the door.

The smell was stronger on the inside, and Mattie could hardly contain herself from wanting everything the baker had to offer. Reeling herself in, she selected a few cream buns from the display case and had them wrapped and boxed to take home, hoping that James would like them.

She paid the baker and then turned to begin her journey back to the ranch. The sun had sunk considerably lower in the sky since she first started her journey to town, and the air had cooled slightly. A breeze floated by, bringing with it a waft of flowers and dust that it stirred up along the road.

"Mattie," sounded a familiar voice behind her, and Mattie's heart sank as she turned in the direction of it and saw Hubert Bird standing there.

He had a pink box tied with ribbon held in his hands, and he was jogging to catch up with her. For a moment, her conversation with Josie rang through her mind, and she wondered if she should just turn and begin walking back toward the ranch. As soon as she finished the thought, however, she realized that while she knew she needed to proceed with caution, she could not bring herself to be outright rude to someone she did not think deserved it. And so, Mattie stopped to wait for him.

By the time he caught up to her, his cheeks were flushed with exertion and his breaths came in short, panted gasps.

"I was hoping I would see you," Hubert wheezed, and Mattie allowed him a moment to gather himself.

He straightened his arms out to her, presenting her with the box.

"This is for you."

Mattie eyed it warily, hesitant to reach out and take it. Not picking up on her reluctance, Hubert reached forward and opened it. At first, all Mattie could see was swaths of blue flowers, but upon closer inspection, she began to make sense of it all. Nestled inside the box was the hat that she had tried on at the haberdashery two days before.

"Oh Hubert," Mattie's breath left her in a surprised, worried rush. "You shouldn't have."

"It's quite alright," he waved her words away, thinking that they were a compliment instead of the admonishment they were. "It looked so splendid on you in the shop, and I thought you just had to have it."

Hubert reached inside the box, extracting the hat. He took a step forward, moving as if he was going to place the hat on Mattie's head, but she took a quick step of retreat.

"I apologize, Hubert," Mattie began, careful to keep her voice kind but firm. "But I truly cannot accept this. It is too much."

Hubert eyed her for a moment, taken aback by her refusal to accept the gift. After a few seconds, he seemed to gather his wits about him. Placing the hat back into the box and securing the lid, he thrust it back out to Mattie.

"I must insist that you take it," he said, his tone inviting no room for argument. "I have no use for it, and it was already purchased, so it is already done."

He nudged it forward again, and Mattie once again harkened back to Josie's warning about Hubert not knowing how to handle rejection. She wondered if she pushed the issue, how far would his persistence go?

"Mattie," he insisted again, giving the box a tiny shake.

Mattie cast a quick glance around them, wondering if there was anyone around that she might be able to call on to help her out of the situation in which she had found herself. But of course, there was no one. Beside James, she only really knew two people in town. One of them was Josie, who she knew was tucked away in Jessup's shop. And the other was standing right in front of her, insistent that she take a gift that she did not want.

Glancing down at the box she reached forward slowly. Apparently, Hubert thought she was taking too long, because he thrust the box forward again until it made contact with the one that held her pastries. Mattie reached forward, arranging the hat box on top of the one from the bakery so that she was able to easily carry both.

"Would you like help carrying them back home?" Hubert offered.

"No," Mattie said forcefully, determined that she would not allow him to escort her.

Not only had she promised herself that she would maintain a healthy distance with Hubert, but she had just gotten back into James' good graces. Mattie would not jeopardize that again and spend another few days fighting with him.

"No," she said again, this time in a more polite voice. Thankfully, Hubert seemed to have gotten the message. "The hat was quite enough. I will not allow you to walk me home as well. You have already been so gracious."

Hubert beamed at her, "it has been my pleasure, Miss Mattie."

Mattie glanced down at the boxes in her hands and then back up at Hubert and felt it as color rose in her cheeks.

"Thank you, Hubert. This was really, quite kind."

He tipped his hat to her as they wished each other goodbye. Mattie's steps became hurried as she began following the road that would lead her to home. But she hadn't been walking long when Hubert called out from behind her.

"You can pay me back with a dance in a few days."

Mattie shivered and she felt his eyes following her until she eventually faded into the distance.

Chapter Seventeen

James sat on the front porch swing, with Amy on his lap, pushing them back and forth as the swing made the occasional creaking sound. He'd been glad to spend the morning with her, feeding her breakfast and playing with her.

He'd been even more glad to know that Mattie was using that time to venture into town and spend time with Josie. He wanted her to make friends here, wanted her to build a life here. Even if he knew that the life she built wouldn't be with him.

Amy squealed with delight and began clapping her hands, and James followed her eyes to figure out what she was looking at. Mattie was walking down the lane, two boxes held in her hands and her cheeks flushed from the brief time spent under the sun.

James stood and placed Amy on his hip as he strode across the porch and down the stairs to greet her.

"Do you need help with that?" He asked, gesturing with one hand to the boxes that she held aloft.

"If you don't mind, would you grab this top one?"

James did, and he glanced at the box as he gripped onto it. It was pink and round, and whatever was inside of it jostled slightly as he held it aloft.

"What is in here?" He asked, giving it a delicate shake.

"Nothing of importance," Mattie answered, waving him off as she held up the other box with a grin. "This is the one you should be concerned about."

James' curiosity spiked as they walked into the house. Mattie instructed him to just leave the pink box on the staircase and she would take it to her room later. He was half tempted to lift the lid to see what was inside, but he did not want to invade her privacy in such a manner. So instead, he set it down and followed Mattie into the kitchen.

The moment he crossed the threshold, she looked at him with a large grin and began opening the box.

"Look!" She said, pulling back the top and exposing the contents underneath.

James stepped forward, peering into it with curiosity. Nestled inside, atop a piece of tan parchment paper, were three, large cream buns. James' mouth immediately began to water at the sight of them, and he glanced at Mattie with a smile.

"These are my favorite," he breathed.

"Are they really?" Her face lit up with hope and James nodded.

"Did you not know?"

"No," she shook her head. "I spent the entire walk home hoping that you wouldn't hate them."

James laughed as he secured Amy in her dining chair.

"Nothing to worry about there, except for maybe that I'll eat your bun and Amy's too."

Mattie chuckled lightly as she pulled the buns out of the box and set them atop a plate. Cutting one of them into small bites, she set those pieces in front of Amy, who immediately began picking them up and eating them. Her face lit with delight at the first bite, causing both Mattie and James to laugh.

"I'll put on some tea as well," Mattie said, turning to walk to the stove.

James waited for her to finish and joined her at the table. They talked excitedly as they ate, with Mattie recounting her day decorating with Josie. James closed his eyes as she spoke, trying to picture the decorations as she described them, and he had to admit that they sounded beautiful. She told him all about the bakery, and everything that she saw tucked within the glass case and James made a mental note of the things she seemed most excited by. He figured it wouldn't hurt to venture in there the next time he went to town, and pick up a few of the goodies she was describing to surprise her.

James took another bite of his bun, savoring its sweet flavor as it exploded across his tongue. A giggle sounded from across the table, and his eyes darted around to find Mattie snickering behind her hand.

"Something funny?" James asked with the arch of an eyebrow.

"You got a little something there." Mattie moved her finger back and forth over her top lip, and James hastily swiped his hand across his mustache to clear whatever it was away.

All that did was illicit another bout of giggles from Mattie, who shook her head and leaned across the table to get closer to him.

"No, here."

James watched as Mattie reached up and swiped her finger just above his top lip. He could feel it stir the whiskers of his mustache and a thrill went through him at how close she was. He worked hard to keep his face neutral and to not react to her proximity, but he feared that he would hear how hard his heart was beating.

"Thank you," James said as he cleared his throat and leaned back in his chair to put distance between them.

Mattie blinked at him as if she was only just realizing how close she had gotten to him. She shook her head slightly before sitting back in her seat and returning to her tea.

James finished his bun and then washed it down with a splash of the mild tea that Mattie had brewed. When he glanced at the clock a bolt of shock darted through him at how much time had passed.

"Mattie," he said as he pushed himself up from the table. "I am so sorry; I have to go out to meet Elmer for a bit of work."

"Not a worry at all," she waved a hand of dismissal at him. "I'll clean everything up and then get started on dinner."

She gave him a sweet smile, and James deliberately ignored the butterflies that it produced in his stomach. He kissed Amy atop the head before turning and striding from the house. The pink box caught his eye once again as he walked past it on his way out the door, and he found himself wondering once more what could be nestled within it. During Mattie's recounting of the day, she hadn't mentioned stopping to do anything else. Perhaps it was something that Josie had given her?

James shrugged it off as he pushed open the door and strode forward on his way to meet Elmer.

It took him no time at all to find the young man in question, his red hair gleaming in the sunlight acting like a beacon. Elmer was looking around him absently and barely heard James approaching until he was only feet away. When the young man turned to find James standing there, he let out a high-pitched, blood curdling scream as his face drained of all color.

James couldn't help it, he immediately doubled over in laughter, unable to get the sight of Elmer out of his mind.

"You should have seen your face," James wheezed.

Slowly, Elmer gained a little bit of his color back before his expression turned from one of shock to one of annoyance.

"Glad you're havin' a good laugh at my expense." Elmer protested with his hands on his hips.

James faced his ranch hand, swiping a finger under his eyes to clear away the tears from his laughter.

"You looked like you saw a ghost, I couldn't help it." James chuckled once more before walking forward and clapping Elmer on the back. "Now let's get to work."

The two took up their typical cadence easily, working in amicable silence. Now that it was creeping into May, the days were growing even warmer, and the sun beat down on James. Before long, both of them had removed their shirts and were still dripping in sweat.

James stopped working for a moment, standing to wipe at his brow and catch his breath from the post holes he was digging.

"There's a dance coming up," Elmer said as he, too, stood to take a quick break.

"There is," James said with a nod.

Setting down his tools, he walked over to where a large canteen rested in the shade of the wagon and picked it up to take a hearty drink of water. Elmer trotted over to join him, picking up his own canteen and doing the same.

"Are you going?" Elmer asked, as he wiped the back of his hand across his mouth to clear away a stray bit of liquid.

"I am." James nodded his confirmation and Elmer's eyes lit up.

"Are you taking Mattie?" Elmer grinned and James rolled his yes.

"Yes," James answered brusquely. "Both Mattie and I will be going to the dance. But we will not be there *together*."

"So she's free to dance with other people?"

"Of course she is."

"Then perhaps I'll ask her for one." Elmer threw him a wink, and James knew that the young man was taunting him.

"You are engaged, so you are none of my concern."

"But you do have concerns?"

Another knowing grin was thrown in James' direction, and he had to fight off a curse. He had played right into Elmer's trap, admitting that there was some part of him that was worried about who Mattie would dance with, and whether she would like them. James admonished himself but refused to let it show on his face.

"She is the governess to my child and someone I consider a friend. It would be natural for me to worry about who she surrounds herself with." James tried to keep his voice nonchalant, but the knowing look did not leave Elmer's face.

"Mmhmm," Elmer hummed. "I'm sure that's it."

James rolled his eyes once more. "We need to get back to work."

There was a part of James that wished that he could admit the truth. That he was excited to go to the dance and was excited to experience it with Mattie. He hadn't been to a dance since before Ruth passed away; the memories had been too painful any time he had attempted to go. But now? The thought of twirling the night away with Mattie brought a smile to his face.

But of course he couldn't spend the night dancing with her. He knew that if he did, he would risk breaking the promise that he had made to Gilbert, and the one he had made to himself to help her find love. But that didn't mean he couldn't have at least one dance with her, did it?

James shook the thought from his mind and threw himself back into his work, and eventually, the physical exertion was all he was able to focus on. Leaving thoughts of Mattie and the dance far behind.

Later that night, James held a sleepy Amy to his chest as he walked carefully up the stairs. He could hear the dishes clinking together in the kitchen as Mattie cleaned everything up after dinner, and the sound grew fainter with every step that he took. The floorboards creaked quietly under his footstep, and he sent up a silent prayer that Amy would fall asleep quickly.

He got to her room and walked her to her changing table. She fussed as he slipped her dress over her head and wrestled her into her nightgown.

"What's all the fuss about, sweet one?" James cooed to Amy. "We'll get you to bed in no time at all."

When Amy was dressed, he walked her to her bed and laid her down. She stared up at him expectantly, nestled cozily into her blankets. Without thinking too much about it, James began to sing softly to his daughter.

"A tree in a meadow,

A soft blowing willow,

A baby blue sky,

Some moss as a pillow," James kept his voice quiet and low, hoping that it wouldn't travel down to Mattie on the floor below.

"And here I will lay,

Dream of her for a day,

And then when I wake,

For her I will pray."

Amy's eyelids fluttered closed, her long lashes lying stark against her pale cheek. As the last few syllables fell from James' lips, Amy's breathing deepened. His song trailed off, and he sat in the seat by her bed for a few more seconds, waiting to make sure she didn't wake again. But when it was clear she was well and truly asleep, James leaned forward and planted a soft, reverent kiss to his daughter's brow before pushing himself up from the seat and making his way back downstairs.

As he descended the stairs, the house was quiet, save for the creaking of the floorboards, and he assumed that Mattie had finished the dishes. He stopped for a moment when he reached the first floor and listened for any other sounds in the house. He didn't think that Mattie had gone to bed; he thought he would have heard her come up stairs. Plus, her bedroom door had been open when he had left Amy's room.

A faint humming drew his attention, coming from the direction of the drawing room. Stepping as lightly as possible, James followed the sound. Once he turned the corner, a grin tugged up the corner of his mouth at what he discovered.

Mattie was in the center of the room, arms held aloft as she twirled around as if dancing with an imaginary partner. Her red-gold hair shone in the quickly fading light that came through the windows, and her skirts swished around her ankles. James paused to watch her, allowing himself a few short moments to admire the beauty of the woman dancing before him.

She turned once, but her eyes were closed, and she didn't see him. Pressing his fingers to his lips, James worked to fend off a chuckle. He shifted his weight to lean against the door frame, and the floorboard under his foot creaked loudly.

Mattie let out a small gasp as she whirled to face the sound, her eyes going wide at the sight of him.

"How long have you been standing there?" She demanded as color rose to her cheeks.

"Long enough," James said with a laugh.

"Well, you should have said something. You shouldn't just stand there watching a lady without her knowing."

She looked away from him, running her hands nervously down the front of her skirt.

"Were you practicing for the dance?" James asked, stepping farther into the room until only a foot separated them.

"What if I was?" Mattie replied, raising an eyebrow at him.

"It's alright if you were," James said with another soft chuckle.

Mattie narrowed her eyes at him, and James stood still. He could tell she was embarrassed that he had caught her practicing, and she was defensive because of it. They had struck such a delicate balance over the last couple days, and he didn't want to ruin it by having her think he was making fun of her.

"Alright, fine." Mattie said as she relaxed slightly, the relaxing her posture. "Yes. If you must know, I was practicing. I haven't been to a dance since the one where Lewis... well, you know that story. But I don't want to make a fool out of myself."

Her cheeks flushed again, and James yearned to reach out and run his finger along her jaw.

"I haven't been to one since before Ruth died," James explained. He took a step toward Mattie, and he was encouraged when she didn't retreat. "Perhaps we could practice together?"

Mattie studied him for only a moment before nodding. James closed the space between them, one hand coming up to hold Mattie's, while the other wrapped around her slim waist to rest on the small of her back. They held each other's gaze for a flash of a second, and James had the briefest thought that perhaps this was not the best idea. But he quieted the small voice inside his head the moment he and Mattie began to move.

He spun her around, the proximity of her body and the feel of her hand in his making his blood warm. James looked down at Mattie, and he hummed loudly as they danced around the drawing room. Mattie's bright green eyes were wide as she looked up at him through long, dark lashes. It took all he had not to tell her how lovely she looked in that moment.

To put more distance between them, he took a step back and spun her. Mattie giggled as she turned, and when she returned to his arms her face was lit with a beautiful, radiant smile. James' pulse jumped at the sight of it. When Mattie's eyes found his, her smile began to fade. The look upon her face turning into one that was much more serious as it began to simmer with curiosity and desire.

James' eyes darted down to Mattie's plump, full lips. The air between them grew thick, and it took James a few seconds to register that they had stopped dancing. When he met her gaze once more, he couldn't stop himself.

As if being drawn by a magnet, James began to lean forward. Inch by inch, he brought his mouth closer to hers. When he was close enough that he could feel her breath coming in short, panted gasps, he smiled.

Right as he was about to close that final bit of distance, a cry rang out through the house, shrill and distressed. Amy's cries broke through whatever haze they had found themselves in, and both James and Mattie jumped back.

"Mattie...I... we.... that..." James stammered, but Mattie just began shaking her head.

"I'll go take care of Amy."

Her voice was strained; her tone laced with forced happiness that immediately set James on edge. She shot him a hurried, panicked look before turning and striding quickly from the room. James wanted to chase after her. He wanted nothing more than to make her come back so he could explain what had happened. Or rather, what had almost happened. And that it was a mistake, but not in the way she thought.

But beneath it all, James knew that it would only make things worse. Instead, he remained in the drawing room as he struggled to return his breathing and heart rate to normal. He ran a frustrated hand through his hair, mussing up the long, dark strands. He could hear the faint murmurings coming from Mattie as she worked to quiet down the cranky toddler.

When Amy's cries faded entirely, he heard Mattie's footsteps across the wooden planks of the hallway. He wondered if she would come back downstairs, and if she did, he wondered what he would say. But he was spared from making a decision when he heard the door to her bedroom shut with a snap.

James hung his head, realizing that he had messed everything up for what felt like the thousandth time. And as he trudged up to his room, he could only promise himself to not mess up again.

Chapter Eighteen

Mattie blinked hard against the bright, streaming sun as she gave a grunt of effort and pushed the pram farther along the main street that ran through Mt. Juliet. She hadn't seen James that morning at breakfast, and as the day had worn on, she had resolved herself to pretend as if the night before had never happened.

"It isn't like anything actually occurred, anyway," Mattie uttered to herself as Amy looked over the side of the pram at the lively town.

Mattie was not going to allow an almost kiss to ruin her day, or her excitement for the upcoming dance. Spotting the seamstress shop, Mattie put on an extra burst of speed and pulled the pram up alongside it.

"Come on, little dove," Mattie said as she reached forward and pulled Amy out of the basket of the stroller.

Amy squealed in delight to be freed from the confines of her blanket, and Mattie ruffled her hair in affection. The bell on the door chimed merrily to announce their arrival, and the older woman at the other end of the shop glanced their way. When her eyes fell on Mattie, they lit with recognition and her face broke out in a wide grin.

"Hello dear," the woman said as she pushed herself to standing and walked over to greet them. "I got your dress finished just this morning."

"I can't wait to see it," Mattie answered, her spirits lifting with anticipation.

The seamstress motioned for Mattie and Amy to follow after her, leading them to the back of the room. When her eyes fell on the beautiful, sage green gown she had chosen and all the adjustments that had been made, Mattie's mouth popped open in surprise.

"It's lovely." Mattie stepped forward and reached out a hand to run her fingers over the delicate fabric.

"Oh good," the seamstress said with a smile. "I am so glad you like it. I'll get it boxed up for you then."

Mattie nodded at the woman, completely at a loss for words. She walked back toward the front of the store and stood, looking out the front window to the street beyond while she waited. She had only been there for a minute or so, bouncing Amy on her hip while they looked out at the passersby, when a glimpse of a familiar face caught her eye.

Mattie's heart began to beat wildly in her chest as she whispered, "it can't be."

Without thinking about it, Mattie darted toward the front door and pushed it open. Standing under the awning of the seamstresses' shop, her eyes raked over the crowd once more, looking for the man she had just seen.

A flash of bright, copper hair caught her eye and she honed in on it. The man turned in a circle, looking around him to get his bearings, and Mattie's face pulled into a cheek splitting grin.

"Gilbert," she called as she rushed forward.

Her brother's gaze fell on her and his eyes lit with confusion, and then recognition.

"Mattie!" He yelled back in greeting as he trotted to close the final bit of distance between them.

Amy cackled loudly at the jostling as Gilbert wrapped them both in an embrace. Mattie clung to her brother with one arm while she held Amy with the other. She let their hug linger a moment, taking in the scent and familiarity of him.

When they broke apart, Gilbert held her at arm's length, taking Mattie in from head to toe.

"By God Mattie, you are looking well. Looks like Mt. Juliet suits you, just as I suspected."

Mattie waved away his praise.

"What are you doing here? How long will you be staying?" She gushed. "Oh I can't believe it."

"I'm here to see you and James, clearly. As for how long, only about a week or so."

Mattie nodded, still beaming at her brother.

"What are you doing in town? I figured you'd be out at the ranch. Thought I'd surprise you both," Gilbert asked.

"I'm here to pick up a new dress for the dance," Mattie explained, hiking a thumb over her shoulder to point at the seamstress's shop. "Care to join me."

"Already out to drain my pockets, eh?" Gilbert raised his eyebrows at her, forcing Mattie to roll her eyes.

"It's already paid for, don't you worry."

Gilbert followed her back to the shop. The seamstress was standing by the counter, a large blue box placed on top of it.

"I was afraid you'd left," the woman said with a smile and a wink. "Thought you'd run off to spare my feelings about how much you hated the thing."

"I would never. I'd tell you I hated the gown first," Mattie joked back, eliciting a cackle from the seamstress.

Mattie began walking forward, but Gilbert beat her to it. Darting past her, her brother reached for the large box and plucked it off the counter.

"What else are brother's for?" He asked her.

She shook her head at him but didn't object. They said their goodbyes to the seamstress and made their way back out toward the street. Gilbert waited patiently while Mattie tucked Amy into the pram and then instructed Gilbert to place the box with the dress and his small travelling bag in the carriage underneath.

Gilbert took over pushing the stroller, and they began making their way toward the ranch.

"Does James know that you were coming?" Mattie asked after they had been walking for a bit.

Gilbert shook his head. "It's a complete surprise."

"Good." Mattie beamed at him. "He'll be so excited to see you."

As they walked, Mattie caught him up on everything that had happened since she'd arrived in Mt. Juliet, leaving out the parts about the fights with James and the moments where she thought he was going to kiss her. When she started filling him in on meeting Hubert and what had followed after, Gilbert looked at her with concern in his gaze.

"Be careful with that man," Gilbert warned. "I've heard enough about him through James to know that he isn't good news."

Mattie nodded at her brother. "No need to worry. I've been fairly warned about him by more than just James."

Gilbert nodded as he accepted her answer. She wished that James would have given her the same courtesy instead of drawing it out into a multi-day fight.

The house came into view, and Mattie pointed it out to him. She knew that Gilbert had been here before, but she was still enjoying being able to tell him about everything she had learned about the ranch, and things that might be new since he had last been there. Amy was fast asleep by the time they made it to the porch, having succumbed to the rocking of the pram as they'd walked.

Gilbert carried his bag and the dress box into the house, with Mattie, cradling a sleeping Amy, following after him. She instructed him on where the spare bedroom was for him to leave his things, and also instructed him where he could leave the dress box as she took Amy to her room to continue her nap.

When she came back down, Gilbert was lounging in the family room, with his arm draped over the back of the sofa.

"I have to get dinner started," Mattie explained. "But keep a look out for James to come back inside. And when you see him, hide in the drawing room. I want to surprise him."

Gilbert nodded his agreement. "Got it. I'm gonna stay here and rest a bit, but I'll keep an eye out."

Mattie grinned at him and then went back to the kitchen, still ecstatic that her brother had shown up. Not long after, she heard Amy stirring in the upstairs bedroom and went to get her. Placing her in her dining chair, she talked happily to the toddler as she cooked.

"It's all very exciting," Mattie said to the babbling child. "And if Gilbert is staying for the week, that means he'll be able to join us for the dance tomorrow! Oh Amy, won't it be grand?"

"Rand!" Amy repeated as she clapped her chubby hands.

"Yes! Grand!"

The sound of hurried footsteps grabbed Mattie's attention, and she glanced to the doorway of the kitchen, spotting Gilbert with an excited look on his face.

"He's on his way!" Gilbert whispered loudly.

"Shoo," Mattie said as she waved a kitchen towel at her brother. "To the drawing room with you."

Gilbert snickered as he disappeared through the doorway. She could hear the creak of the floorboards as he disappeared into the room and forced herself to act nonchalant when she heard the screen door open and close. James came into the kitchen, and Mattie turned to greet him.

"Well hello there James," Mattie said, her voice coming out much too chipper. She shook herself internally, trying to push past her nerves. "How was your day?"

James furrowed his brow at her in question, but Mattie just rearranged her features a little more.

"It was quite alright," he said as he pulled out his chair and took a seat.

He watched her for a moment with a wary look in his eyes.

"Mattie, look. About last night," he began, and Mattie's heart dropped.

In the excitement of Gilbert arriving, she had all but forgotten about the moment in the drawing room the night before. She couldn't have him bringing it up, not with Gilbert within ear shot.

"No, no," she waved him off with a smile. "None of that. We don't need to talk about it."

James cocked his head at her and opened his mouth to speak again, but Mattie quickly cut him off.

"In fact," she said loud enough to drown out the sound of James' voice in case he decided to start speaking again. "I have a surprise for you!"

"A surprise?" James' brows knit together in confusion, and Mattie nodded her head eagerly.

"Stay right there." She commanded, pointing at him. "Cover your eyes."

James gave her a tense look but didn't object as he brought his hands up to cup his eyes. Amy laughed as her father sat there with his palms over his face, and Mattie hurried from the room.

"Keep them closed," she called as she entered the drawing room smiling like mad.

She spotted Gilbert and waved for him to follow her. He nodded and snickered behind his hand and then tiptoed after her back to the kitchen.

"No peaking!" Mattie reminded as she and Gilbert walked back into the kitchen.

"I'm not peaking," James protested. "But Mattie, what is this all about."

"Patience, Mr. Murphy."

Mattie pointed to a spot directly beside her, right in James' line of sight.

"Ok! You can look now."

James dropped his hands from his face, and for a moment his expression was a mask of confusion and disbelief.

"Well, you old fart," Gilbert chided him. "Are you just gonna sit there or are you gonna greet your best friend?"

Finally realizing that it wasn't a joke, and that Gilbert was truly standing in his kitchen, James' face broke out into a wide smile. His blue eyes shone with happiness, and it made Mattie's heart beat faster and her palms began to sweat. She wiped them against her skirt and forced her breathing to remain steady as she watched James rush forward and wrap her brother in a crushing embrace.

"Did you do this?" James asked, looking at Mattie with wide, excited eyes.

"I wish I could say it was me," Mattie explained. "But he showed up all on his own."

"Figured I'd surprise you both," Gilbert answered.

"Well, I'm glad either way." James clapped Gilbert on the back once more before guiding him to the table.

Mattie turned back to the stove to finish supper while Gilbert and James began catching up. She cast a few, errant glances back toward them as she cooked. Mattie couldn't be sure, but along with the happiness that James so clearly felt to have his friend there, she could swear that she also saw a trace of guilt.

She shrugged it off as she brought the food over to the middle of the table and began to load their plates. She listened to the two men as they laughed and joked, recounting stories from their childhood and catching each other up on their lives. Mattie focused her attention on Amy, allowing the two old friends to have their time together. But all the while, she couldn't help but feel that James' answers were stunted somehow. As if he was holding himself back.

Mattie tried to catch his eyes a few times, hoping to give him a glance or mouth the words that he had nothing to worry about, but after a while she was forced to admit that he was ignoring her. If Gilbert noticed any strangeness to the two of them, he didn't let on.

After a bit, Amy began to get cranky, and Mattie stood to take her upstairs.

"I'll do it," James said as he pushed himself back from the kitchen. "I haven't got to see her much today."

Mattie thought about protesting, telling him to spend a little more time with his friend. But he had Amy out of her dining chair and out of the room before she could speak up.

"What was that all about?" Gilbert asked, glancing from Mattie to the doorway James had disappeared through and back.

"Heaven only knows." Mattie shook her head and sent up a silent prayer that James would be able to find it within himself to relax while Gilbert was there.

Perhaps she'd be able to find a moment alone with him to tell him he didn't have anything to be guilty or weird about. She and Gilbert began clearing the plates, and in no time at all they had the kitchen sparkling clean.

"I suppose you're tired after a long day of traveling and now a full belly?" Mattie asked, looking at her brother.

Gilbert just nodded and exaggeratedly patted his stomach, forcing a laugh from Mattie. She shook her head at him, and they made their way up the stairs. She could hear James in

Amy's room, singing to her lightly, and her heart gave a quick tinge of affection.

Mattie shook it off internally and walked to her room. To her surprise, Gilbert followed after her.

"I didn't get a good look at it earlier," he explained as he walked around taking in her furniture and the small splashes of decoration around the space. "It's lovely."

"It was like this when I arrived," Mattie explained with a quick shrug.

"And what is this?" He asked, his hands resting on the hat box she'd been given from Hubert.

Before she could stop him, he pulled it open and took out the hat inside.

"This is quite pretty," Gilbert said, placing the hat atop his head.

Mattie chuckled at how absurd he looked but didn't provide any additional information.

"James must be paying you quite well if you can afford something this," Gilbert took the hat back off and studied it.

Mattie's cheeks blushed, and she looked down at her hands.

"It was a gift from Hubert Bird," she said, keeping her voice low, and Gilbert's eyes immediately snapped to hers.

"You didn't tell me he was buying you gifts," Gilbert said seriously. "Mattie, why did you accept this?"

"I tried not to," she argued, bristling at her brother's insinuating tone. "I told him that it was too much, but he was quite persistent."

Gilbert studied the hat in his hands before setting it down atop the long dresser that spanned the wall.

"And you're sure you have no romantic feelings for the man?"

Mattie answered without hesitation. "I am sure. After everything I've heard, even if I had at first, which I didn't, but if I had, it would all be gone now. I trust Josie, and I trust James."

Gilbert nodded. "I've only met Josie once. But James is a good judge of character. You are right to trust him."

Mattie didn't say anything else, opting instead to let her brother accept her silence as confirmation. Thankfully, it wasn't in Gilbert's nature to continue to press an issue, so he merely patted the hat once and turned his back on it.

"Alright then," Gilbert said. "Off to bed I go. I'll see you bright and early."

"Bright and early." Mattie confirmed with a small smile, recalling the words they used to speak every night before she'd fallen into her sadness after Lewis.

Gilbert smiled at her fondly before exiting to the hall and closing her door behind him. She sat for a moment, listening to the sounds of the house. Mattie could no longer hear James singing in Amy's room, which was next to her own. So, she assumed that he had gone to bed as well.

She stood and began undressing, readying herself for bed. As she pulled her nightgown over her head, the soft scratch of the cotton slipping over her body, she sent up a quick prayer that the strangeness that had fallen between her and James once again would be gone by morning.

Chapter Nineteen

James stared at himself in the looking glass above his dresser and he blew out a hard, frustrated breath. He had not been prepared for Gilbert's arrival, and while he was happy to see his best friend, he hoped that Gilbert hadn't yet picked up on the fact that he was beginning to fall for Mattie.

The revelation had come as a shock to James late the night prior. After leaving Gilbert and Mattie at the dinner table so he could put Mattie to bed, he'd been able to think of little else.

What would happen if Gilbert discovered all the times that James had come close to kissing Mattie? He knew that he'd have to explain himself, but the only explanation that he could come up with is that he had begun to care for her deeply. And with that thought, his mind had begun to spiral.

He'd tossed and turned all night, thinking about Mattie and Gilbert both asleep merely feet away. And by the time the sun's rays had begun to filter in through his windows, James was no longer able to deny the truth of his own feelings, even if he could never act on them. And with that revelation bouncing in his mind, he did his best to avoid Mattie at all costs throughout the day without raising any concerns. But that was all about to change.

He tightened the leather strap that held back his hair and gave himself one final glance in the looking glass before turning and leaving his bedroom. The door to Mattie's room was closed, and he could hear her on the other side singing softly to herself as he passed by. He found Gilbert sitting in the family room with a book propped open on his lap.

His teenage neighbor, Rose was sitting on the floor in the middle of the room, playing a game of peek-a-boo with Amy.

Her parent's owned the next farm over, and he'd asked if she could watch Amy for the evening so they could all go to the town dance. Rose had watched Amy before, and she and his daughter absolutely adored one another. So Rose had happily agreed.

Having heard James' approach, Gilbert lowered the book that sat on his lap and glanced up at his friend.

"Do you think she's about ready?" Gilbert asked, nodding his head in the direction of the stairs.

"I can only assume so," James shrugged.

Gilbert pushed himself off the couch and they both walked toward the entry way and the foot of the stairs. James leaned against the wall across from the stairs and began whistling as he and Gilbert waited for Mattie to finish getting dressed. A few moments later, they heard the door to Mattie's room open.

"Are you all out there?" Mattie's voice rang loudly from the floor above.

"We sure are. Waiting on you while you take your sweet time." Gilbert called back, forcing James to laugh.

"I didn't take my sweet time." Mattie protested, but still she didn't step out into view.

"Would you come down already?" James yelled.

They heard the click of her boots against the wooden floors, and a moment later she appeared at the top of the steps. James's mouth popped open, and his heart began to race at the sight of her. Her golden red hair had been braided and then twisted around her head to form a crown, with soft, tendrilled curls falling down to frame her face. The dress that he'd bought her, while it had looked amazing the day they found it at the seamstress's shop, now hugged her torso closely, accentuating the delicate female shape of her.

A blush rose to James' cheeks, and he was thankful for his beard as she rested a small hand on the banister of the stairs and began her descent.

"Might want to close your mouth," Gilbert said low enough that only James could hear him. "Or else a fly might get in."

James' jaw snapped up so quickly, his teeth clacked together, and he heard Gilbert chuckle lightly beside him. A bolt of shame and guilt washed through him, and he quickly stamped it down.

"Do I look alright?" Mattie asked when she made it to the bottom of the stairs, her hands nervously flitting over her skirts.

"You look remarkable," Gilbert answered as he darted forward and offered her his arm.

Mattie delicately draped her arm through her brother's and then looked at James expectantly.

"I'll bring around the carriage," James stumbled over his words, and a twinge of guilt rocked through him at the disappointment that flashed across Mattie's face.

But James knew if he walked forward and put his arm through hers as she was so clearly wanting, he wouldn't be able to control his reaction to her. And even though he could now admit his feelings to himself, it wouldn't serve him well to put himself in a position that tempting. Especially not in front of Gilbert.

He turned and walked out the door, doing everything he could to ensure his stride remained seemingly confident and unaffected. His body moved automatically as he hooked the horse up to the carriage and then led it around to the front of the house. Mattie and Gilbert were both standing on the porch, arms still linked, waiting expectantly.

James didn't move from his spot on the wooden bench of the wagon as Gilbert helped Mattie climb up the stairs and into her seat. She sat beside James, with Gilbert on the other side of her, and James did the best he could not to focus on the heat rolling off her body.

"Are you excited for tonight, Mattie?" Gilbert asked her.

"Oh yes, Josie told me all about the dance and some of the bachelors that are going to be there."

James tightened his grip on the reigns as the thought of her dancing with other men popped into his head, but he immediately forced himself to relax. Reminding himself that that was what he wanted, for her to meet a nice man who was worthy of her, and for her to fall in love. That way it would allow him to keep his promise to Gilbert and absolve him of any guilt he might be feeling.

He tried as hard as he could to tune out Gilbert and Mattie's conversation, not wanting to hear her musings about who she might dance with and how the night would go. Instead, James deliberately focused on the sound of the horse's hooves hitting the ground, counting each one in turn.

Two hundred and thirty-four hoof strikes later, and the carriage pulled up to the town hall. James expertly guided the horse to a wooden beam where he could tie it up, alongside a few other horses and carriages that belonged to other townsfolk.

Climbing down, he didn't turn around to watch Mattie and Gilbert while he secured the horse, made sure it was comfortable, and had a bit of feed. By the time he'd finished and turned back to look at them, they were both walking toward the wide, wooden front doors of the town hall.

James felt a quick pang of distress when they didn't stop to wait for him, but he quickly shook it off. He knew that he hadn't been particularly good company the past two days, so he couldn't entirely blame them. Breaking into a light jog, James worked to catch up with them.

"The place looks beautiful, Mattie," James overheard Gilbert exclaiming as they climbed the stairs. "You said you and Josie did all of this?"

As soon as James stepped over the threshold of the hall, he had to fight to keep his mouth from gaping in surprise. Mattie had told him about all the decorations that she and Josie had hung, but he hadn't imagined that they had transformed the space quite this much.

The greenery draped over the wooden beams, the beautiful, delicate, wildflowers that poured from vases, the lanterns flickering merrily on iron hooks against the walls. It all came together to create a beautiful, warm atmosphere that called for revelry and laughter.

"Mattie! James!" James heard someone yell and he whirled to find Josie stalking toward them with a wide, affectionate smile.

Jessup wasn't far behind her, watching his wife with eyes filled with love. James felt a small stab of jealousy as he watched the pair approach, and once again he had to work to stifle his feelings. He wasn't entirely sure what had gotten into him, but he knew he needed to get it under control quickly.

Josie threw her arms around Mattie, the two women embracing fondly as James leaned forward to shake Jessup's hand.

"And who is this handsome fella?" Josie asked when she and Mattie broke apart, raking her eyes over Gilbert.

"I'd be Mattie's brother, Gilbert," he answered, shaking her hand and Jessup's as well.

"A pleasure to meet you, Gilbert. And welcome to Mt. Juliet." Josie gave him a broad smile.

Jessup took a few steps, forming a semi-circle with Gilbert and James as Mattie and Josie bent their heads together, both of them whispering and giggling excitedly. James couldn't make out what they were saying, but when Josie's hand rose to point at Vance Tavers, he was sure that he could guess.

"So, Gilbert," Jessup began. "How long are you in town for?"

"About five more days or so," Gilbert answered, sticking his hands in the pockets of his trousers. "Don't want to be away too long."

Jessup nodded. "I bet you're glad to have your old friend up here then, huh James?"

"Thrilled." James had meant the word to sound sarcastic and joking, but instead it just came out harsh.

"You doing alright?" Gilbert asked, furrowing his brow.

"Sorry," James shook himself, trying to get rid of the emotions that were bubbling inside of him. "I'm a little off kilter today."

"I can tell." Gilbert's words were soft, without any bite or accusation, but he still looked at James knowingly.

He tried not to think what that look might mean, and instead turned his attention back to Mattie and Josie. His heart sank as his eyes found them again. In only the few, short minute that his attention had been on Gilbert and Jessup, a small flock of men were already clustered around Mattie, one of them being the aforementioned Vance.

Jealousy roared to life deep in James's chest as Mattie threw her head back and laughed prettily at something Vance had said. Everything within James roared at him to walk over to her and pull her onto the dance floor, hoarding her attention to herself. Thankfully, before he could do anything rash, Gilbert clapped him on the shoulder.

"What do you say we grab a drink?" His friend asked.

"Sounds great." James gave a brief, curt nod.

Gilbert turned to walk toward the other end of the hall, where a small bar had been constructed, with James and Jessup following after.

"How are things going at the ranch?" Jessup asked as they walked, making their way through the throng of tightly packed bodies.

"Calving season is about over," James explained. "So that's good. Have a few that have yet to birth. But most of them have."

"Sounds messy," Jessup said as he scrunched up his nose.

James couldn't help but chuckle at the look on Jessup's face, and it caused his mood to lift marginally. He couldn't imagine that Jessup dealt with much *mess*, as he put it, in his life as a tailor. But he liked that about the man. Where James could be a little rough around the edges and preferred to get his hands dirty, Jessup had a cool, and prim demeanor. James had always thought that it was a good balance to Josie's bright and bubbly personality. But he also couldn't deny that he liked seeing the man disgusted, just a little.

"It is," James answered with a quiet laugh.

They made it to the bar, and James ordered them each a large mug of beer and threw a few copper pennies onto the bar. James grabbed the handle of his mug and brought it to his lips, the foam tickling his mustache as he took a deep, hearty swig. The sour tang of the drink danced across his tongue, and as it washed down his throat, he felt himself begin to relax.

"Want to head toward the dance floor?" Jessup asked eagerly, looking through the crowd and James had to assume he was looking for his wife.

Both James and Gilbert nodded, and the three men made their way back through the crowd once more. He kept an eye out for a flash of sage green, hoping to spot Mattie amongst those standing and watching. But that hope was short lived.

As they made it to the edge of the dance floor, it didn't take long for his eyes to find a flash of pale red hair and have his attention diverted. Mattie stood in the arms of William McTavish, twirling across the wooden floor in beautiful, sweeping circles. James watched as she laughed and smiled at William, and the jealousy that had risen inside him before reared its head out again.

Jessup spotted Josie on the outer ring of the crowd that stood watching the dancers, and handed his beer off to Gilbert before striding forward to ask his wife to dance. Gilbert nodded his head at an empty table on the edge of the dance floor, and he and James took a seat.

James could feel Gilbert's eyes on him as they sat, and he worked to keep his expression neutral as his eyes roved over the dancers. He took extra care to not let his gaze linger on Mattie too long.

"Thank you," Gilbert's voice was clear over the din of the crowd, and James looked in his direction.

"For what?" he asked with a furrowed brow.

"Mattie." Gilbert nodded his head toward the dance floor, where the woman in question was dancing with a new man who James recognized as Luther Baker. "She seems like she's doing well and really coming into her own here in Mt. Juliet. When she left, she looked like a ghost, and now it seems like she might have come back to life."

James' cheeks flushed with pride as he recalled that first glimpse of Mattie when she got off the train. Gilbert wasn't wrong. Because even though Mattie had looked so beautiful that day it had made his chest hurt, there had been a dullness to her. Her cheeks had been hollow, her eyes devoid of the joy and the fire that he had come to know. He was glad that she had started to find some of that again, not that he felt he could take credit for it. And he told Gilbert as much, but his words were waved off by his friend.

"Nonsense. Of course you had something to do with it. Don't get me wrong, I'm sure Josie and Elmer and everyone that she's met so far has had a hand in it, too. Plus, I think it helps that the air isn't so damned stiflin'. But don't count the part you played in it short, either."

James held his friends' gaze and felt a bit of gratitude wash through him. For a moment, he wondered if perhaps he could ask Gilbert's permission to dance with Mattie. He wondered if his friend would be amenable to it, despite the promise that James had made to him those weeks ago. What would it be like to hold her in front of all these people? Just as James worked up the courage and opened his mouth to speak, a commotion kicked up from the middle of the dance floor.

"I said no." Mattie's voice rang clearly over the noise of the townsfolk, and James was instantly alert. He jumped up, his eyes roving through the crowd until a flash of sage green caught his eye and he homed in on Mattie.

Someone had a grip on her arm, and she was struggling against them, telling them to let her go as she tried to take a step backward. He followed the line of the arm to the person it belonged to, and his blood boiled when he realized it was none other than Hubert Bird.

At the same time, James and Gilbert both pushed their chairs back from the table they had been sitting at and began making their way through the crowd toward Mattie.

Chapter Twenty

Mattie cursed internally as she struggled against the grip Hubert had on her arm. His fingers dug into her flesh as she held his gaze.

"Hubert, let go of me," Mattie demanded in a clear, firm voice.

"Now, now," Hubert said in a low tone as he took another step toward her.

He was close enough that she could smell the sourness of beer on his breath and Mattie scowled.

"I bought you that hat, didn't I?" Hubert continued. "And you said you'd give me a dance to repay me."

"I assure you I said no such thing," Mattie fired back. "You assumed, but I did not agree to this. And I do not want to dance with you. So, let. Me. Go."

Mattie annunciated the last three words to try and ensure he got the message, but still Hubert remained unmoved.

"Let go of my sister."

Gilbert's voice broke through the crowd a moment before both he and James pushed their way toward Mattie. Hubert's eyes narrowed on the two men as they approached and then let go of Mattie's arm. The moment his fingers opened; she took several retreating steps away from him until her back bumped against something solid. Glancing over her shoulder, Mattie realized she had backed directly into James and a feeling of protection wrapped around her.

"Are you alright?" James asked her, his deep voice an immediate comfort.

Mattie nodded and then turned her attention back to Gilbert and Hubert. The two men were standing rather close, glowering at each other.

"Who are you?" Hubert asked with venom in his voice.

"I am Mattie's brother," Gilbert fired back. "I assume you're Hubert. What a displeasure to make your acquaintance."

Hubert sputtered at Gilbert's insult, his face turning red. Someone in the crowd chuckled, and Mattie felt a stab of sympathy for the man in front of her. She may not be interested in Hubert, but after her own life experiences she couldn't bring herself to take pleasure in another person's ridicule.

Stealing strength from James' steady presence behind her, she took a step forward.

"Hubert," Mattie began, sure to keep her voice firm but kind. "I am sorry that you arrived here tonight under the impression that I would save you a dance. I should have been clear the day you gave me the hat. It is why I tried to not accept it."

Hubert narrowed his gaze on Mattie. His face, which had already started to flush now became a burning, bright crimson. But Mattie knew that men like Hubert would stop at nothing to get their way, so she could not afford to stop talking now. She needed to make her point clear.

"I would be more than happy to return it to you, and it has not yet been worn. And while your attention and affection has been quite flattering, and I appreciate the friendship that we've cultivated, I need you to understand that I do not harbor any feelings of romance for you."

Hubert sputtered as the final words left her mouth, and his gaze began to swing wildly from person to person until they finally landed on James.

"You put her up to this," Hubert accused as he took a step in the other man's direction.

Gilbert quickly put himself between the two men, puffing up his chest in the process. If the moment had not already been so fraught with tension, Mattie would have rolled her eyes at her brother.

"I did no such thing," James answered, his voice cool and calm.

With the tension dancing through the air, James' unflappability was a balm to Mattie's frazzled nerves, and she found herself feeling stronger in his presence.

"He did not," Mattie stated, repeating James' words. "I assure you; I came to this conclusion all on my own."

A pregnant pause fell over the group, each person regarding the other wearily. After a few moments that drug on, Hubert took a deep, calming breath. Some of the color that had risen high in his cheeks began to fade, and he reached up with shaking hands to smooth down his mousy brown hair.

"You will regret this," he said in a matter-of-fact tone, and the promise that laced his words sent shivers down Mattie's spine.

Before any of them had a chance to respond, Hubert turned on his heel and pushed his way through the crowd. Mattie watched the movement of heads and bodies that marked Hubert's passing on his way out the door.

"Are you alright?" James murmured, still standing close to Mattie.

She nodded, but when she reached up a hand to tuck a stray strand of copper hair behind her ear, it's shaking betrayed her fraught nerves.

"The night is beginning to wind down, anyway," James said. "Perhaps we should all head home?"

He locked eyes with Gilbert, and her brother just gave a quick nod.

"Thank you," Mattie said in a hushed tone, but neither James nor Gilbert replied.

They waited for a few moments, deciding it was best to give Hubert enough time to be well on his way home. They tracked down Josie and Jessup on their way out the door, and the woman gave Mattie a long, hard squeeze before they all turned and began their journey back to the ranch.

James brought the buggy around the building, stopping to pick both Mattie and her brother up. Gilbert extended his hand to Mattie to help her up the steps. She paused for a moment, looking between the two men with trepidation. She didn't want to sit in the center of them, but she couldn't think of a protest that she could make that wouldn't seem odd.

With a sigh, she took Gilbert's proffered hand and allowed him to lead her up. Usually when she and James took the buggy to town, there was plenty of space and Amy was nestled neatly between them. The ride home from the dance, however, would apparently be a different story.

When Gilbert scooted across the bench seat beside her, Mattie was all but forced into pressing her leg against James' to make room. Even through all the layers of fabric between her skin and his, she could still feel the heat radiating off his body.

With a snap of the reigns, James began to expertly lead them toward home, and Mattie tried with all of her might to focus on the road ahead of them and not the man sitting beside her. It didn't help that the heady, musky scent of him, the one that somehow always smelled like coffee and cedar, kept floating up to her on a gentle breeze.

Gilbert and James began talking amongst themselves, reminiscing about their childhood and the very first dance they had gone to together. And Mattie did her best to distract herself from her wandering thoughts.

Turning her mind back to the start of the evening, she allowed herself to bask in the feel of the revelry within the building when she'd walked in and what it had been like to see such much joy being expressed over what she and Josie had created. Mattie glanced at the shops, the homes, and the few people milling about as they passed through Mt. Juliet, and a warm feeling of safety washed over her.

"Mattie," Gilbert's voice came drifting to her through the haze of her thoughts, and she blinked rapidly when she noticed her brother was waving his hand in front of her face.

"What?" She asked, turning her attention to him.

"The dance?" He knit his eyebrows together as he looked at her with worry. "I asked you if you had fun and what you thought of the men you got to dance with."

"Oh, I'm sorry. I didn't hear you." She took a moment to gather her thoughts, wondering how much she should divulge to her brother and to James. "Well, Vance and William were quite nice."

Gilbert raised an eyebrow at her, "they were nice?"

"Yes." She cocked a head at her brother. "What's wrong with nice? It's better than being surly and grumpy all the time."

She couldn't help but glance to her other side, shooting James a pointed look and she felt him stiffen.

"They weren't the only people you danced with though," Gilbert prompted quickly, and she could tell he sensed James was readying himself for a fight.

Mattie cocked her head in confusion. "You mean Jessup? That's the only other person I danced with."

"Is it? I could have sworn you danced with someone else."

Mattie shook her head.

"Well," Gilbert held her gaze, his green eyes that were identical to her own roving over her face, "was there anyone else you wanted to dance with?"

Mattie considered this for a moment. The truth was, there *was* someone that she had wanted to dance with. The entire time she had been in the arms of both Vance and William, she hadn't been able to keep her mind from wandering to James. Multiple times she had glanced across the room, seeing him laughing with her brother or talking with one of the other townsfolk and wondered what he would say if she asked him to dance. But it wasn't as if she could say that.

"No one that I noticed," Mattie said, hoping that neither of them sensed her lie.

"What about you, James?" Gilbert leaned forward, a sly grin tugging at the corner of his mouth. "Was there anyone you had your eyes on?"

"Not a one." James shook his head, never once taking his eyes off of the road before them.

The horse gave a loud whinny, and Mattie turned her attention back to their journey, finding herself surprised and more than a little happy to find them already approaching the house. She wasn't sure how much more of that conversation she could take. A smile flitted across her lips as she looked at the home that had now grown so familiar to her.

The family room windows were illuminated with the lanterns, and Mattie smiled, feeling good to have arrived home after an eventful evening. The porch creaked under the stairs as the three of them walked across it, with James reaching forward to pull open the door.

Rose was curled up on the sofa working diligently on a pinpoint. At the sound of their approach, she looked up and gave them a sweet smile.

"Amy is already tucked in," she explained, pushing herself to standing and dusting off her skirts.

"Thank you very much," James said, stepping forward to press a bit of money into the young girl's hands.

She tried to protest, saying that it was always a pleasure to spend time with Amy. But James waved her off.

"You more than earned it." His voice was kind but made it clear that he wouldn't be accepting no as an answer.

"I'll walk you home," Gilbert advised, stepping forward. "No need for a young lady to be walking home at night."

Rose accepted with a gracious nod. Mattie and James both said their goodbyes to Rose, with Mattie wrapping the girl in a warm hug before she and Gilbert turned and walked out the front door.

Mattie turned, looking at James with a soft smile.

"Quite a night," she said, her voice low and reverent.

"Quite a night," he echoed holding her gaze. "Come on."

He nodded his head toward the door, and Mattie followed after him as he turned and walked onto the porch. She had been too wrapped up in her own thoughts on the walk home to notice much about the night. But when she stepped out onto the top stair, underneath the cover of the porch ceiling, a bright, shining moon glittered above them, and the stars danced merrily.

Mattie stood for a moment, wrapping her arms around herself as she watched the sky.

"It's amazing, isn't it?" James asked as he walked up beside her. "How they're all up there, watching over everything."

"God knew what he was doing when he hung them," Mattie agreed.

"I know you told Gilbert you were alright, but I have to ask again… how are you?"

Mattie turned to look at him and she took a moment before answering, giving herself just a second to really take in his features under the light of the moon. The silver light made his ice blue eyes seem like they were glowing, and she felt as if she could get lost in them.

"I'm alright, I promise," she said softly. "There were too many people there, so he would not have been able to do anything but insist. But I am thankful that you and Gilbert stepped in when you did. It kept it from escalating and becoming more of a scene."

James nodded. "It made me furious to see his hands on you."

He said the words softly, as if the admission wasn't something he made the decision to make, and he was equally as surprised as Mattie when the words left his lips. She chewed the inside of her lip, as a million different responses rushed through her mind.

"Why?" She asked finally.

She studied him as he took a pause of his own, and she watched as he swallowed hard before answering.

"I don't like the idea of any man touching you."

The words hung heavy between them, and Mattie took an involuntary step toward him. Her heart began racing as she did, and his eyes shone in a way they hadn't before.

"Tonight must have been torture for you, then."

A small laugh slipped out of him. "That it was."

Mattie took another step, bringing them so close that all she would have to do is lean forward slightly and her head would be on his chest.

"I wished I could have danced with you tonight," James said, and it caused Mattie's cheeks to flush and her heart to begin racing.

"I wish we could have, also."

James' eyes flitted down, looking at her lips, and like so many times before it felt like they were being pulled together by a magnet. Inch by inch his face crept closer to hers. One moment, she could feel his sweet breath brushing across her cheek, and the next his lips were on hers.

Longing exploded through her, and fireworks danced along her nerve endings when their mouths met. Mattie's eyes closed and she brought her hands up to twine around the nape of James' neck.

His hand came up to cup her cheek, and she leaned into it as the kiss deepened. She had imagined her first kiss a thousand different times, but all of those fantasies and daydreams could not hold a candle to the moment she was currently experiencing with James.

Mattie had no idea how long they stayed like that, with their lips pressed together as the moon shone down on them. But when they finally broke apart, they were both breathing heavily.

Mattie's lips felt swollen from the force of the kiss, but she also felt as if she couldn't get enough. Just as she was about to lean forward to bring their lips together once more, there was the sound of someone clearing their throat from the yard just beyond the porch.

"Well that was quite a show," Gilbert said as he stepped forward out of the shadows.

Chapter Twenty-One

James jumped back, putting as much distance between he and Mattie as he possibly could as Mattie herself let out a yelp of surprise. It was loud, echoing off the porch around them, and apparently it travelled far enough to wake Amy, because a high-pitched wail floated down the stairs to greet them just a moment after.

For just a moment, all three of them stared at each other, with no one saying a word, and James could have sworn that his heart was beating so loudly he couldn't be entirely sure that it wasn't what that had woken Amy up.

"I'll go tend to her," Mattie stammered, and she didn't wait for anyone to reply as she wiped the back of her hand over her lips and rushed into the house.

The sound of Amy's cries only lasted for a few moments before they began to subside and James assumed that Mattie had made her way into the nursery.

"Gilbert, I..." James began but his words failed him as shame and guilt racked through him.

He climbed down the stairs, stopping in the yard once he was only a few feet from his friend. Now that he was closer, he could fully make out Gilbert's features. James had expected to see anger, betrayal, or at the very least a look of hurt. But what he found instead sent his mind reeling in confusion. Gilbert was smiling.

"Don't you dare try to apologize," Gilbert said in a happy, upbeat tone. "It's about damn time."

James' brown knit together as he looked at the man before him. "What do you mean?"

"I could see the way the two of you looked at each other. I do have eyes, you know." Gilbert shrugged one shoulder. "I could tell nothing had happened yet, because of how shy you two were around each other. But all the stolen glances when you thought the other wasn't looking and the way you look at Mattie when she's caring for Amy. It wasn't that hard to figure out. I must admit, though, I was shocked when you didn't ask her to dance tonight."

"You were shocked?" James repeated, thinking that Gilbert had to be playing some type of joke on him.

Because surely he was furious at James. Surely there was no way that Gilbert was alright with the fact that James had just kissed his younger sister, after that friend promised to stay away from her. Surely he was just toying with James before he began yelling? Right? Because nothing else made sense to James. He couldn't wrap his mind around it.

"Obviously, I was shocked," Gilbert said, looking at his friend with concern. "Are you alright there, James? You look a bit confused."

"Of course I'm confused. Aren't you angry?"

"Angry? Why would I be angry?" Gilbert looked at him like he'd lost his mind. "My best friend and my sister? Together? I couldn't have picked a better outcome. I'll admit I'm a bit annoyed that neither of you talked to me about it. Not a big fan of secrets." He shot James a pointed look. "So don't keep secrets from me again. But other than that, I'm over the moon."

James stared at Gilbert again, his mouth gaping open at this unexpected turn of events. Never in his wildest imagination had he thought that Gilbert would be alright with his pursuing Mattie. Had he considered it, had he allowed himself to entertain that one, fanciful thought, perhaps everything would be different.

He would have been able to act on his feelings the moment they began to develop, not pushing them down and trying to keep Mattie at a distance. He wouldn't have had to watch her twirling across the dance floor with men who were not him. It was an entirely new world of possibilities.

"You're certain?" He asked Gilbert, terrified that his friend had changed his mind.

"Absolutely positive." Gilbert gave him a firm, definitive nod and his heart leapt with joy.

"I have to go tell Mattie," he said, looking at his friend with a wide, happy grin.

Gilbert laughed. "Well, go then."

James turned and walked into the house with quick, excited strides. He took the steps two at a time, all the while thinking of the way Mattie's face would light up when he got to tell her the good news. All was quiet when he made it to the top of the steps, and he was glad that she had seemingly gotten Amy back to sleep.

The door to Amy's room was still ajar, the lantern flickering merrily and casting a pool of dancing light on the floor of the room and the hall beyond. James walked into the room, expecting to see Mattie laying Amy back down in her bed.

What he did not expect to see was both of them still in the rocking chair on the far side of the room. Amy curled up on Mattie's lap, her head resting against the woman's chest as both of them dozed peacefully. Mattie's head was resting on the pillowed back of the rocking chair, her long dark eyelashes resting against her pale, beautiful cheek.

James' heart squeezed at the sight of them together like that, with Amy so trusting and comfortable in Mattie's arms. He wouldn't lie to himself and pretend like he didn't want to wake her. But he also couldn't bring himself to do it. The two of them looked so peaceful.

So instead, James crept across the room and grabbed the blanket from Amy's bed. He approached them quietly, making sure he stepped carefully so that the floorboards would not creak and wake them. James draped the blanket over both of them, and Mattie's eyelids fluttered slightly before she nestled further down into the blanket and clutched a still sleeping Amy a little tighter.

"Goodnight," James whispered to the two sleeping forms.

And with that, he turned and strode from the room.

Chapter Twenty-Two

Mattie's eyes fluttered open as the sound of laughter bubbled up from the kitchen below. The sunlight streamed in through the window at an odd angle, and Mattie blinked at it in confusion as she tried to figure out where she was.

With a mind still hazy with sleep, it took her a moment to piece together that she was in the rocking chair in Amy's room and that she must have fallen asleep the night before when she came up here to check on the toddler.

She looked down at the child still sleeping in her lap, and images of the night before came flooding back to her. Mattie stifled a groan as she recalled Gilbert walking up to the porch as she and James shared their first kiss. And she had to admit that Amy waking up couldn't had come at a better time. She had not wanted to face her brother after that moment.

Amy stirred in Mattie's lap, her eyelids fluttering and then opening entirely. Mattie smiled down into the sleepy child's face, and she was rewarded with a wide, toothy grin.

"Good morning little dove," Mattie cooed. "Looks like we fell asleep together."

Amy nodded at her, and wiped sleepily at her eyes. Mattie glanced down, and realized they were both covered in a blanket.

"Now, where did that come from?" She said aloud.

She realized that someone must have come upstairs and draped it over them in the middle of the night, and her stomach gave a swift, nervous twinge. She wasn't sure if she preferred that it had been James or Gilbert. Either option felt particularly horrible and embarrassing after the events of the prior evening.

"Well, I guess we have no choice but to both get up and face the day. Isn't that right?" She asked Amy, who gave her a quick nod. "But first, you'll need to get dressed."

Mattie looked down at herself and realized she was still in her gown from the night before and gave a quick sigh. It looked like she would need to get dressed and spruce herself up as well.

Amy crawled out of Mattie's lap, and the toddler did her best to assist Mattie in both of them readying for the day. It took a little bit longer than if Mattie had done it herself, but she wasn't entirely upset to delay seeing James and her brother. The laughter and loud, excited voices were still bouncing up from downstairs from time to time, and as Mattie pulled a dress over her head, she couldn't help but wonder what they were talking about. She was too far away to make out any words. But if their tone was any indication, the two friends had been able to come to an understanding the night before.

Mattie's heart fluttered at the thought that perhaps James had taken the brunt of her brother's ire.

"Maybe this won't be as bad as I fear," she said to Amy before taking the child's hand and starting the walk toward the kitchen.

When she made it to the bottom of the stairs and turned the corner, the site before her caught her by surprise. James was in his usual seat at the table, a mug of coffee held in his hands. Gilbert, however, was at the stove, spatula in hand as he flipped a large, round pancake in the cast iron. There was a large stack of them on a plate on the counter already, and Mattie watched as he added one to it.

"Good morning," Mattie said hesitantly as she stepped into the room.

Amy let go of her hand and toddled over to her father, her arms outstretched in an indication that she wanted him to lift her. James looked at his daughter with a smile before bending down to pick her up and placing her on his knee. He began to bounce her, the child clapping her small, chubby hands, as James turned to look at Mattie.

His eyes were bright and happy when they met hers. And he looked so handsome that it made her stomach feel like it was going to flip.

"Good morning, Mattie," James replied, his deep voice washing over her like a gentle caress. "How did you sleep?"

A grin tugged at the corner of his mouth, and Mattie knew instantly that he had been the one that had placed the blanket over he and Amy. Mattie's gaze flicked from both James and Gilbert, noting that there was no strangeness between them, nor was there any directed at her as her brother turned to glance at her over his shoulder. Perhaps their plan was to act as if it never happened?

Mattie wasn't sure if the idea horrified or pleased her. Until she decided, she figured she may as well go along with it. She walked across the room and pulled out her chair at the kitchen table and sat.

"I slept well, thank you." She grabbed one of the bronze mugs in the center of the table and poured a bit of coffee in. "What occasion is it that calls for pancakes?"

Gilbert added the final one to the already towering stack and turned around with a flourish.

"No reason at all," he said with a grin as he walked over and placed it in the center of the table.

To go with the pancakes, berries and syrup had been placed on the table before her, and she eyed it all hungrily, despite her nerves. She didn't trust her brother's answer, because he only made those pancakes when he felt as if there was something to celebrate. Which was exactly the opposite of what she had expected after the events of the night before.

Once Gilbert took his seat, they all grabbed themselves plates from the middle of the table and began piling them high with pancakes, fruit, and syrup. Mattie offered to place Amy in her chair, but James waved her off, stating he would feed her from his lap. She watched the two of them interacting, and her heart swelled with fondness.

When Mattie had first agreed to come to Mt. Juliet, she had been prepared to care about the child. But she had never anticipated how deeply that caring would go. And when she added in the affection she held for James, an affection she still wasn't sure how to articulate and was too afraid to look at closely, it made her heart glow as she looked at the two of them.

Gilbert cleared his throat and Mattie glanced over at him. Her brother gave her a knowing look as his mouth tugged up in a grin, and she realized that he had caught her staring at James and Amy. She felt her cheeks flush crimson and turned her gaze to her plate, intent on keeping it focused there as they made their way through the meal.

"So, what do you have planned today?" James asked Gilbert.

"Well, after breakfast I figured little Amy and I can go on a walk, maybe pick some wildflowers." Gilbert turned his attention to the toddler in question. "What do you think about that, you tiny thing, you?"

Amy grinned at him as she munched down on a strawberry, the juice dribbling down her chin. Mattie chuckled slightly as she looked from the toddler to her brother. Breakfast was over quickly, each of them having devoured the pancakes and fruit Gilbert had set out. When they had cleared their plates, Mattie and Gilbert made quick work of cleaning up while James took Amy upstairs to clean some of the syrup off her.

"Hand me those," Mattie said, gesturing to the plates that her brother was carrying over from the table to the sink.

He did as he was asked, and Mattie thrust them into the heated water where she began to scrub. She handed them to her brother when they were done, who quickly dried them and then put them away in the cabinet.

"I'm not angry, you know," Gilbert said as he took yet another dish from his sister and began to dry it.

Her cheeks flushed when she realized what he was talking about.

"I had assumed, since you've seemed fine all morning," Mattie answered, not daring to take her eyes off the water in front of her.

"Well, I just wanted you to hear it from me."

She passed him the final plate just as the floorboards behind them creaked, announcing James and Amy's arrival back in the kitchen. She dried her hands on her apron and then picked up the wash bucket to dump it out in the back yard. By the time she returned, Gilbert and Amy were gone.

James stood in the threshold of the kitchen, leaning his shoulder against it with his hands in his pockets. He regarded her as she walked to the center of the room and then stopped, their gazes locked.

"Why don't you go sit with me on the porch swing?" James asked, his blue eyes sparkling.

"Alright." Mattie nodded and they walked through the house and onto the porch side by side.

They sat on the wooden swing, rocking it gently. She turned her body to look at James, and a soft, May breeze stirred a loose tendril of her hair around her face. She reached up to brush it back, but James' hand beat her to it. She blushed as his large, strong hand caught her copper hair between his fingers, and they ran along the length of her cheekbone as he tucked it behind her ear.

"Gilbert and I spoke last night," James began, not looking away as he held her stare.

"And?" Mattie prompted. "After breakfast, when you took Amy upstairs, he told me that he wasn't angry. But he didn't provide any additional explanation."

James nodded. "He said he'd let me be the one to talk to you. And he isn't mad. He's actually quite pleased about the whole thing."

"Pleased?" Mattie's eyebrows shot up in surprise. "You mean to tell me he approved of you kissing me?"

"Approved is an understatement," James chuckled. "He's actually over the moon about my affection for you."

Her heart began to hammer in her chest. "Your affection for me?"

He nodded, his blue eyes brimming with sincerity. "I've come to care for you quite a lot, Mattie. More than I ever intended. From the moment you climbed off that train, I have been unable to get you out of my thoughts. I told myself that it was just the initial shock and that it would fade. But the more I got to know you, and the more I discovered that not only are you beautiful, but you are funny, and kind, and stubborn, and tenacious, and an entire host of other, amazing things, I became more and more affected by you."

"And I tried to fight it. I tried telling myself that I would be betraying Gilbert's trust by pining after his sister. I told myself that I would be betraying Ruth by caring for another woman. But they were nothing but hollow excuses. Because Gilbert loves us both, and he said he couldn't think of anything that he'd love more than for us to care for one another. He wants us to be happy, and that's really all he cares about.

"And the truth is that Ruth would not want me to spend the rest of my life alone. She wouldn't want Amy to watch me grow up sad, and miserable, and lonely. She would have wanted me to care for someone spectacular, that treats Amy well. Those things that I was tellin' myself were just excuses, because at the end of the day, Mattie, I'm afraid. Afraid to care for someone and lose them again. Of Amy losing someone that she loves. But I know now that that fear won't ever go away. I just can't allow it to run my life, not anymore."

He lifted one shoulder in a shrug and let it drop. Mattie's mind raced to take in all of the information that he had just given her, as her heart leapt with joy and butterflies flapped in her stomach. There were a thousand things she wanted to say, but all of them fell silent before they could reach her lips. So instead, she said the only thing she could think of.

"I'm glad that Gilbert's happy," Mattie gave James a soft smile. "And I care for you quite a lot, as well."

She knew that it didn't cover nearly half of the truth of what she'd come to feel for him. She'd realized it the night before as she had rocked Amy, and subsequently herself, to sleep. When James lips had touched hers, she'd been forced to accept that she had well and truly fallen for him. But, in the harsh light of day, she'd been terrified to examine that realization any closer for fear of what the rest of the day would bring.

But now, knowing that it was safe to express those emotions, safe for her to harbor those affections for her brother's best friend? She couldn't quite process the joy that was coursing through her.

James returned her smile with one of his own, and then ever so slowly his hand came up to cup the back of her neck.

Bringing his face to hers, he whispered, "I am so very glad."

And before she could respond, his lips pressed to hers and she lost the ability to think at all.

***

Later that night, Mattie sat in the drawing room, a lantern flickering merrily in the corner, and she softly picked at the keys of the piano. James had taken Amy up to put her to sleep, and she'd wandered through the house in search of something to busy herself with. Gilbert had gone upstairs for something or another, and left to her own devices, she'd found herself itching to sit at the piano.

As the final chords of the song she'd been playing quieted down, she heard a faint, soft clapping from behind her. Casting a quick glance over her shoulder, she found Gilbert leaning against the door frame, watching her with a smile on his face.

"I haven't seen you play in quite some time," he said, pushing from the wooden threshold and walking across the room.

He sat down beside her on the bench of the piano and looked at her.

"You seem better here," Gilbert said. "Happier."

"I am." Mattie nodded.

"I promised James he'd be able to talk to you first. I assume he did that earlier?"

"He did." She smiled at her brother, and he quickly returned it.

"Good. I just want you to know that if you are happy, then I am happy. That's it. Before you left Bartlett, after everything that happened, it was like the light just drained out of you. But when I got to Mt. Juliet, I could see from the second you found me wandering the street that the life had returned to you, and maybe you were even filled with a little extra. It's all I've ever wanted... for you to be happy."

A lump formed in Mattie's throat as Gilbert spoke, and she forced herself to swallow it.

"I'm very happy," she explained when her brother had finished speaking. "Amy is the sweetest little girl, and it is so easy to care for her. All the people in Mt. Juliet are so kind and have welcomed me with open arms. And to be fair, the weather is a bit more bearable than in Mississippi."

Gilbert chuckled. "And James?"

"James, he..." Mattie flushed as she worked to find the words. "He is kind, and he is good. He's more than a bit stubborn, but it helps to keep things interesting."

"And you care for him?"

Mattie nodded. "Very much."

"Then I am happy for you."

Gilbert leaned toward her, wrapping her in a hug. She squeezed him back, reveling in her brother's embrace and in the blessing that he'd just given her. When they broke apart, Gilbert was grinning wildly.

"Now," he said, "I have some news of my own."

"Oh?" Mattie's eyebrows shot up in question and Gilbert nodded.

"Now that you're all happy and what not, now is the time to tell you that I've been courting someone as well."

"Gilbert!" She smacked his shoulder playfully. "Why didn't you tell me sooner?"

"I wasn't sure if it was real, you're feeling better. And I didn't want you to feel as if I was gloating, or making things worse."

Mattie's heart sank at her brother's words, and she held his gaze as she spoke.

"I don't care how much pain I'm in, or how sad I am. I will never, ever want you to hide your happiness from me."

Gilbert nodded, and reached down to hold Mattie's hand where it sat on the bench between them.

"Our parents would be proud, you know." His voice quivered slightly as he spoke, and Mattie felt happy tears pricking her eyes. "To see us both happy like this."

She nodded, blinking quickly to chase the tears away. And as the words fell from her brother's lips, she smiled, finding that she believed them.

Chapter Twenty-Three

"I would like to ask Mattie to marry me."

The words left James in a rush as he sat at the kitchen table, looking at Gilbert, who sputtered into his coffee.

After breakfast, Mattie had taken Amy upstairs to get her cleaned off and dressed for the day. James glanced at the ceiling now, hoping that she was still up there and wouldn't walk around the corner any second and interrupt the conversation he knew he needed to have with Gilbert.

"I know that it's soon," James explained as Gilbert wiped the coffee off his chin. "But I know more than anyone that when you care for someone, there's no sense in waiting. Life is too short."

Gilbert nodded as he spoke. "That it is."

"And I know that you're set to leave today, but I'd like to ask you to stay for a little while longer," James said, then caught the confused look on Gilbert's face. He continued with his explanation. "Now that Mattie and I are courting, it would not be proper for us to live here together, without someone else residing in the home."

Gilbert nodded again, considering James' words before speaking.

"Thank you," he said after a brief pause. "For considering my sister's honor. And I agree, it would be improper. As far as my permission, I grant it whole heartedly and happily. And I can stay until the wedding, because I'll be damned if I miss the chance to give my little sister away to my best friend."

James' heart warmed at the thought, and he opened his mouth to thank his friend just as a loud creak from the stairs echoed throughout the house, announcing Mattie's arrival a moment before she appeared.

"There we go," she sang merrily as she bounced Amy on her hip. "The little dove is all washed up and ready for her day."

She looked away from Amy, and as her eyes raked over James and Gilbert, her brow knit together in confusion.

"Are you two alright? Why are you both smiling at me like you've gone mad?"

Gilbert chuckled as he pushed himself away from the table and stood.

"Everything is more than alright, dear sister," he said with a grin. He walked forward and held his arms out for Amy, who gladly reached for him. "I'm just going to take this little one outside to play for a bit. It's a beautiful day."

Mattie glanced at her brother warily but didn't object as he took Amy from her and walked toward the door. She watched them as they faded into the distance but didn't try to stop them. When the door to the house shut behind them, she turned to look back at James.

"You're both acting quite odd," she said.

"Mattie." James stood, crossing the kitchen in a few quick strides. "I would like to talk to you."

He saw a look of worry cross her face, and he shook his head.

"It's nothing to worry about," he said quickly, giving her what he hoped was a reassuring smile as his nerves threatened to overcome him. "Let's head to the drawing room."

She nodded and began to turn, but James quickly reached down and grabbed her hand. Lacing their fingers together, they walked through the house until they reached their destination. Inside the beautifully furnished room, James turned to face Mattie, and reached forward to hold both of her hands.

He blew out a quick breath as he tried to calm himself and work through the anxiety now coursing through him. He had thought that getting permission from Gilbert would have been the hard part, but now that he was standing there with Mattie blinking at him in confusion, he realized that he had grossly miscalculated.

Earlier, James hadn't given himself space to consider what would happen if she rejected his proposal. But now, looking down at her beautiful face while her vibrant green eyes regarded him with care and confusion, he realized that the hardest part was yet to come.

"Mattie," James began, willing his voice to remain sure and steady. "I wasn't entirely honest with you yesterday when we spoke."

Her brow knit together with worry, and she opened her mouth to speak. But he carried on before she could.

"I told you that I care for you, and while that is true, it isn't the full story. The whole truth is that I love you. And it terrifies me, but it is true. And I know that life is short, and that it is often uncertain. But the one thing I'm certain about is that I'd like to spend the rest of mine with you."

Her mouth popped open in surprise as he spoke, and he had the urge to lean froward and brush a kiss across her lips.

"Are you... James... what are you saying?" Mattie asked as she regarded him with shock.

"I'm saying," he clarified. "That I love you. And I'd like you to be my wife if you'll have me."

His heart hammered in his chest as he looked down at her. Slowly, he saw the shock written across her lovely features began to transform. The creases in her brow smoothed, her mouth began to close and then the corners tugged up in a glowing, radiant smile.

"Oh," she said so softly it was barely above a whisper. "I love you, too. And it would be an honor to be your wife."

It took James a moment to realize what she had said, to register that she had agreed. But when it did, a wave of happiness rushed through him so suddenly that he couldn't stop himself from rushing forward.

Wrapping his arms around Mattie's middle, he lifted her off the ground and spun her in a circle. A beautiful giggle pulled itself from her as they spun, and James rained kisses down upon her face. When he stopped, both of them swaying with dizziness, he grinned down at her.

"You're sure about this?" He asked, terrified that she might say no but needing to give her the chance to reconsider anyway.

Mattie pressed her small hand to his cheek, rubbing her thumb across the top of his beard as she gazed into his eyes.

"I have never been more certain."

He bent and kissed her, slowly and sweetly. When they broke apart, James filled Mattie in on his plan, to which she eagerly agreed, and they headed out to the front yard to find Gilbert. He and Amy were in the garden, pulling up weeds. In the short time that they were out of sight, both of them got so covered in dirt that James found it perplexing, but he didn't want to bring it up and ruin the happiness of the moment.

When James and Mattie told Gilbert that she'd agreed to be his wife, he had jumped to his feet and rushed forward to hug his sister. James had watched as Mattie threw her head back and laughed and reveled in the moment as she tried to untangle herself from her brother's embrace.

"Would you be able to watch Amy for a little while?" Mattie asked when they broke apart. "James and I will need to go to town to speak to a minister. We don't want to delay you getting home to your sweetheart any more than we have to."

Gilbert agreed eagerly, all but pushing them toward the road and telling them to get on their way. As they walked toward town, James and Mattie spoke eagerly about what the upcoming wedding would be like. The journey passed quickly, and James felt as if it was only the blink of an eye later that they were standing before the small, parish church in the center of town.

They walked up the wooden steps to the building that had been painted a bright, gleaming white, and pushed open the door. Inside, the pine pews had been polished to gleaming, and they shone in the light that filtered in through the windows. The minister was standing at the far side of the room, arranging a few candles at the foot of the dais.

At the sound of the door shutting behind them, he stood up and turned to greet them.

"Hello," he said in a warm, husky voice. "How are you, James?"

The minister reached forward to shake James' hand, and James did so gladly.

"I'm doing quite well; I hope you are also."

"A day on God's green earth means that I am doing well indeed. Now how can I help you?"

James told the minister about the wedding, and about the need for it to be done quickly. The other man nodded as he spoke, shooting quick, happy smiles to both he and Mattie in between murmured congratulations. By the time James was finished, the minister clapped his hands together.

"A joyous occasion indeed," he said with a grin. "And of course I would be delighted to help. I should be able to get you two wed by weeks end."

James felt a rush of joy fill him. They both thanked the minister, but the man quickly waved it off. Excited to tell Gilbert the news, both Mattie and James turned and strode out of the church.

"Can we go to the General Store?" Mattie asked when they stepped back into the sunny street. "I'd like to pick up a few things for a celebratory dinner tonight."

James agreed eagerly and they began to walk in that direction. As they approached the shop, there were a few old men sitting atop overturned barrels and a checkerboard between them. Their eyes did not move from it as they talked to each other, and as James and Mattie grew closer, he was able to make out what they were saying.

"... that Hubert Bird made a fool of himself," one of the men said. "Wouldn't let go of that girl until James Murphy and some other man Dolores said was the girls' brother stepped in."

"It's a right shame," the other man said, shaking his head as he reached forward to move one of his checker pieces. "Embarassin' yourself like that in front of the whole town."

They both grunted their ascent, and James felt a twang of something he couldn't identify as they walked past the men and into the shade of the store. They browsed the shelves slowly, together picking out all of the items that Mattie listed off. It wasn't hard though, for them to hear the whispers of the other patrons in the store. They were all talking about the exact same thing, which was how atrociously Hubert Bird had behaved at the dance.

Days ago, James would have said that hearing townsfolk gossip about Hubert Bird embarrassing himself would have brought him the smallest bit of joy. But now, as he looked at Mattie, the woman that he would soon be marrying, he felt a bit of sympathy toward the man that he had hated for so long. It wouldn't be easy for him once word got out that James and Mattie had gotten married.

After their items were selected and paid for, they were placed in a basket and James carried it as they walked home.

"What if," Mattie said excitedly as they walked, "we go home and see if Gilbert and Amy would like to walk about town? It's such a lovely day."

James nodded as he looked at her, smiling at the joy on his bride-to-be's face.

"That sounds like a lovely idea," James agreed with the dip of his head.

So, they did just that. The moment that they arrived back at the ranch, Mattie went inside to put away the things they bought at the General Store and begin readying Amy's pram. James went to find Gilbert and laughed when he rounded the corner of the house to the garden and found Gilbert and Amy laying on the grass, covered head to toe in dirt, staring at the sky.

"What are you doing?" He asked with a chuckle as he approached.

Gilbert propped himself up on his elbows, shielding his eyes against the bright sun as he looked at James.

"We're looking at clouds," he explained.

"Clow!" Amy said excitedly, pointing up toward the sky.

James darted forward, swooping his daughter up off the grass and tossing her in the air while she squealed excitedly.

"Well," James grinned. "How about we get the dirt washed off and we all walk to town, what do you say?"

Gilbert agreed as he pushed himself to standing. They readied themselves quickly, and before James knew it, they were off again, heading back toward town. All three adults traded off on managing the stroller as they walked, while Amy babbled in delight as she continued pointing at the clouds in the sky. When eventually the flat fields gave way to the first line of houses, James took over managing the pram, allowing Mattie the freedom to flit from store window to store window, pointing out the various things she found.

With every moment that passed, knowing that they were getting closer and closer to the moment of their wedding, James felt lighter. He could not wait for the day to arrive, when he could proudly call Mattie his wife to everyone that would listen. Mattie disappeared into one of the shops and came out a moment later holding a bag of penny candy.

She grinned as she passed a small piece to Amy, who squealed with delight as she popped it in her mouth, and they all laughed. Mattie rested her hand on James' on the handle of the pram, and he gazed down lovingly at her face, smiling.

"Uhm, James," Gilbert said, breaking through his and Mattie's moment of reverie.

James glanced at his friend, who nodded toward something off to the side of them. James followed Gilbert's gaze, and it took him a moment for him to make sense of what he was seeing. But as the realization dawned on him, he had to fight against the urge to groan. At the side of the road stood Hubert Bird, holding an obnoxiously large bouquet of flowers.

Chapter Twenty-Four

Mattie saw the change come over James' face as his gaze drifted across the road, and worry creased her brow. She turned to see what he was looking at, and saw Hubert standing at the edge of the crowded street with a large bouquet of flowers.

"I can't believe…" James began to mumble under his breath as Hubert began walking toward them and Mattie patted his arm.

"Let me speak to him," she said.

He gave her a look that was riddled with apprehension, but Mattie gave him what she hoped was a reassuring smile.

"Hubert is harmless, I promise you."

She did not wait for him to respond as she turned and walked away, heading to meet Hubert in the middle of the road. She was thankful when neither James nor her brother tried to stop her. Hubert's face broke into a wide, excited grin as she approached, and Mattie's stomach twisted into a knot over the thought of what she'd have to do.

"Hello Mattie," he said as she approached, extending the bouquet to her. "I brought these for you when I saw you walk into town. I was hoping to track you down. I'd like to apologize about that nastiness the other night."

She glanced down at the flowers and then back up at him. He was smiling at her, exposing all of his teeth, but she could not read an ounce of true sincerity upon the man's face. And the final thread of patience that Mattie had for him finally snapped.

"Hubert," Mattie held up a hand as she tried to interrupt him, but that only served to make him speak louder to drown out her objections.

"I did not act like a gentleman," Hubert plowed on. "I was upset that I did not get the opportunity to dance with you after I bought you such a beautiful hat. And I thought that we had agreed that you would save me a dance, but I must have misheard, and for that I apologize. I am also incredibly sorry that I scared you, it was never my intent. As I said, I was simply frustrated, and it got the better of me. Please,"

"Mr. Bird," Mattie demanded, louder this time.

Her voice rang out clearly, drowning out the sound of his explanations and grabbing the attention of a few townsfolk that were passing by. She saw them behind Hubert as their eyes roved over the two standing and talking. Recognition flashed across the face of one of the women, and she leaned in close to whisper in the ear of her companion.

Mattie's face flushed crimson. She had heard everyone gossiping about the events of the dance when she and James were out earlier in the day. She had hoped that they would be married soon enough that the talk of their wedding would make its way to Hubert before she ran into him again. Or, at the very least that James and Mattie getting married so hastily would provide the town with something else to talk about.

She had not, however, wanted to have this discussion with Hubert on a crowded street. But it seemed that he would be providing her with no other option.

"You must stop," Mattie said, careful to keep her voice firm. "You must stop with the gifts; you must stop with showing up to try to win my affections. I apologize if I have led you astray in any way, but I need you to hear me when I tell you this. I do not harbor any affections for you. I thought I had made that apparent at the dance, but it appears that I did not."

Hubert gaped at her; his eyes wide with shock as she continued to speak.

"Now, I am very sorry if your feelings or your pride are hurt by my words, as that was never my intent. I had hoped that after the dance you would have bowed out gracefully, but once again it seems as if I was mistaken."

"Ms. Mattie," Hubert said, taking a step toward her. "Surely you cannot mean this. After the things that I have bought you, and the care…"

"No." Mattie shook her head, once again holding up a hand, and this time Hubert fell silent. "Do not continue. The gifts must stop."

She cast a glance over her shoulder, spotting her brother, James, and Amy exactly where she left them. They were watching her closely, both of the men appearing as if they were ready to spring into action at a moment's notice, and the sight filled her with even more courage as she turned to face Hubert once more.

"James and I are set to be married by the end of the week. So, you see, your gifts are not only unwanted, but they are improper." She watched Hubert's face closely as she spoke, seeing emotions flit over his face one after the other.

First, his mouth became a mask of shock, with his mouth gaping and his eyes wide. Then, as he began to process what she had said, his cheeks reddened, and his eyes began to narrow.

"You cannot expect me to believe this," he demanded as he took another step toward her.

Before she could stop him, or even attempt to move out of the way, he was upon her. Hubert's hand clamped down on her bicep, his fingertips digging into her skin and making her cry out with pain. She had thought that he had gripped her hard during the dance, but Mattie realized that he had barely applied any pressure at all.

"Hubert, you're hurting me," she protested as she reached up and attempted to pry his fingers off. But his grip was too strong.

"You cannot be serious," Hubert snarled, spittle flying from his lips. "You cannot choose that man over me; this cannot happen again!"

He raised the hand that still clutched the bouquet into the air, and for a moment Mattie was terrified that he was about to strike her. When Hubert brought his arm down, a startled gasp sounded from somewhere around them, but Mattie did not turn to look at who it came from. Instead of coming in contact with her, his fist opened and released the bouquet, sending them catapulting to the ground.

Mattie was unable to make sense of what was happening. As suddenly as he threw the flowers, Hubert's grip on her arm released and he was suddenly forced back away from her. The lack of him pulling on her forced Mattie to stumble a few steps backwards and it took her a moment to catch her bearings.

When she did, her eyes raked over the sight before her as her mind tried to catch up with what she saw. Hubert was sprawled in the dirt, blood pouring from his nose where he clutched it. James stood above him, shaking out his fist while he looked down on the man.

"You will never, ever put your hands on my fiancé again, do you understand me." James' voice was riotous, ringing out into the crowd of onlookers that had stopped to take in the scene before them. "She tried to tell you, and had you listened to her this could have all been avoided. But instead, you decided to place your grubby hands on her and now look at you."

He sneered down his nose at Hubert, who in return glowered up at James. Loathing roiled in the air between the two men, and anyone with eyes could tell that this moment had been a very long time coming. She cast a look behind her out into the crowd, her eyes searching for Gilbert and Amy. Relief rushed through her when she spotted her brother standing a safe distance away at the head of the pram, making sure to keep Amy distracted from what her father was doing.

"You will not speak to her again. You will not buy her gifts. You will not impose your will or affections upon her in any way. Do. You. Understand. Me."

Hubert's already mean stare narrowed even further on James as he leaned to the side and spit, blood mixing with saliva as it hit the dirt before him.

"James Murphy," Hubert said menacingly, his voice now nasally and congested from the force of the blow. "I said this at the dance, and I'm saying it again. You will come to regret this."

He pushed himself up off the dirt and stood before James, both men's chests heaving with anger as they stared each other down. Finally, James turned away, his eyes immediately finding Mattie and turning soft.

"Come on, Mattie," he said, giving her a soft smile. As if in an afterthought, he cast a quick glance over his shoulder to where Hubert still stood, his tone becoming uninterested. "There is nothing else to see here."

James turned and walked toward Mattie, and she extended her hand to him. Stepping onto the bouquet of flowers that lay on the ground, she didn't dare cast a glance back at Hubert as they joined with Gilbert and Amy and began to walk home. But even though Mattie did not turn back, she could feel Hubert's gaze on their backs every step of the way.

Chapter Twenty-Five

As James pushed the pram up to the house, Amy let out a soft, fussy cry. Mattie rushed forward, cooing to the small child but James could see her hands shaking as she reached out for the toddler.

"I have her," he said softly to his fiancé, stepping forward to gently brush a stray tendril of hair away from her face to try and calm her. "I think she needs a nap. Go sit for a little bit and I'll meet you after I put her down."

Her beautiful green eyes searched his face for a moment, and James gave her a soft, reassuring smile before she turned and strode into the house. He diverted his attention back to Amy, shushing and cooing to her as he extracted her from the swaths of fabric nestled inside the stroller.

When she was secured in his arms, she began to settle a bit, and as he looked down into her sweet face, her eyelids had already begun to droop with the temptation of sleep.

"There, there, precious girl," he murmured, holding his daughter close to his chest as he made his was across the porch and into the house. "Papa is here and we're going to get you all settled in for a nap."

He pressed gentle kisses onto her forehead and face as they walked up the stairs, with James cooing to her all the way. By the time he pushed open the door to Amy's room, she was already fast asleep.

As softly as he could, he moved her small body from where it was nestled to his chest and laid her down on the bed. She stirred for a moment, her chubby hands coming up to swipe at her eyes groggily, and he sat down on the bed beside her.

James began to hum as he stroked his daughter's hair, and eventually she drifted off to sleep once more.

He waited for a few moments, just to make sure she would not wake again, before he pushed himself to his feet and began heading downstairs. Careful to not make the stairs creek too loudly, he crept softly away from Amy's room, not wanting to wake her once more. As such, Gilbert and Mattie did not hear him approach when he went to find them in the kitchen.

"...don't know. He's never told me the full story, but clearly there's something more." Mattie's voice sounded frazzled as it floated to him through the otherwise quiet home. "I wish that I had more to tell you."

"I've never known him to be violent, not like that." It was Gilbert speaking this time, and James did not have to try too hard to figure out who it was they were talking about. "Don't get me wrong, as boys we got into our fair share of spats. But the animosity between those two, that was more than just rivalry."

With a lump in his throat, James stepped into the kitchen where Mattie and Gilbert sat at the table, both of them nursing a mug of hot tea. Mattie's eyes found his the moment he was in the room with her, and he knew that there would be no escaping her and Gilbert's questions.

"Is there still tea left?" He asked, striding over to the stove where the kettle rested.

"Should be," Mattie answered. "I can also put on a pot of water for coffee as well, if you'd like that."

"No need."

James grabbed the last mug from the cabinet and filled it with the tea before turning and walking back to the table. He did his best not to appear anxious as he set the mug and then himself, in between his fiancé and her brother. Mattie stared into her tea, swirling the liquid around with a small spoon, while Gilbert looked at him head on.

A long, hard sigh left Gilbert's lips as he leaned back in his chair, all while his gaze remained hard and fixed on James.

"So," he said after a pause. "We've already figured out that there's more to the story with Hubert than either I or Mattie know, and we think it's time for you to tell us everything, now that things have come to blows."

James took a moment to collect his thoughts, running over his past with Hubert Bird in his mind to make sure that when he began recounting everything to the people before him, two of the people that meant the most in the world to him, he wouldn't miss a thing. Finally, when he was confident that he was ready to begin, he did.

"Hubert and I met when were young, which you both already know." He dipped his head in acknowledgement to both Mattie and to Gilbert before continuing on. "When I was still living in Bartlett but would come to Mt. Juliet for the summer, his father and my grandfather were relatively friendly. So, we were around each other then. When I finally came to Mt. Juliet for good, we were in school together. To be honest, I can't recall a time where Hubert ever actually liked me, or even tolerated me. Unfortunately, as you can likely guess, that followed us well past our school days."

Mattie and Gilbert both nodded. Mattie had now brought her gaze up to study his face as he talked, and James tried to make sure he was glancing between both of them as he did so.

"We inherited the ranches within a year or so of each other, you know. And at first, it was just small things. I'd take some of the cattle to markets and he'd deliberately undercut me in pricing, even if it meant he took a loss for his head. It didn't seem to matter to him, as long as I wasn't the one making the sale. Then, I started to have suspicions about the quality of cattle and crop that he was selling.

"Animals that I would have never had butchered, those that were too sick, too young, or even too old to make good, healthy cuts of meat, that I would have just allowed to continue grazing, well Hubert started to sell them. A couple of my cows that had been clipped showed up on his ranch more than once, and he acted as if it was all just an accident. Suggesting my cattle had gotten out due to a broken fence or a gate left open, and they had just wandered onto his property. Never mind the fact that mud had been strategically smeared over the spot where the brand was, like he was trying to disguise them.

"Things only continued to get worse from there. Parts of my fence that had just been mended were suddenly weakened, my grain stores tarnished with no apparent cause. I could never prove it was him. But I always suspected."

"Did you ever confront him about it?" Gilbert asked, raising a brow in question.

James nodded. "A time or two, right after the more egregious acts had been committed, like the fence tamperin' and the stuff with the feed stores. But of course, he always denied it. He would just tell me he had no idea what I was talking about and that some people just had bad luck. There was really nothing I could do."

James paused for a moment, taking a deep steadying breath as he looked from Mattie to Gilbert. He had never openly talked about what had come next, about what had occurred between he and Hubert after James had met Ruth. And it wasn't always easy for him to find the words.

"And then, there was the dance. The same night I met Ruth was the night that Hubert met her as well. He actually met her first. She had been dancing with him the first time I saw her. And at first, I had wondered if perhaps they were courting, so I asked around. I knew that he hadn't been married to anyone, but for all I knew he could have been preparing too.

"But when everyone told me that, as far as they knew, they were just dancin' I couldn't fight against my interest in her. So, when they were done, I approached Ruth and asked her to dance with me. And she did."

A small, fond smile tugged at the corners of James' lips as he thought about the night he met his late wife. He glanced at Mattie, afraid that the talk of Ruth would make her uncomfortable, but she just shot him a reassuring smile and nodded for him to continue. Warmth and gratitude flooded him as he began to speak once more.

"I fell in love with her that night. As it turns out, so did Hubert. When he found out that I was courting her, he lost it. The antics with my animals ticked up, and a lot of my crops got ruined. That's right around when I hired Elmer. He was really young then, but I hired him and some of the other kids around town to look after my crops and animals in shifts throughout the night.

"The night before our wedding, Hubert came to Ruth and asked her to marry him instead. Despite her telling him 'no' repeatedly, he still tried as hard as he could to convince her. She was forced to be quite rude to get him to take her seriously, and when he did, he left in a huff. At one point, after Ruth's death, Elmer overheard Hubert talking in the saloon about how if Ruth had chosen him all those years ago, she would still be alive today. He's blamed me for every little thing that's gone wrong with his love life and his business since we were kids."

James glanced at the table, hearing Mattie's quick gasp at the final sentence and seeing Gilbert's hands tighten into a fist. That was the end of the story, he didn't have anything left to add, but he hoped that what he had divulged to them had been enough.

"And now he thinks you've taken his chance with Mattie." Gilbert's voice was grim when he spoke and when James glance at his friend once more, the lines of his face were hard. Gilbert was clenching and unclenching his jaw, and James knew that Gilbert's mind was turning over the problem at hand to analyze it from every direction.

"I would assume so," James answered with a quick, terse nod.

"Should we be worried?" Mattie asked, and James swiveled his head to her.

Her green eyes were bright with more than a little fear. James reached across the table to where her hand rested, placing his own on top of it and holding her gaze.

"I don't think so," James began. "The antics that he got up to all those years ago died down a while back, shortly after Ruth died. And they've never started back up. Sure, he's still undermining what I sell when we go to market or to auction, but it's nothing like what it used to be. And should he try anything, I promise you that I'll protect you."

That promise fell over them, weighted like a blanket. And for a moment a chill ran up his spine as the words seemed to spin in the air before them, and James got the sense that God himself heard the promise, and that he took it as a challenge.

Chapter Twenty-Six

Mattie ran her fingers over the bodice of her dress, smoothing down the light blue fabric that was dotted with small, yellow flowers. She focused on pulling a deep breath into her lungs and expelling it slowly, trying as hard as she could to pull her mind away from all the nastiness that had occurred with Hubert. But it was of no use.

James had told her that she didn't have to worry, that even if Hubert did try to retaliate, he would protect her. But Mattie couldn't help but worry that it wouldn't be enough. Having heard the lengths that Hubert had gone to in the past to humiliate James and to retaliate against him had been enough to send shivers down her spine. And she was positive that now that Hubert felt as if he had been jilted for a second time that he would be even more unhinged.

She tried to blow out another steadying breath, turning to Amy who sat on the floor playing with her blocks. Amy blinked up at her with her large, brown eyes and light blonde hair, giving her a wide, toothy smile, and a bit of Mattie's spirit lifted.

"What do you say, little dove?" She asked, looking down at the excited toddler. "What if we go into town to see your Auntie Josie? Maybe that will preoccupy our thoughts."

"Oh-Zeee," Amy repeated, trying her hardest for her uncoordinated mouth to form Josie's name.

"Yes, let's go see Josie." She gave Amy another small smile before bending to pick her up.

The pram was still on the porch from where they had used it to walk home the day before, so it was no time at all before she had Amy nestled into the small mound of blankets. She remembered to run back inside and leave a scrawled note on the kitchen table. James, Gilbert, and Elmer were out moving the cattle to another pasture this morning, and if they came back while she was gone, she did not want them to worry.

She whistled and sang to Amy as she pushed the stroller along the dirt road, pointing out various wildflowers and plants that they passed. Mattie tried her best to coax Amy into saying a few of the words with her, but so far, the words the toddler said were unintelligible.

When they made it to the first row of houses, she let out a sigh of relief. Mattie had begun to feel so cooped up at the ranch, like she was just sitting around and waiting for something to happen. At least by getting out of the house she was able to feel like she was actually doing something.

She made it to the stairs that lead to Josie and Jessup's apartment and untucked Amy from the pram. Placing the toddler on one hip, she climbed the stairs and knocked on the door. Mattie could hear Josie on the other side, bustling about and calling out merrily that she was on her way. When the door was pulled open, Mattie's face immediately broke into a wide grin at the sight of her friend.

"Mattie!" Josie cried excitedly, rushing forward, and throwing her arms around both Mattie and Amy. "I'm so glad you're here, come in come in."

"Actually, I came to invite you to tea," Mattie explained with a grin. "There's a beautiful tea shop just off of Main Street that I saw when I first came to town and haven't gotten a chance to try it yet. And I thought what better time to go then when we have something to celebrate."

Josie's brows knit together in confusion. "Well, I always love an excuse for tea. But what are we celebrating?"

Mattie felt color rise into her cheeks, as she smiled softly at her friend. "James and I are engaged."

The other woman's mouth popped open into an "O" of surprise, and she continued to gape at Mattie, who couldn't help but let out a quick giggle.

"Let me grab my boots," Josie said finally, her words coming out in an excited rush. "And then you absolutely must tell me everything."

She turned and hurried back into the house while Mattie stood on the staircase, bouncing Amy on her hip as she sang to her. Quicker than Mattie would have thought possible, Josie was pulling the door open once more and stepping onto the landing with her friend.

"Is it really true?" Josie gushed as they made their way down the stairs.

"It really, truly is." Mattie beamed at her friend and was glad to see the happiness blossom over Josie's lovely features.

"I am so glad." Josie looped her arm through Mattie's as they walked, with Amy still perched snuggly on her hip due to the short walk.

"When did he ask?"

"Yesterday," Mattie answered. "Right before we came to town."

"Is that what happened with Hubert Bird then? Did he find out and not take it well?"

Mattie winced. "You heard about that?"

"It's a small town, darlin'. Everyone heard about that." Josie shot her a sympathetic glance, but the conversation died out between the two of them as they approached the small tea shop.

The shop was made of wood that had been painted a lovely, dusty lilac. The color of the building had been what had originally drawn Mattie's attention, as it was one of her favorites. There were two, petite spindle tables with two chairs each on the small porch in front of the building, and vases of wildflowers on each one.

As the two women and the toddler pushed open the door, stepping into the shade inside, Mattie inhaled deeply. The aroma of various teas and cakes drifted through the air to her, making her head swim with delight. There was a woman with bright red hair and a tidy apron behind the counter, glancing down at something in her hands.

As they approached, the woman looked up with a smile on her face. She opened her mouth to begin speaking, but when her eyes slid from Josie to Mattie, the smile fell from her plump mouth and recognition glowed in the depths of her blue eyes.

"I'm so sorry," the woman said, the tone of her voice sounding anything but. "You are not welcome here. We cannot serve you."

The red-haired woman's eyes were on Mattie the entire time she spoke, and Mattie blanched. She had heard the woman's words, had understood them clearly. But she still could not get them to make sense. How could she not be welcome in a place that she had never been.

"I beg your pardon?" Mattie asked, her brow knitting together.

"You are not welcome here." The woman clarified, speaking each word slowly and deliberately.

"I don't understand how that's possible," Mattie argued, taking a step forward as her cheeks flushed with color.

"Ma'am, please leave." The woman's voice raised a bit, and her face became flushed as she stared Mattie down.

"Mattie," Josie said under her breath, turning toward her friend and a now fussy Amy. "It's alright, step outside and I'll find out what's going on. I'm sure this is all a big misunderstanding."

Mattie studied her friend's face for a moment, taking in her sincerity and honesty and drawing strength from it. She nodded at Josie before turning and heading back out into the sun, cooing to Amy to calm her down as she walked.

Once outside, Mattie began to pace along the front of the porch, entirely unable to think of sitting still. She glanced out toward some of the people walking past the tea shop along the road, and she could have sworn that a couple of them threw reproachful glances her way.

The door to the tea shop pushed open and Josie stepped out beside her. She wore a sad, concerned expression as she regarded Mattie, and Mattie's heart sank.

"What did she say?" Mattie asked, raising her chin with as much pride as she could muster.

"She said that you are in an inappropriate relationship with James. And that they would not allow someone of such character to be a patron of theirs." Josie's voice shook as she gave Mattie the details, as if she was terrified of what the words would do to her friend.

Mattie felt herself begin to shake. "How is it improper? We are engaged to be married and my brother is living with us to act as a chaperone!"

She began her pacing again, feeling the shame and the anger rise within her.

"Apparently Hubert has been telling people within the town that he had witnessed the two of you alone, kissing, while at the ranch. He had hinted that perhaps it had gone farther, to things that should only be reserved for the marriage bed."

Mattie stopped short, whirling on her friend with her mouth gaping. "Hubert did this?"

"It appears so." Josie nodded.

Suddenly, the errant glances from some of her fellow townsfolk right before Josie had come out of the tea shop began to make sense.

"I cannot believe this," Mattie protested, tears of anger pricking at the corner of her eyes. "Josie, you have to believe me, there is nothing improper or untoward occurring. I would never…"

Josie rushed forward, taking hold of Mattie's shoulder to force her to hold her gaze. "Mattie," Josie interrupted before Mattie could work herself into a tizzy. "You do not need to explain yourself to me. I know that you would never, and neither would James. He is too good of a man to risk your reputation in that manner. No, this is Hubert Bird being a petulant child."

A rush of gratitude washed through Mattie as she held her friends' stare. The tears still pricked at the edge of her vision, but she refused to let them fall while she was out in the open for everyone to see.

"I need to get home," Mattie said to Josie, who just nodded with understanding.

"Let's go get the little one's stroller, and you can hurry home. Don't let this get to you. It will all shake out, I promise."

Mattie nodded and the two women turned, heading back to Josie's house where they had left the pram tucked under the stairwell. Once Amy was settled inside, Mattie pulled her friend into a tight, fierce hug and thanked her for believing in her. Josie quickly waved off Mattie's words and shooed her away, telling her to get home so she could talk to James and Gilbert about what they should do next.

Mattie did just that, heading back toward the ranch and pushing the pram as quickly as she could over the uneven ground. She tried her best to amuse Amy on the way by pointing out more flowers and by pointing to interesting clouds that floated above them, but her efforts were only halfhearted. By the time she and Amy arrived back to the house, Mattie had sweat dripping down her brow and back.

She could hear Gilbert and James inside, both of them talking and laughing loudly, their voices coming from the direction of the kitchen. Mattie took a steadying breath before pulling open the screen door and striding into the house.

"Mattie?" James' voice called, alerted to her presence by the sound of her boots against the wooden floors.

"It's me," Mattie answered, wincing when she heard the panicked edge to her voice.

When she stepped into the kitchen, the smile that had been tugged across James' face just a moment before began to fall. His eyes roved over her, clearly taking in the worry etched across her face and reading that something must be terribly wrong.

Both James and Gilbert pushed their chairs back from the kitchen table and rose to their feet. Gilbert rushed forward with his arms extended for Amy, who gladly went to her uncle and began babbling at him gleefully. Amy's happiness was directly at odds with the cacophonous roaring taking place within Mattie.

In the presence of James, in the safety that she had begun to find with him, she felt the careful wall she had constructed to hold in her feelings about what had just occurred begin to crumble.

"James," Mattie said, feeling her bottom lip tremble as the tears that had been threatening to spill over since she left town finally fell down her cheeks.

"Mattie, what's wrong?" James' brow creased with worry as he stepped forward.

He extended his arms to her, and she gladly stepped into them. When they closed around her, she sighed with relief, sinking into his embrace as the tears began to fall more relentlessly.

"What happened?" James asked again, pressing a kiss to the top of her head.

"Mattie, what occurred? What is going on?" Gilbert's voice came from behind her, and it tugged at her heart to hear the worry it was laced with.

"It's Hubert," Mattie choked out as she launched into a recollection of exactly what had occurred when she'd gone to town to visit with Josie.

She told them about the employee at the tea shop, the pointed glances from the people of the town, all of it, as the shame and the guilt roiled inside of her. Logically, Mattie was aware that she had done nothing wrong. That the accusations of any kind of impropriety were unfounded and nothing more than the wailing of a rejected man. But it still didn't take away the sting.

James just held her while she spoke, whispering soothing words to her as he patted her shoulders and rubbed her back, letting Mattie get all of it out of her. When she finally finished, she felt much better. Not that the problem was over, because it most decidedly was not. But having the burden spread out amongst James and her brother made her feel a little less alone in what was happening.

When she pulled away from James, Mattie wiped a shaky hand across her cheeks, clearing away the marks the tears had left on them. She sought out James's gaze, giving herself a moment to bask in his stormy blue stare. James' jaw clenched and unclenched, but finally he inhaled a deep, steadying breath as he raised his hand to gently cup Mattie's cheek.

Never once looking away from Mattie, James spoke carefully, as if he was promising not just Mattie, but the universe and to God as well.

"I will make him pay for this."

Chapter Twenty-Seven

James worked as hard as he could to control his face while his fiancé recounted the events that had occurred in town. But all the while that she was speaking, he was raging inside. He now ran the pad of his thumb gently over her cheekbone, taking in the face he loved so dearly that was now so distraught, and wrath bubbled up within him.

"I will make him pay for this."

The words fell from his lips before he had a chance to consider them, but as he looked at the woman that he loved and at the hurt and pain that Hubert Bird had caused her, he meant every single word. And Mattie, for what it was worth, did not bulk or shy away from the promise, but instead she just nodded. Giving him silent permission to do whatever needed to be done.

Without giving himself time to think too much, James dropped his hand from Mattie's face and turned to glance at Gilbert.

"Do you need me?" Gilbert asked, stepping forward and ready for action, but James shook his head.

"Stay here with her and Amy."

Gilbert gave James a quick, terse nod. Satisfied, he turned and strode from the house. When he got into the barn, Elmer was there, making his rounds at the feed trough.

"Is everything alright?" The young man asked, brow furrowing with worry as he took in James' flushed face and angry posture.

"No." James said, not providing any additional explanation as he reached the stall that housed his favorite horse.

"I'll grab your saddle," Elmer offered, immediately understanding that James was not in the mood for further conversation.

Elmer disappeared for only a moment before returning with everything that was needed to place the saddle upon the large, brown beast. Working in tandem, the pair was able to get the horse fitted and James mounted seamlessly, and in no time at all he was riding the massive creature out the doors of the barn and into the dwindling afternoon.

He spurred the horse into action, galloping out onto the road in the direction of Hubert's ranch. And with the breakneck pace of the animal below him, it was not long at all before the house came into view.

"Hubert Bird," James bellowed as he pulled the horse up beside the porch of the large white house and came to a stop.

He threw his leg over the saddle and dismounted in a swift, smooth jump as the man in question stomped onto the porch. A smug smile spread across Hubert's face, and the rage that had been simmering within James on the ride over lit ablaze once again.

"Did you insult Mattie?" James roared, the sound of his boots echoed loudly through the open air as he approached Hubert, stopping when their chests were almost touching as he looked down his nose at the man.

"I didn't say anything that wasn't true," Hubert sneered up at him.

"Townsfolk are refusing to serve her or allow them in their establishment because of your lies, Hubert. Just because you were rejected you would ruin a good woman's reputation with lies and slander?"

"Now why would I be upset over a clearly loose woman with shaky morals?"

James' hands clenched into a fist at his side. He wanted nothing more than to punch Hubert again, but he refrained. Knowing that it would only incite the man more and make him feel further justified in the lies he had spread.

"You will not speak about my fiancé again," the words flew from his mouth, anger flaring through them. He took a step forward, and James felt a rush of satisfaction as fear danced behind Hubert's eyes and the man retreated a bit. "You will not tell people that you saw something that you did not see. You will not allow your hatred and bitterness toward me to taint the way this town feels about Mattie. Do I make myself clear?"

Hubert didn't answer James, just stared up at him while James watched as the man tried to rearrange his features to not betray his worry. Not waiting for long, James turned and strode back toward his horse. He felt only marginally better now that he had confronted Hubert, but he still needed to figure out how to repair what Hubert had tarnished with his mistruths.

Allowing the horse to canter, James' mind turned over what had occurred, looking at it from every perspective that he could as he tried to find a way to fix it. An idea struck him, one that he didn't necessarily like but that would get them out from under the current situation they had found themselves in.

He grimaced into the wind when the house came into view. He rode past it and into the stables, spotting Elmer still within it. His ranch hand eyed him wearily as he tried to read James' mood.

"Everything go alright?" Elmer asked, staring at him wearily.

"Perfectly fine," James bit out as he dismounted and passed the reins to Elmer. "Will you get him settled?"

Elmer nodded and James turned, striding toward the house. He was still terribly angry over what Hubert had done and the position that it had put Mattie in. But their wedding was already set for the end of the week, only a few days away. All they had to do was make it through a couple more nights, and then everything would be fine.

His footsteps announced his arrival as he strode across the porch and into the house. Mattie and Gilbert were still seated at the kitchen table, and both of them pushed back their chairs when he strode into the room. Mattie's bright green gaze roved over him with worry before relaxing with relief at finding him unharmed.

He did not pause as he walked forward and took her face into his hands.

"I love you," he breathed, his eyes taking in this face that had become so dear to him. "More than anything. You and Amy are my entire world, now. And I promised you that I would keep you safe."

Her brown knit together in worry. "Of course, James. But I'm not in any danger here. Not with you."

"Hubert is an angry and volatile man, he's shown this in the past and he is showing it again, now. I love you, but I will not have his bitterness over the past he shares with me to tarnish anything for you." James said in a rush, trying to get the words out before he could be interrupted. "I think that you should stay with Josie and Jessup until the wedding."

Mattie began shaking her head. "No."

"Mattie," James began to argue, but she leaned up and pressed her lips to his quickly, silencing him.

"No," she said again when they broke apart. "We haven't done anything wrong."

She held James' gaze as she spoke, her bright green eyes sparkling with emotion.

"We have done *nothing* wrong," Mattie repeated, emphasizing her words. "And I will not be punished for doing nothing wrong. Gilbert is here, he is chaperoning us. We know the truth, and we will be married very, very soon. And then the town will know the truth as well. And I am not going to give Hubert the satisfaction at knowing his words and his actions caused us to be separated, even just for a few nights."

James studied her, looking for any sign of wavering or doubt, but he found none. A rush of relief washed through him. He had not wanted to be separated from her, not even for a few nights. But it had been the only option he could think of.

With a sigh, he pressed his forehead to hers and they stayed like that for a moment, both just breathing in the presence of the others.

"Alright you two lovebirds," Gilbert said, humor lacing his voice. "I'm still chaperoning this, so break it apart. You only have to make it until the end of the week."

James and Mattie let go of each other while Gilbert grinned at them.

"Until the end of the week," James whispered to his fiancé, just loudly enough for her to hear him.

"Until the end of the week," she promised.

Chapter Twenty-Eight

The rest of the week dragged by, and Mattie was glad when she fell asleep each night that it brought her one day closer to her wedding with James. The few times that Mattie had gone into town, she had felt the eyes of some of the townsfolk on her, judging her, and she had wanted to cry. But instead of wilting, Mattie had raised her chin and walked through them on her way to visit Josie or whatever errand she was running, reminding herself that she had done nothing wrong.

Although a part of her couldn't help but feel hurt that some of them had believed the lies that Hubert had spread, more than a few of them had told her flat out that Hubert was jealous and they knew James Murphy better than that, which touched her. And she knew that she would be incredibly glad when all of this was over.

The morning of the wedding, Mattie opened her eyes to sunlight streaming in bright and cheery. She grinned at it, overwhelmed with joy and love that the day was finally upon her. There was a sound on the first floor, and it took her a moment through the haze of sleep that still covered her to realize it was someone knocking on the door.

She heard the door to James' room open and the sound of his boots along the floor as he went to see who was calling on them that early in the morning. She heard muffled talking drifting up to her, and a moment later the creak of the stairs and a knock on her bedroom door.

"Mattie!" Josie's voice called from the other end of the door. "It's your wedding day! Wake up wake up!"

"I'm awake," Mattie laughed, pushing herself out of the bed and pulling on her dressing gown.

She pulled the door open, finding the other woman standing on the other side wearing a wide, excited grin as she rushed through the threshold. She was holding a large, white box and Josie glanced down to it reverently before looking back at her friend.

"I brought something for you," Josie said, her cheeks flushing. "Please don't feel any pressure that you have to say yes, or you have to wear it. I just know that everything was planned so quickly, and I thought perhaps maybe you hadn't had time to get a gown."

She walked over and set the box down on Mattie's still unmade bed before pulling off the lid. It took Mattie a moment to realize that that the beautiful white, folded fabric inside was a gown.

Mattie's mouth popped open in surprise as she glanced between her friend and the box, stepping forward to brush a shaky hand over the delicate fabric.

"Josie," Mattie whispered reverently.

"It's my wedding dress. We're about the same size, so it should fit fine. But again, you don't have to…"

Her words cut off when Mattie threw her arms around her friend, wrapping her in a tight embrace.

"It's beautiful," Mattie said. "Thank you. I would be honored to wear it."

Josie returned her embrace, and then the two women broke apart wearing matching, wide grins.

"Now, it's time for us to start getting you ready for your wedding." Josie swiped delicately at her eyes, and Mattie realized that her friend had begun to cry for her.

An entirely new wave of gratitude crashed over her, and she wished that she could express just how much she appreciated the woman who was standing before her.

Mattie nodded, tears pricking at her own eyes as she and Josie quickly made Mattie's bed and then she walked over to the small desk with the looking glass at the far side of her room. She could hear James and Gilbert playing with Amy while making breakfast down in the kitchen, and she hoped that they were getting along alright without her.

Josie began braiding Mattie's hair skillfully, wrapping her copper tresses around Mattie's head like a crown. She then pinned in beautiful, small white flowers and tiny gemmed butterflies at carefully selected intervals.

She wasn't sure how long had passed, but eventually she heard a knock on the door and an announcement that James would be heading to the church, and he would meet her there. She wished that she could see him, could peer out the door to lay eyes upon the man that in a few short hours would be her husband, but they would not go against tradition.

A little while later, Josie spun her to view her face in the mirror. She had pinched her cheeks and bitten down on her lips to bring color and plumpness to them. As she gazed at herself in the looking glass, her eyes went wide.

"I look... lovely." She said reverently, reaching up a shaky hand to touch her porcelain skin.

"You absolutely do." Josie said, smiling at Mattie's reflection. "Now up, time to get you in your gown."

She waved Mattie over to the other end of the room and began helping her through the corset and the many layers of fabric.

"Hold your breath," Josie commanded as she put the final lace on Mattie's corset, pulling her figure in tight.

When the beautiful white gown went over her head, Mattie was happy to find that it fit her perfectly. The long, beautiful sleeves and the high collar were ruffed with a delicate lace, and while Josie worked on the pearl buttons that lined Mattie's back, she couldn't help but run her hands over the delicate gown.

When she was fully finished, she couldn't help but stare at herself in the mirror for a few moments. She had dreamed about this day for a very long time. When she had been a girl with her crush on James Murphy and she had imagined it would be him at the other end of the aisle someday. Mattie wished that she could talk to her younger self now, and chuckled lightly to herself when she thought of how giddy she would have been at that age.

"Are you ready?" Josie asked, stepping back to look at her friend in all of her bridal glory.

"I'm ready." She smiled, her heart beating wildly.

Gilbert was standing at the foot of the stairs, waiting for them to join him. He glanced up at the sound of his sister's bedroom door opening, and an affectionate smile tugged at the corners of his lips.

"Well don't you clean up nice?" He asked as Mattie and Josie descended the stairs.

She heard Amy in the other room, playing with Rose who had agreed to watch her for the wedding. Mattie thought briefly of going in to say goodbye to her, but she was pretty sure they were already running a little bit behind schedule.

He extended his arms to her, allowing Mattie to step into a warm affectionate embrace.

"You don't look too terrible either." Mattie joked, hugging him a little tighter before releasing.

He was in a green shirt with buttons down the front that complimented the bright shade of his eyes, pressed black trousers, and a pair of black suspenders. His copper hair had been slicked back away from his face, and his beard had also been combed. If he hadn't told Mattie about the woman he had fallen in love with back home, she would be pressing him to meet some of the ladies here in Mt. Juliet.

Gilbert stood in between Mattie and Josie, looping his arms through theirs as he led them out the door and to the carriage that waited for them. He stood at the foot, extending his hand to help both women up and into the wagon, before he himself climbed up, took his seat, grabbed hold of the reins, and just like that, they were off.

Mattie was fidgeting with the dainty, white lace gloves she had slipped over her hands, and the closer they got to the small church, the more nervous she became. She stared down at her lap, her heart racing more and more with every passing second.

Another gloved hand placed itself on top of hers, stilling her movements and Mattie glanced up to find Josie grinning at her.

"It's alright to be nervous," Josie whispered to her, the sound barely carrying over the clopping of the horse's hooves and the creaking of the wagon beneath them. "I was so nervous the day of my wedding that I thought I would lose my breakfast."

"I'm more excited than I am nervous," Mattie explained, color rising into her cheeks. "I only wish that my parents were here."

Gilbert cleared his throat next to her, keeping his hands on the reins as he glanced at his sister sidelong.

"I know they would want to be here with you also," Gilbert said, his voice thick with emotion. "They would be so proud of you, Mattie."

The church came into view, and Mattie worked to clear her throat from the thickness that had formed there, as happy tears threatened to spill from her eyes.

"Oh, look at me," she giggled, waving a gloved hand in front of her face. "Already a mess."

"A beautiful mess, though." Josie grinned at her, forcing a laugh from both Mattie and Gilbert.

The carriage rolled to a stop before the small parish church she and James had visited just the other day. And with her heart hammering so loud she thought for sure her brother and Josie would be able to hear it, she and her companions climbed down from the wagon. She stared at the closed front doors, knowing that just inside was the man who was set to be her husband.

The doors to the church were pulled open, revealing the minister she and James had met with earlier in the week. He smiled when he saw Mattie, Gilbert and Josie walking up the stairs.

"Right on time," the man said with a kind, swift nod.

Mattie stared at the church and the closed doors just beyond the foyer that would lead to the small nave. James was on the other side of it, and at the thought her palms began to sweat. Josie rushed forward into a small room before returning and producing a small bouquet for her.

"I asked James to store it here for you," she said with a soft blush.

Once again, Mattie was overcome by the woman's thoughtfulness. She and James had decided that they only wanted their wedding to be them and the people they considered family. And as Mattie had wracked her brain, the only other person she had thought of that she had wanted by her side during the service was Josie. And now, she could see just how right that decision had been.

"Thank you," Mattie said sincerely, meeting the woman's gaze and holding it. "For everything. You've been a Godsend this entire day."

Josie dipped her head, waving off Mattie's thanks. The minister advised Josie that it was time to go take her place up near the altar, where she would stand as a bridal matron for Mattie, and then they both disappeared through the door. Mattie draped her arm through her brother's, as she took deep steadying breaths to wait for the moment that it was time to open the door and lay eyes on her husband.

The sounds of a piano being played drifted through the door to them, and Mattie tried to calm herself as they crept closer to her cue. When the music swelled, Gilbert looked at her and gave her a wide, happy grin.

"Are you ready?" He asked, and when Mattie nodded, Gilbert's smile widened, and he reached forward to pull open the door.

The small church was empty, as she had expected it to be. But what she hadn't expected was a spattering of wildflowers in vases scattered around the space. Immediately suspecting Josie's handy work, her eyes widened, and she shot her friend a pointed look. Josie just snickered behind her hand.

Gilbert and Mattie began to walk forward, and when her eyes finally landed on James, she felt as if the entire world had come to a halt. His blue eyes held hers, a smile lighting his face so bright she thought that it could rival the sun. Suddenly, all her nerves fell away, and she could not get there fast enough.

"Slow down," Gilbert whispered with a laugh. "You're going to rip my arm off."

With that, Mattie realized that her steps had become hurried, and she had begun pulling Gilbert along with her in her haste to get to the end of the aisle and to her soon-to-be husband. Mattie felt her cheeks flushed and she slowed her steps, but still, she did not take her eyes off of James.

It felt like an eternity before they arrived at the end of the aisle and came to a stop before Josie, the minister and James. But when they did, the music from the piano faded into the background, and the minister smiled down upon them.

"It is my pleasure to receive you all today on this most joyous occasion." The minister's voice rang out loudly throughout the space.

Mattie glanced behind James, her eyes locking on her brother's for only a moment, and he gave her a heartwarming smile that caused tears to prick at the corner of her eyes. She turned her gaze back to James, who was looking down at her with so much love she felt as if her heart might swell and be too large to fit in her chest.

"It is a beautiful thing," the man continued, "when two people can find love such as James Murphy and Mattie Walsh have. It is an honor to God, and to country when you act upon the love that He has placed within your hearts, and you honor Him today."

He smiled down at them, but Mattie could not take her eyes away from James, nor could James take his eyes from her.

"It is time to recite the vows and exchange rings."

There was a brief flurry of activity while Josie darted forward and placed a simple, silver band in her hand that was intended for James, while Gilbert placed Mattie's ring in James' palm. The cold of the metal ring in Mattie's hand was comforting, like it was the one thing keeping her rooted to the ground when she felt so happy and filled with love that she might float away.

"Now, Mattie," the minister's voice carried through the chapel, bouncing off the pews and filling the space. "Do you take James as your husband in the holy sanctity of marriage? To have and to hold, to honor and obey, in sickness and in health, through triumph and strife, for as long as you both shall live?"

Emotion rose thick and heady, blocking Mattie's throat, forcing her to swallow past it. A smile lit up her face, so broad and so wide she feared that it might split her face. She held James' gaze, not daring to look away as his own eyes crinkled with the force of his own grin.

"I do." Mattie spoke as loudly and as clearly as she could, not wanting a single speck of dust to go without hearing her proclaim her vow to James Murphy.

"And James," the minister turned his pensive gaze to her soon-to-be husband. "Do you take Mattie as your wife in the holy sanctity of marriage? To have and to hold, to honor and protect, in sickness and in health, through triumph and strife, for as long as you both shall live?"

James paused for a moment, pretending to be rethinking his vows and causing all of them to laugh before saying clearly and as loudly as Mattie had, "I do."

The words reverberated through her, filling her with such a ferocious joy she thought that she might combust with it.

"Then by the power vested in me by God Almighty, I now pronounce you man and wife." The minister paused, giving them both a sly, knowing grin before saying the final words that Mattie had been waiting for, the one's that she had longed to hear from the moment they stepped foot in the church. "You may now kiss your bride."

Gilbert and Josie erupted in applause, with Gilbert going as far as to yell out his joy for his best friend and his sister. But Mattie hardly heard a thing. As James reached up to cup her face, tears shining in his bright blue eyes, Mattie almost wilted when his lips touched hers.

My husband, she thought the moment their lips pressed together. She could hardly believe it, wanting to pinch herself just to feel the prick of pain and reassure herself that it was all real and not some fanciful dream.

By the time they broke apart, Mattie was flushed, breathing hard and she had to work to regain her composure. James glanced behind her, seeming to search for something. And when Mattie followed the line of his gaze, she noticed Josie giving her husband a quick nod.

"What is going on?" She asked, glancing between the two.

"Well, I know we wanted the ceremony to be a small affair, but we never said anything about the rest of our day." James smiled at Mattie sheepishly. "There will be people waiting for us at the ranch."

"People?" Her eyebrows shot up in surprise and James nodded his confirmation. "How many people?"

"I guess we'll have to go see." He shrugged one shoulder, and Mattie scoffed at him.

They thanked the minister while Gilbert readied the wagon once more, and then the four of them piled into it to begin their trek back to their house. The entire journey back, Mattie felt as if she was viewing everything through a haze of happiness.

When the large, brick house that had become her home came into view, Mattie's mouth popped open in surprise. There were people milling about the lawn, a large number of them. And as they got closer, she began to make out many familiar faces.

"That must be..." Mattie began, her voice filled with awe.

"Nearly the entire town," James finished for her, grinning as they pulled the carriage alongside the house and climbed out. "Everyone but Hubert was invited."

"And it looks like most of them showed," Josie said with a wink.

James, Mattie, and Josie climbed down from the carriage. The moment their feet were on solid ground, Mattie linked hands with James, wanting nothing more than to touch her husband to assure herself that he was here; to know that this was all real. Just then, the woman from the tea shop walked by, carrying a large platter as she made her way to the house.

The moment she caught sight of Mattie, she came to an abrupt stop. Mattie's heart began to beat wildly, and she felt the color rising to her cheeks as a sheepish look flashed across the other woman's face. Mattie did not have expect to see her here, not after everything that had occurred in town.

"I'm sorry," the woman said in a hushed tone, the apples of her own cheeks blushing pink. She could hardly meet Mattie's eyes, opting instead to bounce between glancing at her own feet, up to Mattie, and then back down again. "I should have known that he was lying. I've known the man almost my whole life, never known him to take those kinds of things with any kind of grace. I should have known..."

Mattie dropped James's hand and stepped forward, causing the woman's words to cut off mid-sentence and for her to finally meet and hold Mattie's gaze.

"I accept your apology," Mattie said clearly, making sure that the woman understood that as far as Mattie was concerned, they were square. "As you said, you've known him for a very long time. It's understandable that you would believe him over someone that you barely know."

The woman held Mattie's gaze for a moment more before giving her a quick, solemn nod.

"I brought you cakes." She dipped her head to the platter in her hands that was decorated in small, delicate desserts topped with strawberries. Mattie's mouth began watering at the sight, and she took them for what they were—a final, sincere apology in the best way the woman knew how to provide it.

"They look lovely," Mattie said with a smile.

"I'll just put them inside with all the rest."

There was an awkward pause before the woman turned back toward the house and shuffled off. A chuckle sounded from behind her, and Mattie turned to find James grinning at her with amusement.

"I knew they'd let all this ugliness drop," James mused with a slight shake of his head. "But I didn't think anyone would get themselves in a tizzy quite like that."

He walked forward, draping his arm around Mattie's shoulder. At the casual touch, it once again washed over her that he was her husband now, and she did not have to hide her affection for him in public. Mattie nuzzled into his side, allowing the warmth that radiated off his body to envelop her in a moment of peace, as what felt like the entire town rushed in and out of their house.

The sound of a horse neighing behind them caught her attention, and Mattie turned in enough time to see a few more people arriving. Elmer rushed out onto the porch and began directing people where to go. Many of them carried trays and plates of food, offerings for the newly married couple.

For what felt like the thousandth time that day, gratitude rose inside of Mattie. The wave of it was so large and so fresh that she felt she might break down in tears of happiness right there on the lawn.

Just then, Mr. Tavers from the feed supply store walked by, catching sight of the new couple.

"Hello to The Murphy's," he said with a smile and a dip of his hat. "A pleasure to see you both here."

The old man winked before walking into the house, causing Mattie to laugh. James laced his fingers through hers, and he kept her steady as they walked into the home. It felt like every few steps, someone stopped them.

"Congratulations," an old man that she'd only ever seen on the porch of the saloon said as they walked by, raising a clear glass with amber liquid that Mattie could only guess was whiskey. "A fine young couple, fine young couple."

"I knew that Hubert Bird was jealous from the moment the rumors crept about," slurred the old man's friend from beside him, his own glass sloshing dangerously.

Mattie and James thanked them both as they continued to make their way into the house, though she couldn't help but wonder exactly how early they all arrived and began drinking.

"They probably came directly from the saloon," James whispered as if reading her mind.

When he spoke, he leaned over and pressed his mouth close to Mattie's ear, causing her to break out in goosebumps as a shiver raked down her spine.

"Now let's get some food in you," he murmured before leading her toward the table of platters and offerings that had been compiled by the townsfolk.

As if on cue, her stomach gave a loud rumble that could be heard over the din of the crowd and James laughed. Mattie hadn't had the chance to eat before leaving for the ceremony, and she had been so nervous that she didn't think she would have been able to regardless. Now, however, with the amazing spread before her and with herself properly married to the man that she loved, Mattie found herself famished.

After Mattie had eaten her first plate of food, someone sat down at the piano. With the windows open, the music drifted out to them on the front lawn, and James pulled Mattie into her arms as they began to dance.

"This is exactly how I wanted to dance with you that night in the town hall," James whispered in her ear before bending to kiss her sweetly for the first time for everyone to see.

When their dance had ended and they were once again spending time with their guests, she heard Gilbert's name being called by a lilting, beautiful voice.

Mattie spins on her heel to look through the crowd, almost immediately spotting a beautiful woman with long, bright red hair. She watched as her brother turned to face the woman, and his entire face transforms into one of pure joy and adoration.

As her brother's face broke into a cheek splitting grin and he rushed forward, Mattie had no doubt who the woman that had just arrived was. The moment Gilbert reached her, his arms wrapped around her, picking her up and spinning her around.

"And who on earth is that?" James asked, his head bending to Mattie's ear.

She shivered as her husband's breath stirred against her skin before turning toward him with a grin.

"Gilbert told me last week he was courting someone. It appears that she made it just in time for the wedding."

James' face lit up. "He didn't tell me!"

"That's the privilege of being his sister. I get to know everything first." Mattie joked, hitting his hip with hers.

"Apparently being a lifelong best friend counts for nothing," James huffed, crossing his arms in mock outrage.

The pair stopped their joking as Gilbert and the mystery woman approached, hands laced together.

"Mattie, James," Gilbert said with a grin still plastered on his face as he approached them. "I would love for you to meet Rebecca Lawrence. My fiancé."

Mattie gasped at the word, glancing from her brother to the beaming woman.

"Fiancé!" She exclaimed, darting forward to wrap the woman in a hug. "You didn't tell me you had proposed. Oh, Rebecca, it's a pleasure to meet you."

Rebecca laughed as she returned the embrace warmly, tossing her long, red braid over her shoulder.

"Gilbert said he wanted to wait until I met you to announce it," she explained.

Up close, Mattie was able to take in the fine features of Rebecca's face. Her red hair was striking, and she had a spattering of freckles across her straight, regal nose. She had a proud air about her, one that instantly led Mattie to believe she would not let her brother get away with much. And she liked the woman immediately.

"Well, it's a pleasure to meet you," Mattie grinned, dipping her head toward Rebecca. "And we will be delighted to have you added to our family."

Mattie felt a tug on her shoulder and turned to find Elmer behind her, grinning widely. "It's time for cake."

Her heart leapt as she, James, Gilbert, and Rebecca all followed after Elmer toward where a large, beautifully decorated cake was waiting for them. Everyone gathered around to watch the new couple cut into it, and as Mattie stared out into the crowd, eyes roving over all the people she had come to know and love since moving to this town, Mattie finally felt like she had truly made a home.

Chapter Twenty-Nine

"Someone was looking for her Papa," Josie's voice carried over the crowd, grabbing James' attention as he turned to spot his previous governess walking through the guests with Amy propped on her hip.

Rose had been watching her for most of the day, but that hadn't stopped people from stopping in to play with her, and from James himself going in to make sure that she was eating and being taken care of. But Amy had been so enamored by the revelry taking place around her that she hadn't paid much attention to him any time he'd been in her presence.

Now, however, she was reaching for him, an excited look on her face.

"Pop pop pop," she was repeating, her eyes lit with joy when they landed on him.

"Hello there sweet thing," he said, darting forward to take her from Josie and thanking her.

Josie just waved off his words before darting back out into the cleared space they had been using as a makeshift dance floor. Gilbert was dancing closely with his fiancé, Rebecca. James couldn't help but shake his head as he watched his childhood friend look at the woman he twirled around the grass. In all is years of friendship with Gilbert, he had never seen him look at anyone the way he was gazing at Rebecca in that moment. And as his own happiness washed over him, James spared some for his friend and for the life he knew Gilbert was going to create as well.

"My boy," a voice said from behind him, and he turned to find Mr. Tavers standing only a few feet away. "Mighty fine wedding you've had. And a mighty fine wife."

James followed Mr. Tavers gaze to the dance floor, where Mattie was twirling around in circles with an excited Josie.

"That I do," he said with a smile, shifting Amy on his hip.

"I'm glad for you," Mr. Tavers said, his voice soft. "I've worried about you since Ruth. We all have."

The old man gestured to the townsfolk around him, and as James thought about the fact that they had all shown up, despite the horrible lies that Hubert had spread about him and about Mattie, his heart swelled with appreciation.

"We're glad that we finally get another opportunity to celebrate something good with you," Mr. Tavers said, and the honesty in his voice made James' throat thick with emotion.

"Thank you," James said, inclining his head to the man in gratitude, but it was quickly waved away.

"Just thought you should know." He pointed toward Mattie. "Now you should go dance with that woman of yours. Otherwise, I might."

The old man winked at him, forcing a laugh to bubble up past James' lips. But, as Mr. Tavers turned and walked away, James turned his attention back to his wife, and he found that he couldn't think of anything he wanted more than to dance with the woman that he loved and his daughter.

"What do you think, little one?" He asked, glancing down at Amy who gave him a wide smile. "Want to go dance with Mattie?"

She nodded eagerly and he was all too happy to oblige. He began making his way to the crowd, and Mattie caught sight of him and Amy as they approached. She broke away from Josie, turning to face them with a wild, infectious smile on her face.

He'd been around her all day, and yet he still couldn't get over how radiant she looked.

"Can we have this dance?" James asked with a bow, Amy's hair tumbling into her face as she erupted with giggles when she flipped with the bend of James' body.

"I would love to dance with you, James and Amy Murphy," Mattie called, smiling as she darted forward.

James kept Amy propped on his hip as he placed the other hand around Mattie's waist, pulling her in close so that she pressed against Amy. The toddler clapped and yelled with joy as all three of them began to move to the music.

Mattie threw her head back and laughed, followed shortly by Amy doing the exact same thing. And James couldn't think of any melody that he wanted to hear more than the sound of their joy.

He wasn't sure how long they kept dancing, but he knew that they had been out there for several songs before they finally were breathing too hard for them to continue in their revelry. Eventually, the crowd begin to clear. People began to come up to them and give them their congratulations as well as their goodbyes, and as more and more people left, James and Mattie began to start cleaning up.

A very tired Amy tried to help, but when Mattie turned around and found her asleep leaning up against her toy box, Mattie had laughed and told her that she would take her up and put her down for a nap. James stepped out onto the porch, noticing a handful of people still milling about, staggering drunkenly from too much whiskey.

Spotting Gilbert and Rebecca sitting on the front porch swing, James walked over to them.

"How would you feel about giving them a ride home in one of the buggies?" James asked, inclining his head to the people still left.

Gilbert nodded and looked at Rebecca. "Care to go with me?"

She grinned at him and nodded eagerly before the two stood and walked out, hand in hand, to begin readying one of the carriages. Knowing that the last of the partygoers were in good hands, James turned and strode back inside to finish cleaning up.

As he washed the dishes, he heard the whinnying of the horse as the carriage with the last of their guests rode by the house, and James couldn't help his sigh of relief. From the moment he had woken up that morning he had wanting nothing more than to call Mattie his wife. Now that he could, now that he could kiss her when he wanted, and hold her hand, and do all of the things he had longed to do since the moment she had stepped off that train, all James could think about was being able to enjoy time with his wife, in their house, alone.

The sound of a floorboard creaking loudly echoed behind him. Thinking that it must have been Mattie returning from putting Amy down to sleep, the corners of his mouth tugged up into a smile.

"I was just thinking about you," James said, placing the dish he was scrubbing back in the basin of water and reaching for a towel to dry his hands.

"Well, isn't that sweet."

At the sound of the voice James' blood ran cold. Because it wasn't Mattie. It wasn't even a woman.

Slowly, ever so slowly, James turned, the rest of the kitchen coming into view bit by bit before his gaze finally landed on the person standing on the other side of his kitchen.

Hubert Bird was standing with his feet spread evenly apart, his shoulders squared directly toward James, and his face wore a smug, triumphant smile. Horror rushed through James when the entire sight registered in his mind. Because the reason that Hubert was smiling, was because that he held a gun in his hands. A gun that was pointed directly at James.

Chapter Thirty

Mattie sang softly to Amy, running her fingertips absentmindedly over the little girl's arm. She had long since fallen asleep, but Mattie was craving just a little bit longer of the privacy and solitude this room provided. And Amy was sleeping so peacefully, Mattie couldn't help but be envious of the small form curled up tightly in the bed.

As she sang, her mind wandered over the events of the day. Recalling the wedding, the people, and getting to meet her brother's fiancé. She could not have imagined it going any better than it had.

Finally, when Mattie didn't think she could stall any longer, she pushed herself up off the bed. Hoping that by the time she got downstairs, everyone but her family would be gone, she pushed open the door.

She paused in the hallway for the briefest of moments, giving herself the opportunity to listen to the sounds of the grounds around her. When no noise rose up to greet her, she sighed with relief.

She walked down the stairs, careful to tread lightly so that the wood underneath her wouldn't creak and wake up Amy. When she reached the bottom floor, she looked around, wondering where James had gone off to.

"James," she called softly as she walked from room to room.

But, by the time she had made it through each and every room, including the upstairs, and still had not caught a single glimpse of her husband, or anyone for that matter, a tinge of worry began to rock through her.

The sound of horse's hooves rang out from in front of the house, and she strode quickly to the window. She spotted Gilbert and Rebecca, her tell-tale red hair glinting brightly in the quickly fading twilight, and she rushed out onto the porch to stop them before they could get too far.

Gilbert quickly spotted Mattie waving her arms like mad and tugged on the reigns, bringing the horse to a halt as she crossed the front yard.

"Have you seen James?" She asked, but Gilbert just cocked his head in confusion.

"No," he said, glancing to Rebecca and then back to Mattie.

"He had us take the last of the people home, the ones that were too drunk to walk." Rebecca explained, her own beautiful features beginning to crease.

"I can't find him anywhere," Mattie said. "I went upstairs to put Amy to sleep, but now he's nowhere to be found."

"We'll look for him." Gilbert's words were quick and sure as he snapped the reigns once more, guiding both horse and buggy to the side of the house. He tied off the horses' reigns, giving a quick promise that they'd come back for him before all three of them turned and strode back into the house.

"Be careful," Mattie hissed. "Amy is asleep."

Rebecca and Gilbert both nodded before they began to walk between all of the rooms, softly whispering James's name. Mattie knew that it was likely futile. She herself had already been in and out of every room in the house during her own search and knew that James wasn't in any one of them. But she also didn't know what else to do.

She knew that he wouldn't have left without telling her, or at the very least leaving a note. The only person on this earth that he cared enough about to leave without a word if something was wrong with them was Amy, and Mattie knew that the child was upstairs sleeping soundly.

A sound echoed through the air outside, quick, and loud as a whip. And at first, Mattie's brain couldn't make sense of what it was. But, when Gilbert and Rebecca came rushing back onto the porch, faces ashen when they spotted Mattie, her stomach plummeted with panic.

"What was that?" Mattie asked, glancing toward the stable, which was the direction the sound had come from.

"Mattie, that was a gun shot."

The words rock through her, sending her heart hammering in her chest. Without thinking Mattie took off running, her legs moving as fast as she could make them. She heard Gilbert call for Rebecca to stay back with Amy, and then she heard the sound of his feet hitting the grass behind her.

Mattie pumped her arms hard, and her lungs began to burn with the effort. She cursed the wedding dress she still wore, the heavy fabric impeding how quickly she was able to move. Gilbert pulled ahead of her a bit, and she used that as fuel to push her legs faster. Everything in her body was screaming. And as the front of the stable came into view, Mattie's lips began to move, sending up a prayer to God that whatever was going on inside of those walls, that she would not be too late.

Chapter Thirty

James fell to the ground with a hiss of pain, his hand coming up to cup his opposite arm where the bullet had grazed. He sent up a silent prayer of thanks that Hubert was such a terrible shot, but he knew that that relief would be short lived.

"Damn it," he heard Hubert curse angrily, the man's feet scuffling over the dirt floor of the stable.

James felt the rush of warm liquid as blood trickled between his fingers, and he closed his eyes, waiting for the other bullet to come. He could hear Hubert gearing up for it, hear the sound of him huffing and puffing as he tried to talk himself into just doing it. But what he didn't expect was to hear the sound of two pairs of feet running into the stable and a startled, feminine gasp.

James' eyes flew open, and he propped himself up on his elbow, eyes immediately landing on Mattie and Gilbert standing in the doorway of the barn. Mattie's face drained of all color as she took in the scene before her, and Gilbert immediately swept out an arm, pushing his sister back to stand behind him.

A wave of gratitude washed through James as Gilbert met his eyes. His best friend's face was a mask of horror, but James was still glad to know that after all of this, at least Mattie would still have her brother.

"Well, isn't this just lovely," Hubert snarled, his voice dripping with wrath. "Come to save your husband, did you?"

Hubert spat the word husband like it was something dirty, and James watched as the man's face contorted even further with rage.

Gilbert took a step forward, beginning to raise his hand but Hubert immediately whirled on him.

"Do. Not. Move." The man yelled as he waved the gun around hysterically.

"Alright," Gilbert said, his voice tight with fear.

James watched as Gilbert raised his hands in front of him, deliberately showing Hubert that they were empty and that he and Mattie were no threat to him.

"I told you that you would regret this," Hubert spat as he began to pace.

James followed the man with his eyes, looking for any moment that he or Gilbert could possibly seize to rush the man and possibly get the gun. But Hubert was doing too good of a job maintaining his distance and glancing between James and Gilbert quickly, so that any move that they made would be detected before they could even get close.

"I told you multiple times, even back when Ruth was still alive that you would come to regret the day that you snubbed me. All those times that everyone in school would fawn over you. 'James Murphy' this, and 'James Murphy' that. Everything was always about *you*."

Hubert whirled back toward James, pointing the pistol at him for emphasis and James' heartbeat ticked up notch.

"Well, no more!" Hubert's tone took on a hysterical voice as a small laugh bubbled up past his lips. "No more! It's my turn. I'm not gonna live in your shadow anymore. Your ranch flourishes without you even trying. All you have to do is wink and you get the woman, no, the *women* that I loved first. They all come crawling to you James, malleable putty in your stupid, ungrateful hands. But I know the truth."

Hubert turned his gaze fully on James now, taking a few more steps closer to him. James' eyes locked on Mattie, and he felt his heart break. Her green eyes were wide with fear, and he couldn't help but regret that he had brought her into this.

He did not regret loving her, did not regret that he had married her. But the fact that Mattie was about to go through what he did after losing Ruth, that she would have to grieve him, and it would be his love that would cause her to endure that pain? His heart shattered for her and for what was left for both her and Amy at the end of all of this. He could only hope that God would allow him to continue to watch over them from heaven.

"It is my turn," Hubert whispered loudly. "And the only way it can really be my turn is if you, James Murphy, are dead."

His voice was dripping with malice as he pointed the gun at James' head. James closed his eyes once more, not wanting to see anything else that happened, wanting the last thing he ever saw in this lifetime to be Mattie's face.

As James took a deep, steadying breath he began to pray. And then the sound of a gunshot echoed off the walls of the stable.

Chapter Thirty-Two

A scream tore itself from Mattie's lips, so high pitched and visceral that for a moment she felt as if it would tear her throat wide open. The moment that Hubert's finger pressed the trigger, the sound of the gun firing making her ears ring, James rolled. The bullet missed him by a fraction of an inch, burying itself in the ground with a puff of dirt.

Relief rolled through her, fleeting as it was, when she realized that somehow, through all of this her husband was still alive.

Hubert roared with anger; his attention fully focused on James. And she saw the tension ripple through her brother a moment before he threw himself toward the man with the gun. Mattie bit back a yell of surprise, not wanting to alert Hubert to the fact that her brother was now hurtling through the air toward him, and when their bodies collided Hubert was caught off guard enough that they both went tumbling to the ground.

Mattie's heart raced as she watched her brother and Hubert rolling in the dirt, limbs flying so quickly that it was hard to make sense of it all and to track who was hitting who. The gun was suddenly dislodged from Hubert's hands, and it went skittering across the dirt.

Right when Mattie realized what had happened, Hubert freed himself from her brother's grasp and bolted to his feet. He raised his booted foot over Gilbert's head and brought it down hard and swift. A sickening crunch sounded throughout the space, and Mattie couldn't help the sob that wracked through her as her brother's body fell limp.

Hubert stood over Gilbert's prone form, chest heaving, and Mattie felt tears leaving wet tracks down her cheeks. An idea struck her, and her eyes dipped to the gun at the same moment that Hubert's did. She rushed forward, reaching for it, and hope flared brightly in her chest as she got close, oh so close to wrapping her fingers around the cold steel. But then a hand darted out in front of her quicker than she could react, snatching the pistol up so that when her hand closed, there was only dirt and air left for it to wrap around.

"You didn't think you'd get off that easily, did you?" Hubert sneered at Mattie, pointing the gun at her as he retreated a few steps.

Movement flashed in the corner of her eye, and Mattie turned her head to find James trying to climb to his feet.

"Absolutely not," Hubert said, turning the gun from Mattie to James, who immediately stopped in his tracks.

"Is this what it takes, hmm?" Hubert asked, pointing the gun once again at Mattie while he kept his hateful gaze on James. "Do I need to shoot her first? Will that be what it takes to finally get the payback that I deserve?"

His mean eyes flash as they turn back to Mattie, before darting back to James. Over and over again he looked at the two of them, never once moving the gun from where it was pointed at Mattie's chest.

"It would be fitting, would it not? For you to have two wives die on you before you finally meet your maker. I think I quite like that."

A crazed laugh tore itself from Hubert's lips as he took a step toward Mattie. Her hands flew up, showing her open, empty palm in surrender. Her own gaze flicked to James', and she could see the fear and the pain written so clearly there.

"I'm sorry," she mouthed to him. "I love you."

She watched as James faced crumpled before she turned her attention back to Hubert.

"What do you think happens after this?" She tried her best to keep her voice calm. "Do you think you kill me, James and my brother and no one will think that it was you?"

Mattie raised her eyebrows at Hubert, watching as the man's chest rose and fell with rapid panting.

"I am sorry that you are hurting, Hubert. Truly I am. No one deserves to feel the things that you felt. And if you lower this gun and allow us to walk out of here, I will even help you find a beautiful, amazing wife who will love you and cherish you. That's what you want, isn't it?"

Mattie cocked her head at Hubert, hoping that the offer would entice him. But her blood ran cold when all he did was laugh and shake his head.

"You know," Hubert said, a sick and twisted amusement lacing his words. "Maybe it really is best if you die first. It's what you deserve for being such a little tease."

Hubert yelled the last word, brandishing the gun wildly in Mattie's direction causing her to let out a yelp of fear. He chuckled, low and dark in his throat.

"You two deserve each other."

Mattie watched with horror as Hubert's finger tightened on the trigger, constricting more and more. She turned her gaze back to James, wanting more than anything for him to be the last face she saw. She was sorry that her time would be cut short with him. Sorry that Amy would have to lose someone else that she had grown to love. But still she could not bring herself to regret the decisions that brought her here, to this man and to this life. Because for the first time she had found what it had meant to be really and truly loved, no matter how short lived it may be.

The sound of a gunshot echoed through the space once more, cracking through the air around her. She expected to feel a flash of pain, closed her eyes tight as she prepared for it. She heard a scream as it tore itself out of James' throat, ragged, raw, and full of terror. And her breaths became quick and rapid as she waited for the bullet to find her. But it did not.

Chapter Thirty-Three

James' scream cut off short, his throat already raw from the force of it as he watched Hubert's form crumple to the ground. He blinked in confusion as the man seemed to fall in slow motion, clutching at his right side as a red liquid began to seep through his fingers.

James' brain tried to make sense of what he was seeing, tried to figure out how this was happening, when finally, his eyes landed on a form standing at the door of the stable with a rifle raised to his shoulder.

Whoever it was lowered the gun, and James let out a sigh of relief when he caught a flash of auburn hair. An ashen faced Elmer took a few more steps into the stable, glancing at Mattie, then to James where he still laid on the ground, to Gilbert's still slumped and unconscious body.

"I heard gunshots," Elmer stammered as he crossed the space in a few quick steps.

His movement snapped Mattie into action, and she rushed forward, arriving at James' side a moment later.

"Are you alright?" She began to fuss, moving his arm so that she could see the graze wound the bullet had left in his bicep.

A groan sounded from Gilbert, and they turned their attention to see the man rolling onto his back and blinking up at the ceiling.

"What the hell?" Gilbert groaned as he rolled over to his side, forcing a disbelieving laugh from James' lips.

He turned to look back at Mattie, at her beautiful face still so contorted by fear.

"Let me fix this," she said, reaching down to the hem of her wedding gown. The bottom of it had frayed just enough that she was able to pull at the fabric, causing it to split.

She reached forward to grab his arm, trying to wrap the fabric to bind his still bleeding arm, but James waved his hand at her.

"Go to Hubert," he said, nodding his head in the direction of the man that had just threatened all of their lives.

Mattie blinked at James in surprise, taking a moment to process the request before she just gave him a brief, quick kiss and then strode across the room to where Hubert lay. The dirt below him was growing dark with the spreading pool of blood, and the man panted in pain as he looked up at the ceiling.

James saw Mattie crouch down beside him, but he couldn't quite hear what she was whispering to him as she reached down and moved him around so she could begin binding his wounds. She didn't do it gently, and the scream that wrenched itself from Hubert's lips gave James more satisfaction than he would ever admit out loud.

"I heard gunshots and came to see what was goin' on," Elmer echoed again, and James turned to glance at him.

The young man was clearly in shock, staring down at the rifle in his hands with panic filled eyes and a pallid reflection.

"Come help me out, would ya," James grunted as he tried to push himself up to standing with his good arm.

Figuring that Elmer needed a job to focus his mind on, he immediately had the lad helping him out of his shirt so he could use it to bind his arm. By the time he got it secured, Gilbert had struggled to his feet and made his way over to finish helping Mattie bind Hubert's wounds.

James turned back to Elmer and put his hand on the rifle.

"Go get the sheriff," he said, wrapping his hand around the barrel and taking the gun from the boys shaking hands. "I'll watch over everything here. But be quick."

"A horse and a carriage are still tied at the side of the house," Gilbert called over his shoulder and Elmer nodded.

Some of the panic in the boys' eyes seemed to lift as he turned and ran toward the house, the sound of his footsteps fading into the now dark night. James turned his attention to Hubert, loathing unfurling in him as he glared down at the man who had threatened his family.

"Do not move," James said, levelling the rifle at Hubert.

The man's eyes were wide with fear and pain, swiveling wildly from person to person. Gilbert, sensing that James could use a little assistance, pushed himself to standing and walked over to where the pistol lay on the ground. He turned, and pointed it at Hubert, who's eyes widened even further.

"If you move so much as an inch," Gilbert warned. "We will shoot you. And trust me, I'll be more than glad to be given a reason to."

A wild, feral grin tugged up the corner of Gilbert's lips and James had no question that if it wasn't for Mattie, his best friend would have shot the man already.

James heard a sniffle from Mattie's direction, and he turned his attention toward her. He saw her swipe a shaking hand under her eyes, brushing away at the tears that had begun to fall. His heart gave a squeeze as he shuffled over toward her, never once taking the barrel of the gun off Hubert.

When he reached Mattie, he tucked her under his arm and pulled her into his body. She wrapped her arms around him, burying her face into his bloodied under shirt and he could feel her entire body trembling.

"It's alright," James murmured, trying to make his voice as reassuring as he could. "We're alright."

He whispered the words over, and over, again, saying them like a prayer. Eventually Mattie began to calm down, and her shaking began to subside, but her tears did not stop. And they stood in silence, with nothing but Hubert's terrified panting to fill the space, while they waited for the sheriff.

Epilogue

The sound of horse's hooves outside of the stable helped rouse Mattie from her trance. She extracted herself from underneath James' arm and peered around with worry, letting out a sigh of relief when she spotted Elmer with the wagon carrying the doctor, and the sheriff on his own horse, come riding into the light.

The sheriff's eyebrows shot up in surprise at the sight before him before both he and the doctor snapped into action. The space became a flurry of activity after that, with the doctor barking out orders to everyone around him as he worked to get Hubert stable enough to transport to his house.

Finally, when Hubert was bandaged properly and the bleeding staunched, he pushed himself upright with the help of the doctor and the sheriff.

"I'll need him to be taken to my house," the doctor said, turning to look at Elmer. "Think you can take him in the carriage and get him loaded inside."

The ranch hand nodded, and Gilbert stepped forward, offering to help.

"Tell Rebecca I'll be back as soon as he's at the doc's house." Gilbert said, climbing into the wagon.

"We'll need to get your wound looked at, too." The doctor said, shooting James a pointed glance.

James nodded, and Mattie's heart fluttered with relief that her husband was going to get treated. They all began the short walk back to the house, Mattie unable to untangle her fingers from where they were intwined with James'. She was terrified that if she let go of him, if she loosened her grip at all, that he would somehow be taken from her, exactly as Hubert had intended.

When they all stepped onto the porch, the door was immediately pulled open by a frantic looking Rebecca. Her bright eyes roved over each of them, taking in the dirt covered Mattie, in a now-torn and slightly bloodied wedding dress, the addition of the doctor, the sheriff, the ranch hand, and a now bleeding James.

"Gilbert is transporting someone to the doctor's house," Mattie said quickly before Rebecca could begin to panic. "He should be back shortly. There was a fight and he's a little banged up, but he is going to be alright."

Rebecca let out a sigh of relief and gave Mattie a grateful nod before stepping back and allowing everyone to walk past her. They led the doctor to the kitchen, where they lit as many lanterns as they could find so the man could begin cleaning James' arm and stitching the torn flesh back together.

Mattie was forced to let go of her husband's hand so that the doctor could work, but she didn't stray far, always making sure that she stayed within his line of sight.

The sheriff came up to her and asked for her statement first, and Mattie got the distinct impression that he was trying to distract her while her husband hissed with pain. She told him everything she could recall, doing her best to make sure that not a single detail was left out.

When her statement was done and James' stitches finished, the doctor said goodbye to them and left to go tend to Hubert. The sheriff, however, turned to James and asked him for his version of events.

Mattie wandered to the doorway of the kitchen, spotting Rebecca perched in a reading chair by the large window at the front of the house, keeping vigil as she waited for Gilbert to return. Mattie paused for a moment, listening for any sign of stirring coming from Amy's room, but all was quiet. By an act of God, the toddler had slept peacefully through all of the commotion.

Right as the sheriff took the last of James statement, the man thanked them both and assured them that once he was all sewn up, Hubert Bird wouldn't be going anywhere but to a jail cell. The man turned to leave just as Rebecca shot to her feet.

Mattie knew what the woman had seen and was not surprised when she threw open the door and launched herself at Gilbert as he climbed the stairs. Mattie smiled at her brother as she caught his eye over the top of Rebecca's shoulder, and she became overcome with relief that somehow all three of them made it out of this relatively unscathed.

As the sheriff told Gilbert to come in and give his statement, Mattie and James said that they were going to go upstairs and try to get some sleep. They laced their fingers together as they crept up the stairs, careful not to wake the still sleeping child.

For a moment, Mattie almost went to her old room, habit taking over in her brain. But, when James gave her hand a gentle tug, she remembered that they were married, and from this night on, they would share a bed. In the haze of everything that had happened, the fact that it was her wedding night had completely slipped her mind.

She glanced down at the now ruined wedding dress, and a stab of sympathy filled her. She would have to figure out some way to make the loss of it up to Josie. Mattie glanced from her body up to James, who's eyes were filled with patience.

"I haven't moved my dressing gown and everything over. Is it alright if I have a moment to use the washbasin and clean myself off for bed and then join you?"

James gave her a soft smile before nodding. He leaned forward to press a kiss to her forehead.

"I'd like a few minutes to gather myself as well. I'll be here when you're ready."

With that, he turned and strode through the bedroom door that now belonged to both of them. Mattie's heart began to race for an entirely different reason as she walked into her old room. It was still filled with her things, and she knew that in the morning it would be time to move the clothes that filled the armoire into the room that she would now share with James. But that night remained reserved for spending time with her husband.

She walked over to the wash basin that someone had thoughtfully filled for her, and she began the arduous task of washing herself off. The ritual of it all calmed her still panicked body, the images that she had seen that night plaguing her every so often.

When she was sufficiently cleaned and changed into her sleeping gown, she took a quick steadying breath and then padded out into the hallway. She paused for a moment outside of the bedroom door, wondering if perhaps she should knock, but she quickly dismissed the idea.

When Mattie pushed open the door, James was sitting up in bed with a book open in his lap and a lantern flickering merrily on a small table not far from the bed.

His chest was bare, and Mattie caught sight of his rippling muscles and his softly curling chest hair. James looked up from the book when he heard the door open, his eyes softening with love as they fell on her.

He placed the book down beside the lantern and patted the mattress next to him. With a smile, Mattie padded across the room and pulled back the large blanket before climbing in beside him.

He draped his arm around her, pulling her body snug against his. And as his warmth radiated around them, trapped by the covers that lay atop them, she snuggled into him.

"I love you, Mattie." He whispered in her ear, his breath stirring the hair that fell down around her shoulders.

"I love you, too," she answered with a grin. "But can you promise me something?"

"What's that?" He asked as he pressed a kiss to her temple.

"Can we just have a normal life from now on? No more shootings?"

She felt the laughter rumble through James' body, and she rolled over to face him. His eyes gleamed as they roved over her, and another rush of gratitude for her husband washed through her.

"I promise." James agreed, dipping his head to press his mouth to hers.

Mattie brought her hand up to cup James' face as the kiss deepened, and in that moment, despite all they had been through and all they had almost lost, Mattie found herself entirely overcome with happiness and love.

Extended Epilogue

One year later

"They're here!" Amy's small voice rang out loudly through the space, grabbing Mattie's attention from where she rested in the large reading chair.

She turned to glance out the window, noticing the carriage making its way up the lane and she smiled. Amy ran, her bright blonde curls bouncing wildly as she went to find her father.

"Be careful," Mattie called after her as she struggled to push herself to standing while not waking the swaddled baby sleeping peacefully in her arms.

The baby, a beautiful boy that they had decided to name Thomas after James' grandfather, had arrived just a month earlier, and Mattie still found herself delirious with the love that she felt for the children she and James shared.

Amy appeared in the room again, her small body pulling on her father's arm as she tried to steer him toward the door. Mattie laughed and shook her head at them as she walked over to them.

James planted a kiss on her lips before reaching for the doorknob and pulling it open right as the carriage came to a stop in front of their house. Gilbert beamed at them from the bench seat, and a massively pregnant Rebecca rubbed a slender hand back and forth over her belly.

They had gotten married barely a month after James and Mattie, not wanting to waste any time after the shooting, and now their family will have grown by two more within the next few weeks. Gilbert climbed hopped down from the wagon before turning to help Rebecca while Elmer grabbed their bags from the back of the buggy.

"Are you all going to the dance tonight?" Elmer asked as he trotted up the stairs and into the house.

The other four adults shared a look before Mattie shook her head.

"No, we'll be staying in," she answered, shooting a knowing glance at James.

"Dances only lead to trouble, anyways," James said, winking at his wife.

They all helped Rebecca get settled in the kitchen, everyone filing in to sit around the new kitchen table. When Gilbert and Rebecca had announced that they wanted to come to Mt. Juliet for Rebecca to ready for the baby, Mattie had been over the moon. The first thing that she had done was ask James for a new kitchen table, one that was big enough to accommodate the entire family, as well as Elmer and his new wife, Laurah. It had been a request that James had been more than happy to oblige.

After Elmer finished helping get Gilbert and Rebecca's belongings up the stairs in the room that had once been Mattie's, he announced that he was going to pick up Laurah and that they would be back for the celebratory dinner before they both went to the dance. Then, the young man had all but run out the door.

"So, no dance?" Rebecca asked, her stomach still tracing absent minded circles on her protruding belly.

"Well," James said, the corner of his mouth pulling up in a smile. "Maybe there will be some dancing."

He crossed the parlor floor in a few quick strides, stopping in front of the piano and when Mattie realized what her husband was doing, she couldn't help but grin. Rebecca held her arms out for the baby, and Mattie nestled Thomas snuggly into his aunt as she turned and picked up Amy.

As the first chords of music floated through the air, Gilbert smiled as he began dancing with his sister and his niece. Laughter filled the air, and eventually even Rebecca pushed herself up to standing as she and the baby waddled around in circles.

Breathless with happiness, Mattie looked around at the people she loved the most. At the daughter that she did not give birth to but loved as much as if she had. At the son that God had blessed her with not long after a night that could have ended so tragically. She took in the sight of her brother and sister-in-law who brought so much joy and laughter into her life.

And finally, with her heart already flooding with love and emotion, she looked at her husband. At the man she had known since she was just a girl. One who she had been proud to call a friend before she had ever called him anything else. He was someone who in one of her greatest times of need had provided her with a safe haven to call home, and then eventually had provided her with more love and acceptance than she had ever dared dream possible.

Mattie did not know what she had done to deserve the life that she had been gifted, but she knew she would spend every day of it being grateful.

THE END